Death of an Ordinary Guy

Jo A. Hiestand

Jo A. Hiestand

HILLIARD HARRIS PUBLISHERS

Published by

HILLIARD Harris PUBLISHERS

P.O. Box 3358
Frederick, Maryland 21705-3358

This novel is a work of fiction. Names, characters, places and incidents either are the product of the author's imagination or are used fictitiously. Any resemblance to actual persons, living or dead, events, or locales is entirely coincidental.

Death of an Ordinary Guy Copyright © 2004 by Jo A. Hiestand
All rights reserved. No part of this book may be reproduced or transmitted in any form or by any means, electronic or mechanical, including photocopying, recording, or by any information storage and retrieval system, without the written permission of the Publisher, except where permitted by law.

First Edition

ISBN 1-59133-060-2

Designed by HILLIARD HARRIS

Cover Illustration © S. A. Reilly
Release Date: August 1, 2004
Manufactured/Printed in the United States of America
2004

To my parents, Carol and Douglas Hiestand, who always knew I could.

Acknowledgments

This novel is the work of many people besides the author: professionals and supporters. Among the professionals, I thank Inspector Tony Eyre and Detective-Sergeant Robert Church of the Derbyshire Constabulary, who guided me through the intricacies of British police procedure; Dr. Robert Paine, for medical information, Margaret Elliott, who helped me to my first break; Shirley Kennett, who showed me the importance of subplots and a side-kick; Nicole St. John, the Sister who's been there/done that and offered advice on what not to do; Alan Bamford, Brian Coombs and Jed flatters, for Guy Fawkes celebration information; and to Brian Coombs and David Doxey for keeping the English language pure.

Supporters are equally important, supplying emotional support and encouragement throughout the novel's birth. I thank my sister, Babette Hiestand; friends Chris Eisenmayer, Paula Fontaine, and Anne Sharfman; and my Sisters in Crime—especially Louise Rosen, who was never too tired to lend an ear or shoulder and never jealous of another's potential success.

I am grateful for everyone's help. Any mistakes in facts, however, are entirely mine.

Jo A. Hiestand

Chapter 1

"THE LAST FOUR to die included Guy Fawkes, 'the great devil of it all.' Having asked the King for forgiveness, he crossed himself and was hung. A pathetic ending to a daring plot."

Quiet born of distress and shock stifled the listeners, who clustered on the village green, mesmerized by the waiting woodpile. Morning was slipping into afternoon and the November sun shone through the leafless woods to the west. Two rooks, their black feathers opalescent in the bright sunlight, had settled on a limb of a grandfather oak at the fire circle and surveyed their domain. A stand of pines in the churchyard swayed in the breeze, dropping their dried needles onto the lichen-crusted graves beneath them. I suddenly wondered if Guy Fawkes had such a grave in another quiet corner of England, and if it was the scene of subdued visitations.

One of the Americans murmured something in response and the speaker said, "The plot was discovered when one of their group, a Catholic peer, was warned. His absence from Parliament led to Fawkes' exposure and death."

The speaker was Byron MacKinnon, a ginger-haired Scotsman in his late 40s, secretary to the local lord-of-the-manor. He was good at his job, I had heard, and from what I could judge, good as a guide, showing the manor's bed-and-breakfast guests the delights of the English countryside. And the lord-of-the-manor was delighted with the guests, for not only did they bring a few pence to his pocket but also underscored his decision to buy the manor.

Right now, that decision seemed indisputably good, for his B-&-B wing was fully booked for the week, and Byron was conducting tours nearly daily. The three Americans stared at the peaceful fire circle, then at each other, and then back at Byron.

Jo A. Hiestand

"And you do this because Guy Fawkes and his conspirators almost assassinated the King," the woman said, taking notes so she could relate the story to her friends back home. Her breath came in white puffs, matching her hair color.

Even though the afternoon was sunny, it was cold, with a slight wind that stirred the dried grass and flower stalks. They rustled near the open fringes of the fire circle and rattled against the boulders bordering the creek. The woman blew on her fingers, then went back to her note taking.

"Thirty-six barrels of gunpowder," Byron repeated, eyeing the skating pencil. "November 5th, 1605, plotting to blow up Parliament during the opening ceremony. Aye." He paused and I could see the Americans looking at each other. Some topics just hit too close to home.

Byron either didn't notice the uncomfortable glances or was immune to them, for he continued. "The conspirators hoped to kill James I and eradicate the entire government, clear the way for a Catholic coup over the existing Protestant majority."

A group of elementary school-aged children ran across the green, their chant echoing off the buildings opposite us. "Remember, remember the 5th of November. The poor old Guy. A hole in his pocket, a hole in his shoe. Please, can you spare us a penny or two? If not a penny, a ha'penny will do. If not a ha'penny, may God bless you." The end of the rhyme faded into laughter as the children ran into the woods.

The copse was the remnant of an ancient forest that had encircled Upper Kingsleigh, a sleepy village whose only claim to fame — to date — was its location in the heart of England's Dark Peak District. There were worse places for patrol duty, and normally I would have wallowed gloriously in the quiet, but I was itching to prove myself with something more energetic — a burglary or missing person case. Something for which I, a newly-made detective-sergeant, could get noticed. Something more dynamic than nursemaid to a stack of wood and a straw-filled effigy. But we were few on the ground that November weekend, and a policewoman's lot is not always a happy one.

I therefore ignored the fact that any constable could handle this barmy assignment and prepared for the problem of kids hiding fireworks in the bonfire. And kids did. Or seeing that big brother didn't push little sister into the fire. Which might not have been all

Death of an Ordinary Guy

that bad, considering some of the little devils I've seen. I'd do anything for some quiet.

And it was quiet. No car horn blasted, no radio blared, no human voice yelled into the calm. In spite of my urge for action I admit it was a refreshing change from the Constabulary's sectional headquarters in Buxton, an active city of 22,000. I stood, just listening, letting the silence wash over me, and took a deep breath of winter savory and pine. A moment later the silence shattered when one of the Americans laughed.

I stared at the group, wondering what I had missed.

Byron, straight-faced, gestured to the huge oak. "That's why we make a straw-filled effigy of Guy Fawkes, which we call The Guy. It's hoisted at the beginning of the celebration, the note listing his offenses to the Crown and warning other potential traitors is then read aloud —"

"I won't be able to understand a word if it's in Old English," one of the men said, screwing up his mouth. He was middle-aged and destined towards fat in later life. Already he was developing the jowls of an English bulldog. He pulled his baseball cap farther down on his head before shoving his hands into his sweatshirt pockets. "All those thee's and thou's and hear ye's...."

"We've put it into modern English," Byron said, exhaling loudly.

"Nothin' turns me off faster than thee's and thou's," the man muttered, gazing at me.

"The Guy is then lit with a torch —"

"Hope there's no dead grass around. All that straw and clothing falling down might start a fire. You got pails of water handy?"

"I think, Dear," said the woman, a matronly type, white-haired and wrinkled. Though her hands were smooth, it was her face that gave her age away. That or years of sun worshiping, I guessed. "They've probably thought of everything. They've been doing this a long time."

"Four hundred years," Byron replied, standing a bit taller. "Each November 5th."

"So there's nothing to worry about, Tom," she said, squeezing his arm.

Byron continued. "And then the bonfire is lit with the torch."

"All this over this religious thing?" asked the woman, gazing towards the spot where the children had disappeared from sight.

"Religion or politics," the other man answered. He looked to be the same age as the first man — aging baby boomers relinquishing their fight to retain their teenage physique and succumbing to the pleasures of couch and cuisine. Yet the battle was not quite over. While his stomach shook slightly when he walked, his shoulder muscles screamed of weekly workouts. His hair, too, had refused to shift tones. All in all, he had not gone to seed as quickly as Tom. And he seemed less bothered by the cold — his nylon jacket unzipped, his head bare. "In those days they were pretty much the same thing, weren't they?"

"Steve, let Byron tell —"

The husband waved her into silence. "Steve knows a lot of history, Carla. Majored in it, if you don't remember."

"I thought it was American history," Carla returned.

"Close enough," Tom said. "You learn about King George, you learn about us shaking him off. He tried oppressing the Pilgrims and what did it get him?"

The man called Steve said, "Nothing much changes, not even in four hundred years, Carla. You know, like today's President and Congress. Same thing. Same political odds, though they aren't as violent about their oppositions as this Guy Fawkes thing was."

I could see Byron's knuckles whitening. There was a tensing of his jaw muscle.

"Damned injustice, I call it," Tom said. "You've got a Catholic king so all Catholics get favor at the court. A few years later, when the Protestants are in vogue again, *they* get the royal handouts and titles."

"Doesn't really seem fair, does it?" Carla said, looking at Byron.

"The plot was discovered," Byron said, taking control of the conversation, "when one of their group, a Catholic peer, was warned. His absence from Parliament led to Fawkes' exposure and his eventual hanging."

"And that's why you hang this Guy," the woman said, nodding. "A sort of resurrection each year for Mr. Fawkes."

Steve laughed. "Bring the old guy out of the history books, trot him out for public scrutiny so no one'll forget. We oughta do that with Benedict Arnold. Ya know?"

Ignoring Steve's jest, Byron said, "The Queen's Bodyguard, part of the Yeomen of the Guard, still searches those cellars below the House of Lords on the eve of Parliament's opening. They've never found any terrorist armament."

Death of an Ordinary Guy

"Sounds nutty," Steve said. "Looking for gunpowder for 400 years."

"It's not so much the *search*," Byron said, his voice hardening, "as it is the *tradition*."

Steve asked if they used bloodhounds. "Those dogs are trained to sniff out different odors, ya know."

Tom said, "Write 'em a letter, Steve. They'd be glad of the suggestion. Save 'em a lot of work." He hitched up his sagging slacks, pulling in his stomach as though he were going to help with the labor of building the bonfire, which already towered above us.

"I hope the cellars are modernized with electric lights."

The woman made the mistake of asking why.

Steve said, "'Cause if they have to light a candle to look —" He made a face and yelled "Kaboom!" He laughed while Carla looked embarrassed.

"Least it'd save having to do it each year." Tom yawned, simultaneously trying to say something.

"I can't understand you, dear," the woman said, glancing at me and smiling. Probably thinks I'm a tourist. It's the lack of uniform that confuses them.

Recovered from his boredom, Tom said, "When's this start again?"

"The program begins at 7:00," Byron said. "Then there's the hoisting and lighting of the Guy — the straw effigy — lighting of the bonfire, and the eating of the roasted potatoes."

"Sounds nice," Carla said, smiling and pulling the men in the direction of the newsagent shop across the street.

"Sounds nutty," Tom said. "All this way for a glorified weenie roast."

A PALE MOON shimmered in the fading sky, painting the giant oak and everything within the perimeter of the fire circle in silvery tones. One or two early stars winked in the blackness, confirming their existence. Lanterns, already lit and dotting the bonfire area, seemed to mirror heaven's arrangement. The magical atmosphere broke when Arthur Catchpool, owner of Catchpool Manor, walked up to Byron, who was standing near the unlit fire. Both men were dressed in tweeds and corduroy, lending a decidedly "country squire" air to the coming drama.

"I see the *omnium gatherum* has already begun," Arthur said, looking at the people milling around the stack of wood. "Night looks clear, too. Nice for once, no rain."

Arthur Catchpool, a slight man in his early 40s, could have easily been mistaken for the straw Guy in the lantern-lit darkness, had it not been for his obvious vitality. Though not a lord of the blood, he had bought Catchpool Manor some years ago, saving it from the wrecking ball and the village from a slow death. Now manor, lord and village survived, if not prospered, and enjoyed the influx of tourists who came for the three day celebration of the Catchpool Dole, Mischief Night, and Guy Fawkes festivity. Hardly surprising, for there were few villages — or towns — left that celebrated Guy Fawkes as thoroughly as Upper Kingsleigh did.

Arthur was about to move to the torch area when Byron grabbed his arm.

"What do you —" Arthur began, only to follow Byron's nod. He groaned as he saw Talbot Tanner, the village odd jobs man, walking up to him. "A hell of a time for this," he said, glancing at his watch.

"It's almost 7:00," Byron said. "You want me to —"

"No. I'll shake him off as quickly as possible. Another minute more or less...."

"Trouble is, he rabbits on more than a minute." Byron stepped back as the older man stopped inches away from Arthur and tapped his forefinger against Arthur's chest.

"I just seen the other third of your Trio," Talbot said, his eyes narrowing. "And up *you* pop. Speak of one, as they say."

"What are you on about," Arthur asked.

"This little yearly problem is easily fixed, if Your Grace orders it."

"How do you suggest we remedy it, Talbot?"

"Turn over the dole to me, that's what you can bloody well do. No one need know."

Not unless they were deaf, I wanted to add, amazed the older man would air his grievance so loudly and publicly.

"Not exactly ethical," Byron said, stepping closer to the man. "According to Henry Catchpool's will —"

"Will be damned!" Talbot exploded, grabbing Arthur's jacket.

I took a step forward, wondering if the man wanted me to intercede now that Talbot had become physical. Byron saw me and shook his head.

Death of an Ordinary Guy

"I'll prove it," Talbot said, releasing Arthur's jacket. "I'll prove to you and the whole village that I'm entitled to that dole money. I'm goin' to search tonight, and when I find the proof, I'll see who my real friends are. Aw, hell!" He turned quickly, spat on the ground, and strode toward the oak where the straw effigy lay.

Byron eyed me, silently mouthed 'thank you,' and guided Arthur to the torch area. Minutes later the program began. It was typical of most village entertainment: this year's songs and dances cutely interpreted by the pre-teen group, jokes and riddles by the younger set, and a painful violin solo by an older man who — explained the vicar — had just begun lessons that month. The vicar then said a prayer and thanked that year's hard workers.

Before the applause died, the vicar bent over and tugged at the wooden torch pushed into the ground near the woodpile. Cotton batting, covered in layers of paraffin-soaked gauze, topped the stick, giving it the grotesque appearance of a giant cotton swab. He held the wooden torch as high as he could, letting everyone see and snap a few photos if desired. Then, from somewhere in the darkness behind him, a match scraped against something rough. The smell of sulfur filtered downwind, and a small blue and ochre flame bored a hole into the blackness. The flame moved forward as if floating through the gloom. There was a stronger scent of parafin as the cotton batting ignited, and the vicar's thin face leapt out of the dark, bathed in crimson, gold and yellow. He slowly walked forward, his ink-black robes one with the night, his jet-black shadow bobbing behind him while the torch flames danced. The instant he struck the torch into the base of the gigantic wood pile, the crowd cheered.

"It's like a homecoming," the American woman said to Tom. She pressed her hands together as the man agreed there was something about the bonfire that was better than Independence Day.

Without a word, the vicar walked over to the huge oak. He stood patiently while Byron unwrapped the free end of the rope from the tree trunk. In the bonfire's blaze I could first see the whiteness of a triangle appear from the background, then the figure of a woman. Her left arm was cradled in a fabric sling, yet she climbed the ladder positioned beneath the overhanging tree limb easily enough. When she reached the top rung, Byron pulled the Guy Fawkes dummy off the ground.

"Can you manage the torch, do you think?" Byron asked over the cheering crowd, concern etched into his face.

"If you'll stand by me, in case the torch proves to be too much...."

Byron stepped back into the blackness beyond the fire. When he returned seconds later, the vicar was handing the burning torch to the woman. Her slender form was silhouetted against the blackness of the night sky, the effigy languidly rotating from the massive oak limb that held it in mid air.

From her position near the top of the ladder, the woman grabbed the torch from the vicar. By the yellow light she paused to read the declaration scribbled on a slightly wrinkled square of paper stretched across the Guy's chest and held upright by an old knife. Its wooden hilt and naked blade gleamed in the firelight and threw hideous shadows across the whiteness of the paper. The crowd cheered louder, urging her on as she leaned closer to peer at the effigy's face. Ebony and saffron-yellow alternately washed the face as shadow and firelight flitted across the form. At another vocal urge, the woman raised the torch to peer at the face before her. A moment later her scream rose against the clamor as she fell in a faint.

Death of an Ordinary Guy

Chapter 2

HE KNEW WHAT to expect. Even so, it was difficult to believe the straw-filled effigy sprawled on the ground was really a dead man.

I had related the facts — skeletal as they were — to him via the phone. I had imagined him picking up the phone, cursing its interruption, yet glad of the respite from his paper-choked desk. He would have leaned back in his chair, adapting his long, thin frame to the chair's unyielding one. His legs would be stretched across the desktop, his brown eyes staring at nothing while his whole being was focused on my voice. I had seen him like that dozens of times and at first I assumed he was idly chatting up his wife or friend, passing the time until his shift ended. That was before I knew him better. I would never make that mistake again.

When I had told him the facts I could imagine him leaning forward, the front legs of his chair thudding onto the linoleum floor as they reclaimed their original position, his forearms bracing against the edge of his desk as he grabbed for pen and paper. I had heard his throat clearing, which always announced he had finished cogitating and was ready to act. He had. He arrived in thirty minutes.

"They call it a necktie party in the States, don't they?" I said.

"That, or the tie that binds." He was looking at the corpse, memorizing the details. The deceased wore a tan, plaid jacket, hiking boots, blue jeans of no particular name recognition, and a sweatshirt proclaiming Yale University. His callused hands and weatherworn face held the physical hardships of his 50 years. Fifty years that lead to this spot and this finish.

He lay on his back. Clumps of straw haphazardly protruded from the cuffs of the jacket, obliterating his hands. Straw, pale and casting thick, black shadows under the intense police lights, fringed the lower edge of the jacket. Straw escaped from beneath the dusty straw hat, angled at a rakish angle, and mingled with his blond hair. A small knife plunged into the corpse's chest secured a square of paper. It looked like a try-out for a Ray Bolger role gone horribly wrong.

We, no doubt, looked just as bizarre in our facemasks, paper jumpsuits, and polythene shoe covers. Required apparel to keep the crime scene as pure of outside contamination as possible. Fat chance outside, I thought. Still, we played by the rules.

"But that was in the old days, right? I mean, necktie parties — aren't they illegal now?"

"You're asking me *that* at a crime scene? I thought *murder* was illegal. How'd you make Sergeant rank, TC?"

I colored. I hadn't yet learned for sure when he was joking, for we had been working together for only a month. But I *had* learned when to keep quiet. And to watch Detective Chief Inspector Geoffrey Graham note the surroundings before we examined the body.

Upper Kingsleigh was one of those spots tourists seek out for an authentic British experience, world-weary workers gravitate to on retirement, and local teens escape from in droves. We stood just outside the police cordon, which enclosed the bonfire area of the village green. Within its confines, Scenes-of-Crime Officer Dean Hargreaves and other experts prowled, their bodies half illuminated by the ebbing bonfire, half submerged in night as they stepped into or out of the light. Ancient oaks and junipers jumped out of the anonymous darkness of the November night as Hargreaves moved a flood lamp.

"So, Taylor," he said, abandoning my nickname and switching to my last name. "The Derbyshire C.I.D. is called in again to restore and resolve. England expects each man will do his duty," he quoted, then hastily added, "Sorry, Taylor. Man and woman."

I mumbled an acceptance of his apology, past caring that every sentence had to be politically correct.

"Upper Kingsleigh. A mere 500 souls perched on the fringe of Wormhill Moor." He seemed to stare through the evening's blackness, envisioning what lay beyond the village. His voice softened, nearly inaudible. "Five hundred people clinging to life on the 'spine of England.'"

I nodded, picturing the great snaking mountain chain of the Pennines, the 300-mile link of towering tors, dales, desolate moors, caverns and streams stretching from midland England northward to the Scottish Lowlands. Giant vertebrae. Derbyshire's Peak District was part of the Pennine progression, comprised of Dark and White regions. The White Peak, characterized by its white limestone, gave way in the northern section to the Dark Peak, named for the dark Millstone Grit running through the moors, cliffs and peat hags. Upper Kingsleigh indeed hung onto life, as Graham noted, precariously balanced between the moorland at its front door and the forests and mountain faces at its back. A village nestled into its environment, secluded and tranquil, where not long past in its history the most difficult aspect of life was getting 'over the tops.'

As if reading my mind, Graham said, "This is usually a peaceful place, Taylor. Very few call outs. But it seems to have had quite a jolt tonight."

"Yes, sir. When I was growing up, our village celebrated Guy Fawkes with roasted potatoes, and making and hoisting the dummy. The biggest leaning toward a law offence I can remember was my friends and I lighting the leftover straw and pretending they were cigarettes."

"What a radical you're revealing yourself to be, Taylor! I wouldn't have taken you for a smoker."

"I gave it up after my mum persuaded me to do otherwise." I rubbed my buttocks. It was an automatic reaction when that subject came up. "Anyway, we didn't finish the evening off with murder."

"Murder on a Sunday evening," Graham said. "Dark deed on a dark moor. Forgive the poetic license."

I murmured it was close enough, for Wormhill Moor began a scant quarter mile from the edge of the village. And it fit with the Dark Peak, I wanted to add, but he was looking across the village green.

Ivy-wrapped stone buildings, their gray slate roofs glistening from dew, stretched the length of the road. Beyond the cluster of shops, homes alive with light pinpricked the black evening. A great stand of sycamore at the base of the church hill swayed in the gentle breeze, their bare branches grasping at the moon like a net thrown at a fish. Moonlight danced on the rooftops and in the depth of the pond, gurgled over stones in the stream, painted the foliage with silver.

Someone let a door slam and the magic evaporated. Graham wondered aloud if the baker's shop across the street would have anything left from the day's sales.

"I don't think they're open, sir," I said, pointing out the darkened windows.

"Like a cop, Taylor. Never around when needed. I'm hungry."

I told him I probably had a slightly crushed granola bar in my purse, if he could wait until we finished with the scene, but he declined gracefully. "Despite the urging of my stomach, murder calls. Rather good title, that. *Murder Calls.*"

I nodded while Graham slipped on his face mask and stepped into the brightness spotlighting the corpse. The metal milk crates used to protect the ground and give us access to the body and scene seemed to hover above the dark soil. Like earth-bound clouds against a midnight sky. Graham walked carefully along this path, his head down as though he was focused on every detail the land could give. Which may not be much, considering the barren hardness of the rock-and-soil composition. No such thing as a muddy footprint, in other words.

Graham squatted at the corpse, lifted a corner of the impaled paper with his pen, and peered beneath it. He seemed to speak to the body. "That knife would give anybody chest pains. But that whacking great rope, yet! Hung up very much like your cattle rustler. What a nasty thing this is, TC."

"Quite nasty," I replied and then explained that the police surgeon and the superintendent had already looked at the body. No one liked the look of it. "Deceased is a Steve Pedersen," I said while Graham went on with his cursory look. "American. Fifty years old. Tourist who had just entered the Kingdom a few days ago."

"Traveling with anyone, or free and unencumbered?"

"He was with his brother-in-law and his wife. Arrived about the same time as a number of other tourists."

"For their three days of revelry, I expect. It is that time of year, isn't it? Dole, Mischief Night, and the Fawkes Celebration. One tends to lose track of the calendar, TC."

I nodded, wishing I could have come up with a list of attractions or statistics about the village that would impress him. Instead, I stood there, looking at the corpse, and said, "They do very well in the tourist trade, yes, sir. At the moment they host several Britons and several Americans. But besides playing the tourist, Pedersen was here to see friends."

"So that's why he didn't melt into the vastness of London or Blackpool, say. I suspected there must be something other than jacket potatoes to lure him here." Graham nodded, his mind now

Death of an Ordinary Guy

fully absorbed in physical details. The deceased's left palm had recently sustained an injury, the skin on the heel was cut, and there was a large gouge approximately one-quarter inch square that was red and fringed with broken skin. Several cuts ran parallel to this gouge and appeared dark red, nearly brown. A large, purple bruise covered the heel. I leaned over the chest in order to view the right hand. The palm showed no such injury.

In general, the facial skin was as pale and cold as that of other corpses we had attended. Bruises at the side of the throat were overwrapped in places by abrasions and a ring of redness that followed the jaw line. There were bruises, nearly black, on the left jaw and side of the neck. A thick patch of hair near the left temple was matted with dried blood. The eyes stared vacantly at nothing, though the left pupil had dilated larger than the right one had.

"Have a look, Taylor. Let's see if you spot the same thing I did."

"I don't know what the rest of the lads mean when they talk about pressure in his job." Especially for a woman, I wanted to say, but adjusted my face mask and silently took Graham's place by the body. I had learned Graham's meticulous nature and his impatience with sloppiness. It was a wise partner who stayed alert, responsible and showed superior intelligence. Graham could make or break any rising career. Moments later, I said, "You referring to the head injury, sir?"

Chapter 3

"NOT BAD FOR a refugee from university, Taylor. What were you reading?" He congratulated me on my observation and turned away before I could say I had considered taking a degree in archaeology. He would have laughed. Here I was 20 years later, involved with a different type of dead body.

I said, "Wanted to be sure Pedersen was dead, from the looks of it. Attacked, hanged and knifed. What do we have — a lunatic, or an annoyed trio?"

"I assume Pedersen was knocked out first — that's what the head wound suggests to me, at any rate — then the rope slipped around his neck for the hilarity of the bonfire. Note the bruises at the side of the neck, near the ear, Taylor," Graham went on, gliding over my editorial comment. "And the flap of skin and scalp where the blood has clotted. Classic signs of head trauma. I hate to assume it's a skull fracture, but...."

"From the wounds on his left palm.... Could he have fallen, sir?"

"Looks like it. His palm took the brunt of his fall. Ahrens will tell us if his knees or hip are bruised — that'll tell us, certainly."

Dr. Hugh Ahrens is the Home Office pathologist who will conduct the post-mortem. Karol, the local police surgeon, was here, hovering in the background while Graham spent a few more minutes over the body. Satisfying himself as to its condition, he handed me his pen as he stood up. I took it out of habit, clipping it onto the neckline of my jumpsuit, and watched him follow the milk crates to the oak.

The lads had dispensed with the usual tent we would normally erect around a corpse outdoors. A waste of time, that, the Super had said on viewing the scene — a jumble of grass, gravel, wood chips,

Death of an Ordinary Guy

fire ashes, straw, dry leaves and twigs. A hundred people coming and going all day, milling about at the bonfire, contaminating the area beyond any defense that the tent could tender. I shuddered as a gust of wind dusted the air with a handful of ash. A Scenes-of-Crime Officer's nightmare, this — bonfire debris, hair, lint and other foreign objects. No, the tent would be ridiculous.

Graham stopped beneath the great, overhanging branch and looked around the tree's base, ready to give the area the same intense observation he had given the corpse. Glancing at the rope that swayed slightly above the corpse, Graham said, "No one in our happy group of revelers, I take it, thought anything of the knife? Part of their Guy Fawkes tradition?" His voice sounded tired and he rubbed his eyes, looking remarkably like a small boy who had stayed up past his bedtime. "I agree with your childhood recollections, TC. The effigies of my childhood had some sort of note pinned or stuck to the dummy, the knife borrowed from one of the villagers' households. We'd always thrown our effigy onto the fire, though. This hanging is a bit unusual, though in keeping with the historical end of Guy Fawkes."

I stared again at the wrinkled white paper, lifted from the jacket's dark background by the intense flood lighting. The note seemed to float above the corpse — except for its center where it was cruelly affixed by the knife.

"Well, sir," I said, hating to break into his contemplation, "it's the sort of thing they do each year. Knife in old Guy, note stuck to his chest. No one took any notice. When Ramona Van Dyke — that's the woman who discovered the body — started to light the dummy, she noticed it wasn't. A dummy, I mean."

"Must have given her quite a fright," Graham noted, staring at the rope that ran over the overhanging oak limb. The slowly swaying form, washed by shadow and firelight, with the knife blade winking at the villagers, shimmered before my mind's eye. "Fright?" he revised. "Hell, she would have been *terrified.*"

"No doubt. Anyway, no one noticed a thing. The dummy's been out in plain view since Thursday."

"Three days ago." When Graham turned toward me, I could see his interest.

"Yes, sir. There was nothing extraordinary, it seems, about the dummy. The villagers passed it every day, whether to bring more wood for the fire, or just to see how the fire building was progressing.

They were used to seeing it, so they really didn't see it, if you take my meaning."

Graham mumbled that unfortunately he did know what I meant. "I most likely wouldn't have noticed anything unusual about the dummy, either. How many would?"

"I wouldn't. You see what you expect to see. Especially if you've no reason to expect otherwise."

"Especially if you've seen it year after year with no disastrous results."

I agreed. It was difficult to imagine someone substituting the corpse for the effigy, but it was clever. "I bet they think of this next year, and give their effigy a good going-over before hand."

"You think it likely lightning will strike twice in the same place?" Graham eyed me.

"Not likely. But it'll cross their minds when it comes time to light it. That's certain. Someone'll have a good look, just in case."

"Perhaps." Graham sighed. I knew he was annoyed with the hour, the murder, and the obvious tampering with the scene. He looked again at the tree branch that stretched overhead like the arm of an ancient crossroads gibbet. "Who would have thought that the mundane practice of lighting bonfires, begun on the evening in 1605, would evolve into a tradition still observed nearly 400 years later?" Graham said.

"Or that Guy Fawkes would evolve into the arch villain of the gunpowder plot? Ought to be Robert Catesby."

He looked at me, either surprised I knew my history so well or unsure of his own. Silently I yelled *Carpe diem*, then said, "Catesby, the leader of the gunpowder conspiracy — *not* poor Guy Fawkes, whom we love to revile."

Graham regained his composure and said, "No wonder you turned to detection, Taylor. Your memory of the smallest detail does either your ancestral genes or your police schooling proud. How'd you like Hendon, by the way?"

I avoided his gaze, afraid I would color. "Seems a pity to hang the blame on the wrong lad. Like sending the wrong man to the dock." It had a strange ring of contemporary cases and left me feeling uneasy.

"Do we have any measurements, yet, on height of the tree limb and all the rest? I see they used a stepladder." He indicated the impressions of the ladder's feet in the earth, then gestured to the rope that ran from the limb to the deceased. The rope was about an inch in diameter, creamy white and very new. "Effigy must have been damned high if they resorted to a ladder."

"Yes, sir. They raised the dummy first, then read the note aloud. You'd have to be at chest level to read it. That's when Miss Van Dyke discovered the effigy was Pedersen."

"A face-to-face identification. So, Van Dyke had the honor — or horror — of discovering the corpse. I can't see her scrambling down the ladder to undo that whacking great knot. How'd Pedersen get down?"

"Well, sir, you know how it is...."

"I probably do," Graham replied slowly as he steeled himself for some horrendous account of crime scene destruction. "But let me have it at once so I get over the shock."

I was glad of the mask covering my nose and mouth. He couldn't see my smile. "Well, just like anybody, their first thought was to get him down in case he might still be alive."

"With that ruddy *knife* in him?" Graham exploded, his eyes mirroring his astonishment. Shaking his head, Graham said, '*Ora pro nobis'* to the universe.

I agreed that we needed all the help we could get, but inwardly doubted God would send a flaming chariot of avenging angels, no matter how diligently Graham had served his collar. And, from the office gossip, he had, even if he had been Chapel and not C of E.

In the silence following his vocal plea, I could hear two constables complaining about the evening's cold. Their voices must have jarred Graham, for he said, "Sorry, TC. Go on."

I hesitated momentarily, altering a few words from my previous statement. Best to make this exact and succinct. Save our blood pressures. "Well, they lowered him to the ground, hoping he was still breathing. He wasn't."

"Another body moved before we can examine it. Bloody helpful." Graham snorted, his eyes back on the disarray of the corpse.

"Can't really fault them, sir. Natural reaction."

"I suppose. But I *don't* suppose Ahrens will do the dance of joy over it. When's he going to get here?" He looked at his watch. "Two hours, if he makes good time."

"We can't get a measurement of the height of the body from the ground, no, sir. But we can estimate it fairly accurately. We know his height, and the rope should show signs of —"

"Bloody helpful," he repeated. "Who actually lowered the body? Do we know that?"

"Talbot Tanner. Village odd-jobs man, sixty-two years old —"

"Fine." Graham waved aside the rest of my rendition.

Thinking he would find it interesting as well as pertinent, I mentioned Talbot had been in charge of constructing the bonfire, but that Ramona Van Dyke had overseen the straw dummy.

"Were either Talbot or Ramona responsible for the knife?" said Graham when I had finished.

"Haven't got that far, sir." I hesitated, wanting to recite some fact about them or the bonfire or the lack of fireworks, but they would be taken for what they obviously were — a feeble display of non-essential knowledge. I didn't know what to say to regain his respect.

"Of course not. Early days yet." Graham bent over the body, the knife fascinating him. It seemed to whisper to him, taunt him. "Looks incredibly familiar, but I can't place it. Do you know, Taylor?" He stepped aside, motioning me to join him at the body.

I squatted, peered at the knife from several angles, then stood up and said that it seemed like a scout knife. "Found in many homes, scout-aged children or not residing. Could just as easily be a remnant from a current university student or a jumble sale. Doesn't get us anywhere."

"Probably won't find any dabs on it, either," mused Graham half aloud, taking in the knife's short blade, the metallic rivets pimpling the wooden handle. "Well, one of the SOCOs will have to deal with it. And I hope whoever does it won't make a bloody mess of it this time."

"Yes, sir," I said, uncertain it was a joke, sympathetic to the as yet unchosen Scenes-of-Crime Officer.

Shielding his eyes from the brilliance of the working lights, Graham looked around, as if to see whom he could trust.

Unfortunately, I knew what he meant. An eager constable attached to a previous case had packaged a blood-stained knife in a paper bag, remembering the bit about allowing it to dry first, but forgetting the bit about tying the knife to the interior of a cardboard box, which prevented movement — and removal of blood — during transport. I swallowed, pitying the SOCO if he mucked up this one.

Evidently giving up for the moment, Graham said, "All the fun of a fair for Hargreaves."

Death of an Ordinary Guy

"Murderers are a bit more clever these days," I agreed. "Unless done on the spur of the moment, they plan ahead about the fingerprints."

"Gloves were never one of my favorite bits of wearing apparel. Well, if we're not told otherwise, I don't think Steve Pedersen was stabbed to death. Has Karol expounded anything yet, do you know?"

I replied that Karol hadn't said anything to me, but she was still there if Graham wanted to talk to her.

"Wouldn't dream of disturbing her work." Graham held his hand out to me and I, as though a sister in an operating theater, placed the pen in his palm. With a nearly inaudible 'thanks,' he carefully lifted the left edge of the deceased's plaid jacket. As though addressing Pedersen's chest, Graham muttered, "I'll give you three guesses, Taylor. Three's the magic number. Associated with all sorts of things, so you can take your pick and invoke the Trinity, shamrock, musketeers, or whatever. But if you don't get it in one, I'll be quite disappointed with you, and strongly suggest a refresher course in Elementary Detection."

Even though I assumed he was joking, I wanted to shine, to win back my top-of-the-class status. Of course I wasn't expected to solve this case single-handedly — I mean, that's why I was partnered with him. To learn as well as to complement his skills. But I wanted him to think I had promise. I nervously pulled all police schooling from somewhere deep within me, afraid to speak, as he gestured toward the light blue sweatshirt front that was bunched up slightly where the knife blade had pulled bits of it into the wounded flesh. Aside from a strand of straw and a bit of blood — hardly noticeable — on the knife, there was nothing unusual about the shirt or jacket.

"Well, Taylor?" he said. "What about it? Does this lack of abundant blood speak to you?" I must have made some sort of face, for he said, "Should I be worried about your dinner?"

I could delay it no longer. Praying that I wasn't about to demote myself or look like an idiot, I said, "Bit of a giveaway, yes. Stabbed after death."

I must have answered satisfactorily, for there was a hint of a smile in his eyes. He let the jacket edge fall back into place, got to his feet, and gave me the pen. "Can Ramona Van Dyke talk now?" He turned toward the area where she, her fiancée, and the vicar had been moments before. The grassy spot was empty.

I let Graham swear under his breath after I explained that Karol had given Miss Van Dyke a sedative just before he had arrived. "She needed it. Fearful shock, this whole thing."

He stood, clenching his fingers, staring at them as though they had held the knife. Hands were important to him, I knew from office chatter. He was a serious amateur musician. Some sort of keyboard instrument, I vaguely recalled. What was there besides piano or organ? Neither sounded quite right, and I stood there, trying to recall what the chatter had said. I had just decided to ask him when Graham sighed. "Well, there's nothing for it but to proceed with Plan B, Taylor. You can let Hargreaves and the Clan have their fun. Murder makes their jobs so much more interesting." He muttered a hurried apology and stepped out of Hargreaves' way. "Evening, Hargreaves. Sorry about the hour."

Dean Hargreaves, a short, thirty-something-year-old who excelled in still photography, maneuvered around one of his own tripods, and replied that he didn't mind the time. "The Cop apologized earlier." Even though I had now made sergeant grade, my mates still called me The Cop, or TC. I reveled in the nickname that doubled as a Right of Passage in a male-dominated occupation and as a trophy of a once-vicious taunt. The only woman in my police class, I had endured the course and my colleagues' snide remarks, finally proving myself worthy of being a cop and working with them. Dean continued. "I've just had a cuppa, so I'm in good shape."

Graham nodded, taking in my nickname without a second thought. "Hot tea sounds awfully good. As soon as TC and I sort things out, we'll have to find some."

Hargreaves stepped in front of a floodlight, eclipsing the deceased and silhouetting himself at the same time. From my position at the side of the forensic activity, Hargreaves' features stood out with the boldness of a relief map. The more his black hair thinned, the fuller Hargreaves wore his mustache. I wondered if the mustache would mature into a beard if the photographer turned bald.

I exited the crime scene and took off my work clothing as Graham and Hargreaves talked. From the darkness of the eastern woods I could hear Rams Dyke Creek rushing downstream to join the River Dove. I silently thanked the saint or Olympian god who ruled such things that we weren't dealing with a drowning. I had seen enough water-eaten corpses to fill the rest of my career. Which I hoped would be long, if I didn't do something stupid in front of

Death of an Ordinary Guy

Graham. He could be your best friend or as cold, hard-hearted, and unyielding as the police manual if he was crossed.

I shook off the water-bloated image that claimed my mind and wondered what had pulled Graham into the Force. I had progressed to fantasizing about revenge for a murdered sister when I saw him approach. His step was light and quick, full of self-assurance; his tall, lean body silhouetted against Hargreaves' work lights.

All this time I had been patiently waiting beyond the police tape, and lifted it as Graham joined me. His footprints were dark smears on the frosted grass, a straight trail that spoke of his completion with the scene and his determination to begin the next phase. I collected my purse from where I had stashed it near a straw bundle and asked, "You suppose the knife will be all that difficult to trace?"

Graham disrobed quickly and handed the paper apparel over to a constable, who promptly stuffed it into a paper bag. The evening's chill had gripped him, and although he did his best to ignore it, he looked as though he was cold. And hungry. He tugged up the zipper of his suede jacket and pulled on his gloves, which were of the same color leather. I hugged my arms to my chest, glad of my down-filled jacket. We watched the frozen breaths of the constabulary team shrouding the scene, white against the glare of the police lamps. He turned back to me. "No one will own it, Taylor. You've been a copper long enough to know that. I suppose you better phone up the video team from Chesterfield. Or...." Graham stopped in his directive to study my face. My expression must have told Graham what he had suspected. "Should know better than to tell you something so obvious. They're enroute, are they? Drum roll, please."

In spite of my wish to bottle my feelings, I smiled. It passed unnoticed, for he was concentrating on the job.

"Now, whom should we talk to first? Who's not overcome with grief or drugged beyond sensibility? I don't mean that as cruelly as it might sound. I'm just tired. What time is it?" He consulted his watch, saw that it was 9:00, and swore. "Not particularly late, but it *will* be before we unpack our pajamas."

"Well, since you asked for my vote, I suggest Arthur Catchpool. He's something of the local lord, though there's no claim to a peerage. More of a lord-of-the-manor thing."

"Great benefactor of the village, then?" Graham stared absentmindedly ahead of him into the dark village. A few lighted-up windows spoke of the houses' occupants still awake. Probably chattering on about the murder over hot cups of tea, Graham acquiesced, and murmured something about slices of jam-covered bread, fat rascals, and blazing fires. He spoke of it as one would of a loving memory.

"Couldn't be more of a benefactor than if he guided each villager through life, to hear some of them talk. Pays for half the drinks at the bonfire, for starters."

"And who provides the potatoes?" replied Graham, kicking one of the tubers that had rolled out from the fire area.

I felt suddenly sad, knowing these villagers had been cheated out of their evening revelry. Maybe not such a disappointment to an adult, but to a child it was probably an earth-shaking tragedy. I heard a chestnut pop as I stepped on it. "You will ask embarrassing questions, sir."

He smiled slightly, the skin over his jaw tightening so that the scar was more visible. It was the only flaw in his otherwise lead-actor looks. "Nasty habit of mine. Sorry. Continue with your most interesting discourse."

"Well, Arthur is a likely place to start our investigation. He's converted a section of the venerable pile into a bed-and-breakfast, so we might find some of the tourists who were here at the bonfire getting ready to nest for the night. Save on returning tomorrow to question them."

"I applaud your efficiency, Taylor."

"Thank you. Anyway, even if the tourists are soothing their frayed nerves at the Broken Loaf — that's the local pub — Arthur is still the key player. He emceed the pre-fire program, handed out laurels to workers, oversaw the straw bundle delivery, paid for the chestnuts...."

"Busy man," Graham added. "And apart from observing village hierarchy...." His voice trailed off. Was he envisioning the bonfire, the light-streaked faces of the villagers eagerly anticipating the food and fueling of the Guy? "Very well, Taylor. Let's see if Mr. Arthur Catchpool is still awake and, if so, if his benefaction will extend to two cups of tea."

Death of an Ordinary Guy

Chapter 4

ARTHUR CATCHPOOL WAS indeed awake, and so were the others beneath his roof — family, house staff and tourists. And true to Graham's hope, Arthur *did* offer us tea after he settled us in his study. I grasped the cup in both hands, feeling the warmth from the china invade my cold-stiffened fingers. The tea smelt of hot lemon, and there was an aroma of fried pork and apples hanging in the air. I inhaled deeply, as though the fragrance would appease my growing hunger. It didn't, and I drank deeply of the tea. It nearly scalded my throat, but the temperature shocked me awake.

The room was what I had expected of a country great house — wood paneling, walls of books, accessories and portraits that went back generations. But Arthur was entirely *un*expected. Instead of a robust, rotund country squire, we found a slight man in his early forties, soft-spoken and dogless. I hoped my astonishment wasn't noticeable.

I reluctantly traded my cup for pen and paper when Arthur began his narrative.

"I'm afraid that's all I can tell you, Mr. Graham." Arthur sat opposite us, his legs crossed, his elbow on the edge of a small table. He was dressed in wool slacks and patch-elbow tweed jacket. The knees of Arthur's slacks were still wet from where he had knelt on the damp earth, aiding Ramona Van Dyke during her faint. Lord knows it was understandable — finding a corpse instead of a straw dummy staring at you. A wisp of straw, just discernible, had lodged under the tassel of his moccasin. Probably even now not aware of it. Arthur's voice, though high from apprehension, filled the room.

"The vicar lit the fire, then handed the torch over to Ramona. Of course, we had no inkling that the dummy wasn't — Well...." He paused to swallow, looking quite uncomfortable. "For all that went on here tonight, Mr. Graham, Upper Kingleigh's *still* quieter than Lewes." He offered the village comparison with pride, as though he had to find something good in the night's horror. I could imagine the Sussex town, the lighted dummy dangling from a noose, the noise swelling until every corner of the town seemed filled with the bedlam. Arthur abruptly abandoned his speech, grabbed his shirt collar, and pulled at his tie. Was his imagery too graphic, inducing the feeling of the noose that had strangled Steve Pedersen? He looked definitely paler than a few minutes ago. I was about to find him some water or brandy when he spoke again. His statement now was embellished with the bulwark of village safety statistics.

I watched the man's fidgeting, the clasping and unclasping of his hands.

Arthur swallowed loudly, his fingers intertwined and squeezed together as though he was in earnest prayer. Somewhere within the bowels of the mansion a grandfather clock erupted in a deep-voice to announce the hour. The chime echoed faintly from the opposite end of the hall.

"How could we know? It was dark. Seven o'clock. We weren't particularly interested in it. Well, why should we be, having seen all the other dummies Ramona had made? That's Ramona Van Dyke," he explained, his eyes watching my note-taking. I smiled, thanking him.

Graham asked, "You didn't know the deceased, then."

Arthur seemed to relax somewhat, now that the focus had shifted from him. The flesh of his fingers returned to its normal hue, the top leg ceased its agitated bounce.

"No, I didn't," he confessed rather too quickly, I thought. I glanced at Graham, but his face revealed no hint of emotion or opinion. Arthur continued. "That is, I knew he had been a guest here. Part of the house is a B-and-B. It brings in a few bob a year, so it helps with the household accounts. Plus, there's no other larger accommodation close by. Buxton's a good half hour away."

He seemed to need to justify his commercial venture to us, as though we would find it illegal or ethically immoral.

Graham agreed that every little bit of income was handy these days.

"You're so right. This place costs a bloody fortune to run. That's why I started taking in paying guests. The house has way too many rooms for our current lifestyle. Who can afford nanny and governess and all the rest of the frou-frous our forebears enjoyed?"

Death of an Ordinary Guy

I ventured that even if I could afford them, I would feel uneasy about employing others for what I could do myself. Graham winked at me while Arthur counted himself lucky in only having an uncle to support. And in being childless. "But it's home, and I wouldn't let it out of the family if I could."

"So while you lodged Steve Pedersen..." Graham prompted, guiding the questioning back to the murder.

"Other than greeting him as I do everyone when they arrive, and inviting them to tea the first night... Well, why should I know he was going to —" He stuttered and looked at the carpet. "Anyway," he said when he had calmed somewhat, "Byron knew who Pedersen was, of course, and told me after it — Well, just before you arrived. That's Byron MacKinnon, my bookkeeper and secretary — personal as well as social. My private life's not that demanding, so Byron fills a portion of his 40 hours by keeping the books for Evan Greene, the publican, and the Conways, owners of the gift shop. Met them yet? Grand folks. Anyway, Byron had a business 10, 15 years ago. Then came to work for me."

I asked why a man enjoying the freedom of his own business would trade that to be someone's employee.

Arthur shrugged and slowly answered, "I hate to gloat over another's misfortunes, but it wasn't until his own business failed that he came here."

"Hard cheese."

"What? Oh, yes. Rough go. He's a real hard worker. Invaluable man. Also emulates the Buxton visitor's centre. Keeps the pamphlets plentiful, plans day trips to local sites, lets my guests know what's happening throughout the area. Takes a group photo, which people are free to buy or not. Nice holiday reminder. They seem to appreciate the kindness."

"Invaluable man, indeed," Graham agreed, then caught my eye. "We'll have to see if this paragon of secretaries can tell us anything of Mr. Pedersen."

"Of course you're free to question Byron," Arthur returned. "Or anyone associated with me. I'm all for helping the police."

"It's a pity there aren't more people like you, Mr. Catchpool."

Arthur stumbled over his words, momentarily flustered. "Oh? Yes, I suppose it *would* make your jobs easier. It's been a dreadful shock. Simply awful. I've just seen to my guests, actually, and they're taking it quite well, if you can call dealing with murder 'well.' I suppose it *is* murder...." He glanced from Graham to me as my pen stopped. As Graham nodded, Arthur grimaced, either the word or idea abhorrent to him. "Yes. I thought so. There's a comfort in wanting it to be suicide or an accident, isn't there. I mean, it shifts the horror of an unknown lunatic lurking among us to a self-inflicted event."

"But the burden of suicide," Graham said, the minister escaping from within him, "is that the survivors carry the guilt of the death. They eternally accuse and punish themselves with non-answerable questions of 'Why didn't I help more? Why didn't I spend a bit more time with him?'" He tilted his head, looking wise and paternal and otherworldly. I wondered if his words were mere ministerial dogma or pain from personal loss.

Arthur replied quickly, the subject evidently distressing him. "I hope you catch this berk. Do whatever it takes to find him." He settled back in his wing chair, as though waiting for the jail doors to clang shut on the criminal.

In the silence I sank my fingernails into the chair's velvet upholstery, scraping them against the nap to create little roads in the smooth blueness. Like the villagers' lives, I thought, staring at the uneven fabric. An event hits and ruffles everything. I smoothed out the fabric with the flat of my hand. I wondered how it would feel to sleep against such softness and had begun calculating the cost of sewing a small comforter when Graham said, "I would have thought that Pedersen would have stayed with his friends, the Halfords." He looked at me for confirmation of the name and when I nodded, he said, "Or don't they have the space for a guest?"

"Actually, he did stay with them. Oh, yes," he added as Graham's eyebrow shot upward. "After his second night here he left us. I don't know why he didn't go straight to Kris and Derek, but that's where he ended up."

"Nothing like mother-in-law come to visit?" I suggested.

"The only mother-in-law is in America, and she hasn't been over for ages."

"Fear of flying, then?"

"I have no idea, Sergeant. If you want to know anything in that vein, ask Kris. I don't know her mother very well."

"So." Graham set the teacup on the table and leaned forward slightly, his brown eyes bright with interest. I knew his mind was as alert as his body. "Pedersen checked into your B-&-B Thursday, correct? He stays Thursday night, then checks out —"

Death of an Ordinary Guy

"Saturday," Arthur said. "He had breakfast, then checked out. I think that's right.... Yes. Sorry I'm so muddled, but the murder...."

Graham said we quite understood, and that perhaps this was a bad time to talk.

"No, no. Perfectly all right. Just on edge. Pedersen stayed here the two nights, I believe. Well, Derek, Kris or Byron can tell you. Fortunately, Derek and Kris remodeled a bit a few years back. Would've been a sticky wicket trying to squeeze a guest into that cottage of theirs. But it turned out to be worth every pound I lent them. The house is quite nice. Roomy enough for several guests now. Anyway, we had the graveside dole on Friday. Pedersen presented himself to the Halfords afterwards." Arthur seemed a bit flustered sorting through the progression of days and events.

"I've heard about it," Graham said. "But I don't know particulars. Could you...."

Arthur giggled nervously. "Nothing much to it. My great-grandfather set it up. We assemble every November third in the churchyard. Derek and I are the principal performers, if you will. *A maximis ad minima*," he murmured. "We're also the last performers in the succession of this fantastic tableau. Have been since — Well, I suppose I should start at the beginning if you're to make any sense of the whole thing."

Graham assured Arthur that we would appreciate it.

"This whole thing began," Arthur explained haltingly, alternately blushing and blanching, "almost a century ago—1899, actually—when great-grandfather ran over Derek Halford's grandfather. Well, not *himself*," Arthur corrected as Graham registered bewilderment. "My great-grandfather's *carriage* ran over Derek's grandfather. Broke his leg. Damaged the carriage somewhat, too. Unfortunate."

I offered my opinion that it was very unfortunate for Derek's grandfather also.

"What? Oh, yes. Rough go for Halford. Great-grandfather had him seen to, of course. Best medical attention, and all that. But for some reason, the leg refused to set properly, and Halford limped the rest of his life. Great-grandfather, of course, felt just awful about it." Arthur shifted slightly in his chair to study a portrait of a white-haired older man. The painting hung, gilt-framed, next to an equally white-haired man who bore unmistakable family resemblance. Arthur's likeness was two frames down the line, presumably next to his father. I wondered what would happen if Arthur had no children — or the wall became filled. "He had this consuming sense of duty," Arthur continued, looking again at Graham. "The whole thing haunted him terribly, so on his death bed he provided in his will for Halford. The family was to get £300 annually, payable on the date of great-grandfather's death. It was to run for three generations." Arthur bent forward and lowered his voice, the parentheses almost visible. "I suppose great-grandfather figured the remembrance of Halford's accident would be passed down through successive generations. Vivid enough, certainly, for a father to relate to his son, never mind village gossip helping it along."

"And the son," Graham ventured, "is the present dole recipient, Derek Halford?"

Arthur nodded. "That's why this dole is so unique. Most run on to perpetuity. Ours will die out with Derek."

"Interesting," Graham murmured, resettling into his chair. "So what happens? You hand Derek Halford his money and you all go celebrate in the pub?"

"Nothing quite so normal. No. We gather in the church yard, Derek recites a verse great-grandfather wrote — A foolish bit of scrap, but according to the will it has to be said."

"And it is...." Graham prompted.

Arthur looked at the carpet, as though pleading it should open up and receive him. He breathed deeply, then said, "First the crutch to heal the bone, then the purse will me atone. As the bone and mind set, so must do the man. Sire to son this passes on. Son to son will see it gone till the last of three my charity will span." He looked at Graham, as though waiting for judgment. When Graham merely smiled, Arthur said, "Derek holds up a pair of crutches over great-grandfather's grave — a symbolic gesture, you understand. Merely a stage prop. Though it's oddly prophetic because Derek *did* need crutches for a while. Years ago. Still limps. The vicar then hands me a small brown leather pouch with the dole in it. I hand it to Derek. Then we all troop down to the bonfire area and Derek throws the crutches on the woodpile, ready for the bonfire lighting on Guy Fawkes night. Silly, isn't it? There's all the bother about getting the money from the bank, driving to Buxton or Chesterfield or somewhere to buy a pair of crutches, digging out the leather pouch.... Silly. Whole thing only takes five minutes, but we have to perform."

I said I thought it quite a nice, civilized ceremony. "Refreshing to hear someone has enough moral fiber to stand accountable for his actions."

Death of an Ordinary Guy

Arthur silently consulted great-grandfather's portrait again before replying, "Anyway, Friday we had come down to the bonfire for the last bit, and when it was all over, Pedersen pops up in front of Kris and announces he just happens to be alive and here. I must say," Arthur said, recrossing his legs and looking rather upset, "he chose a bloody awful way of doing it, but there you are. Kris fainted from the shock of seeing him. Well, she *would*, wouldn't she, after believing he had died years ago? Anyway, Pedersen went home with them, I understand, though he returned here to sleep. Then he checked out Saturday and spent the rest of his time with them. What an unpleasant way for a holiday to end."

"Bad way all around," I agreed. "Mrs. Halford enjoys their friend's stay, then winds up being present at his death, as it were. Very unpleasant."

Graham said, "Have you any thoughts why Pedersen should be murdered?"

"*Who's* murdered?" Though decidedly slurred, the statement was understandable, and drew our attention to the newcomer in the doorway. Propped up like a limp sack of potatoes from the bonfire, Uncle Gilbert, as he was begrudgingly known to and called by Arthur, slumped against the door jamb. One hand was wrapped around the edge of the door, the other hand wrapped around a glass. He uttered his question again, this time to the door.

Obviously embarrassed and annoyed, Arthur rose quickly. Glancing at us, he mumbled an introduction. "My uncle, Gilbert Catchpool. He's visiting for a few days."

As if editorializing, the wood-cased clock on the mantle belched the half-hour, then settled into silence.

Uncle Gilbert lifted the glass to his lips and, as though using the glass as odd binoculars or telescope, staggered into the room, barely consuming more whiskey than he spilled. He paused at the couch as Arthur rushed up to him.

Remarkable. No family resemblance at all, I thought, scanning the paintings on the wall. The Catchpools were, without exception, angular, bony people. Brunets and redheads. There were several noses that seemed to pass themselves from father to son, and an occasional cleft chin, but the verification of Catchpool splendor and lineage rested in the eyes. Dress altered with the generations, but those large, close-set eyes linked them. And Gilbert Catchpool either echoed the maternal line or was a throwback to an earlier branch, I thought, for everything about him was round. But his round hazel eyes had taken on a definite red hue, as had the circular spot of pale skin at the back of his head. An emphatic stomach rolled down his substantial frame, threatening to overflow the confines of his belt.

Gilbert's free hand dug into the back of the sofa for support, giving him the appearance of someone leaning into a cyclone. He swayed slightly, alternately blinking and pulling back his eyelids, trying to focus his eyes and mind. Like a bully clamoring for a fight, he demanded our names and to know who had been murdered.

"Steve Pedersen's been murdered," Graham replied evenly from his chair.

Gilbert squinted at his nephew, as though the name and circumstances nagged at him from somewhere within his mental morass. "Do we know him? Did I murder him?"

Chapter 5

BLUSHING INSTANTLY, ARTHUR laughed nervously, glanced at Graham — who wasn't laughing — and said, "No."

To which question, I wondered.

Turning to Graham, Arthur said, "He gets like this, I'm afraid. You mustn't pay him any mind."

I stood up and made a move toward them. "Anything I can do, Mr. Catchpool? Help you get him situated?"

"What?" For a second, Arthur blinked as wildly as his uncle, then pulled a smile from some inner resource. "Thanks all the same. I'm accustomed to this, unfortunately. He's used to me. It might confuse him if you —"

Nothing would confuse that old sot, I thought. What you really want to say is that it'd be embarrassing for me, being a woman, to help tuck Uncle into bed.

"Thanks anyway, Sergeant."

I nodded, reclaiming my chair, and scratched Gilbert's name in my notebook.

"Was your uncle at the bonfire tonight?" Graham's question, ridiculously simple, halted the Catchpools' progress across the room.

Arthur turned slightly toward Graham, his hands on his uncle's shoulders, his mouth open. Gilbert stood facing the door, continuing his mumbled questions while Arthur related Gilbert's activities. "I don't know *precisely* when he was there. I *know* he was there *before* the fire was lit. I saw him. So did most of the people, I suppose."

"His question about killing Pedersen —"

Arthur laughed again, and quickly said it was just his uncle's drunken talk. "He — It's just piffle. He's just talking nonsense.

He's had too much to drink. He didn't even know Pedersen. Uncle's staying with me in this section of the house. I doubt if he even knows who my B-and-B guests are."

"Will he remember anything about his evening when he wakes tomorrow?" I knew Graham wasn't going to bet anything on Arthur's answer or Gilbert's recollections.

"Should do," Arthur replied, glancing at Gilbert. "Depends. Some nights he drinks more heavily. You know how it is. He might wake up and remember everything about tonight."

Graham thanked Arthur, asked again if we could help, then watched the two leave the room. He turned to me, eager to play 'what if.' "In the mood to risk a small wager, Taylor?"

"I've grown quite fond of my wages, actually."

"Could just be the idle talk of a drunk..."

"Could be just an act, too. Wanted to know what we've deduced so far, so he thinks he'll barge in here, maybe crash in a chair and eavesdrop. Only his upstanding nephew —"

"He could've eavesdropped at the door outside the room," Graham reminded me.

"Couldn't hear as well. We weren't exactly shouting."

"No doubt about his having a pull or two. He didn't get that complexion by standing in moonlight."

"Arthur was in an awful hurry to get Uncle G away from us. Embarrassment, fear, or change of plans?"

"There you've got me, TC."

Quarter of an hour later, Arthur was back in his chair, decidedly less flushed and breathing normally, and replying to Graham's original question about motive for Steve Pedersen's death.

"Haven't a clue. As I said, he didn't know anyone except the Halfords. Byron can get you a list of the guests' names, if that would be helpful. Perhaps he had made an enemy among them. I don't know. People do get a bit uptight and on others' nerves when they travel. I probably sound like I'm talking through my hat, but something could have happened like that, I suppose."

"We can suppose almost anything at this stage," I mumbled as Graham stood up.

Arthur quickly got to his feet. He seemed relieved the grilling was over. "Would you like a work area? I've got any number of rooms that might be suitable. I *suppose* you'll be needing something like that." His voice trailed off now that he was in the unfamiliar territory of police procedure.

Death of an Ordinary Guy

As I moved toward the door, Graham thanked Arthur for the offer. "I'll see if we can get a room at the pub. That usually suits our purpose. We really prefer to work away from anyone's home. Not that we don't appreciate the gesture, but we come and go at such unorthodox hours."

"Yes. Less disturbance all the way around. Well, if there's anything more I can do...." He saw us to the door and waved enthusiastically as we got into our car.

"What'd I say about eavesdropping?" I asked. "Probably offered the room so that Uncle G could keep an eye and ear on us. So he'll know how to change his story when we question him."

"Anyone ever tell you you've got a detective's mind?"

"First I've heard it mentioned, sir."

"Well, don't go by my word. I'm only a detective-chief inspector. Well. Not the most helpful interview we've ever had."

Graham's fingers lay loosely across the steering wheel, drumming out a steady beat. I wondered if he was mentally playing a favorite piece of music. I glanced out the window, not wanting him to know I was curious about him. A faint fragment of a tune escaped his lips. So, he likes Handel. And the keyboards in Handel's day were the organ and harpsichord. Was that the instrument office gossip had joked about? I recalled catching the tail-end of one joke as I entered the canteen one day — Graham in a white wig and asking about key information and if anyone could handle it — but at the time I had assumed it was linked to his ministerial career. Graham at the harpsichord was a different image than I would have conjured up. I glanced at my own left hand, surreptitiously pressing the fingertips against my thumb. The calluses from years of guitar playing were hard, unlike the softer touch needed for stroking harpsichord keys. I knew that much from my brother. I looked at Graham's hands again. Did harpsichord and guitar sound good in duet? I was about to ask Graham when he said, "It's not too awfully late, Taylor. Just gone 10:00. What say you sharpen your detecting skills and tackle the Halfords. Think of it as Sleuthing A levels."

In spite of my determination to prove myself capable of the assignment, I panicked. I knew that if I made a hash of it, I'd be renewing my acquaintance with the constables.

I thanked God for the countryside's darkness, for Graham couldn't see my face flush. He was busy expounding. "The female link is vital at times, Taylor. Women convey sympathy, understanding, patience. He'll probably pour out his heart to you.

I'll see about that incident room. Hope I didn't just turn down the only available space in the village."

"We can always plead stupidity. Wouldn't surprise a lot of people."

Derek Halford showed no surprise when I identified myself at his door. He's probably expecting the entire village to be interrogated, I thought as he hurriedly straightened the afghan covering an upholstered chair.

The room carried the house's exterior harmony inside. A wall of bookshelves, flowered draperies, and pastel colors blended to soothe the senses. A large picture window looked out into the Halfords' back garden. I began with my usual apology at having to bother Derek at his hour and under these circumstances, and then inquired about their emotional state.

He crossed the room quickly and turned off the telly, cutting off the actor in mid-sentence. He blushed, as though normal human activity was a sin under the circumstances. Mumbling that he had needed to distract his mind from the murder, he picked up the evening's newspaper and his jacket from a chair and motioned me to it. He dumped the items on the floor near the couch, seemingly oblivious to the small table near my chair, and sat down.

"I suppose we're all right. Though it was a hell of a shock." He glanced at the staircase leading to the upper floor.

I nodded, wondering how many more times in this investigation I'd hear that phrase.

"I was dumfounded, of course, when Steve came up to us at the dole. We'd just about got over that — the shock and joy of his resurrection, I guess you could call it — only to find him like this at the bonfire. Kris —" He shook his head.

I could only guess at his wife's emotions. I had been there, and it had jolted me. Kris had known him. What she — and Ramona — were suffering was more than grief on hearing of a death. I stared at the used mugs on the table and wondered how Derek had forced Kris to drink anything. She had been hysterical at the bonfire before Karol had given her a sedative.

"She was in a pretty dreadful way," Derek continued, as though reading my mind, "but those tablets from your police surgeon.... Thank her again for me, won't you? It's been a hell of an evening, and tomorrow's not going to be much better. Kris will be awake, and the memory...."

Death of an Ordinary Guy

I nodded, knowing the grief that would settle on Kris. The sudden loss of anyone is hard to accept. Still harder to accept is murder. There's no easy way to deal with grief.

I was wondering what Graham would say about it when Derek added, "We'd only known Friday evening that Steve was in the village. We invited him over after the dole." He paused to see if I knew about the dole. When I asked no question, Derek continued. "We got on so well together, and there was thirty years to catch up on.... Well, it was natural that we asked him to bed down here."

"And that was...." I nudged, waiting to see if I would get the same answer as Arthur's.

"Saturday. We had two days with him." Derek's voice broke, and he reached for his handkerchief.

I let him wipe his eyes before I said, "I understand Pedersen was both your and Mrs. Halford's friend. You had no idea he was coming, then?"

Derek shook his head. He muttered that they had known Steve when they had all attended university in America, but they had no idea he had scheduled a visit to the U.K. "We thought he had been killed in Viet Nam during America's war. That's what makes this so devilishly hard. We just got him back, you see, and lost him again."

Only this time there's no mistaking his death. "And you hadn't seen him or heard from him for — what did you say? — thirty years? A very long time. I can well imagine your shock at his reappearance."

"Just walked up to Kris after the crutch bit of the dole. Just said hello, as if we'd just parted yesterday. Hell of a hello," Derek said bitterly. "What if Kris had keeled over from a stroke?"

"Why had he keep quiet all these years? Lose your address?"

"He explained that," Derek said, stuffing the handkerchief into his jeans pocket before grabbing a photograph from the end table and handing it to me. "That's Steve." He stopped suddenly, as though he was aware that I'd seen Steve Sunday afternoon. "Anyway, he said that he'd landed in Nha Trang in 1965 and was captured three months later. Years later we discovered he'd been listed MIA, but at the time he thought of himself a POW. He got back to America in 1973."

"That's an eight year-hole in his life."

"When he returned he was hospitalized."

"Wounded?"

"Mentally. Spiritually. Emotionally. However you want to put it. Aphasia."

"It's hard losing your memory."

"Harder getting it back," Derek corrected sharply. "Easier in some ways than having your leg hacked off, so you won't be confined to crutches or stared at the rest of your life as a handicapped —" He stared at the photo, then at me. I was watching him as he rubbed his left thigh, and remembered his slight limp as I had followed him from the door to the sofa. "I'm sorry. Sometimes this damned leg hurts like hell."

"Recent injury?"

"Car accident. Not as life shattering as many." He tapped the top of the photo's frame. "Steve explained his aphasia. It was brought on by the trauma he'd gone through being POW. Though he appeared to be perfectly normal, he said he couldn't remember much about that segment of his life. He said while in hospital he was like a mental vegetable — couldn't speak or write. Like living inside a glass bottle, not making sense of anything."

"So that's why he couldn't contact you. What took him so long to locate you? Had he just been released when he arrived here?"

Derek shook his head. "He was released in '76 with a clean bill of health, a hearty handshake and a sincere 'good luck' from the physician."

"Even a criminal gets a new suit when he's released," I said, then regretted my joke. We could hear the clock ticking in the silence. Wood flooring in the hall popped as the house cooled. In reply, the fridge gurgled. Derek seemed oblivious to the sounds, having lived long with the nightly symphony. His eyes fastened again on the photo. "So when he returned home..." I suggested, feeling the tension in the room.

"He learned from his mother that Kris and I had married the previous year. He smiled bravely, counted his blessings, took a deep breath, got married and started a business."

"Takes guts. What did he go into?"

"Local, commercial deliveries. He owned a couple small jets and a fleet of vans. The smaller shipments from small companies who wanted stuff flown overnight. In Missouri, Illinois. Oh, I don't know where all."

"And Steve came over here without his wife?"

"Gail? Steve told us she had died a few years ago."

Death of an Ordinary Guy

I slowly relinquished my study of the photo and looked at Derek. "He brought this with him, I take it?" When Derek nodded, I handed it back. "It's a nice remembrance."

"We don't need to remember right now. I'm near to shoving it into a drawer. I don't think Kris —" His face reddened as he sought an explanation. I wanted to tell him I understood, that it's sometimes more painful seeing the loved one daily and not being able to be with him. I let my elementary counseling slip by the wayside as Derek said, "In a month, perhaps, when all this is less painful, I'll dig it out, but now...." He shrugged and practically slammed the photograph onto the cushion beside him. "At university we were inseparable — a Three Musketeers thing. Hard to say for a while who Kris loved more, but I finally decided it." He took a deep breath. "There was a fourth to our party. Kris' roommate. I was rather keen on her at the time. Thought of marriage."

"And did you marry her?" I said, attempting to get relationships correct.

"No. My infatuation wore off, though I thought I was headed that way. We were a constant couple — an 'item,' as they say. Anyway, Kris naturally teamed up with Steve, didn't she? They were planning to wed, but then he leaves for Viet Nam and is captured."

"Rough."

"She waited ten years for him, but never had a hopeful word. This is so hard on her, so *unfair*. After all this time." His voice hardened as though all the injustice of the past and this terrible evening had conspired to wreck his wife's life. "This dreadful affair coming on the shock and delight of recovering Steve. And of course, there was the perpetual row earlier tonight over the dole money. That's expected, but it's none the less stressful on the both of us."

"Perpetual row?" I asked, my mind racing back to Arthur's scant information. "I was lead to believe it was a short little ceremony. Shouldn't warrant stress or a row, I wouldn't think."

"Well," Derek sighed, "you don't know much about Talbot Tanner. He makes a Sunday school picnic an ordeal."

I mentioned that I had heard a bit about Talbot.

Derek shook his head. "What you haven't heard is how hot and bothered he gets each year."

"From the dole?"

"That and his renewed surge of patriotism, I guess you could call it. He walks around the village, cornering people, reminding them that we owe our present way of life to Guy Fawkes and the ensuing events. That we should put more emphasis on thanking our forebears than on the festivities. Says we've turned it into a carnival."

I wondered why he didn't dress in some type of costume for the event, like a doom-declaring prophet in long robes. I was just about to ask when Derek said, "But he's totally daft about the dole. He claims he, *not* me, is the rightful recipient of the Catchpool dole. He'll yammer to anyone who gives him the least concerned look. Bit of a pain, but there you are. Something we endure. Unfortunately, if I want the dole, I have to keep a stiff upper and ignore Talbot's rantings. Gets downright ugly at times."

"Must be worth a fair amount," I said, "for you to put up with an annual whine like that. I think I'd be rather tempted to chuck it. Can't stand conflict in my life."

"Well, I think it's worth the few days of grief. £300 may not be a king's ransom, but it's very nice."

"Very nice," I agreed. "So Talbot thinks —"

"The man's a *lunatic!*" Derek snapped. "He side-stepped normality years ago. Claims some type of relation to me, but of course he's never bothered to bring forth any evidence of this fantastic yarn. Instead, he continues to gripe and complain that it should be *him* up there every November third. Honestly, the man wants mental care, the way he talks on about it. I don't mind so much for myself, but I'm concerned about my wife. She hates any kind of emotional outburst in public, and that's Talbot's forte. The man's totally round the twist."

"Not violent, is he?" I said, wondering about this new development. Villages aren't as peaceful and cozy as they appear. They hold all the human emotions harbored in cities.

Derek snorted and leaned forward, his hands on his knees. "Who's to say, if Talbot gets angry enough? We've seen the occasional temper tantrum, heard the string of vulgarities, but usually Talbot's an easy-going chap."

"Except around November third," I reiterated, wondering if a full moon made it worse.

"He seems to have it in for me personally. *And* for Arthur, though Arthur's as innocent of the dole's regulations as I am. We just show up, do our bit, and I collect the money. Yet Talbot looks at the *both* of us like it's some huge conspiracy against him. I tell you, Sergeant, I wouldn't be surprised if some Mischief Night or Guy Fawkes Night I fall into a trap that Talbot's laid for me. He's a queer one."

Death of an Ordinary Guy

Maybe *Pedersen* wandered into some trap Talbot laid for you. I made the suggestion to Derek. "Since he was a close friend of yours, would Pedersen have felt some kind of honor or duty to protect you from Talbot? I assume he was in the village long enough to hear Talbot's usual ravings."

Derek considered the question for a few moments. "I suppose so, though I don't recall Steve overhearing the row. Most recent one was after dinner tonight. Outside the pub."

I nodded. No wonder I hadn't heard it. "Do you know where Steve was?"

"Can't recall off-hand. You see, Steve's war experience scarred him. He has —" He colored. "He *had* a real fear of sudden noises. They evidently pushed him back into that war mode. *We* never saw that, but I don't doubt his word. Why lie about it?"

"Why, indeed. Plenty of men have that affliction, unfortunately. It's a common occurrence of war. I believe it used to be known as 'shell shock' in the first world war."

"Must be awful, knowing anytime you could lose your equilibrium."

"I've heard it takes some of them like that—a fragrance, a scene, a sudden noise — just waiting to trigger a memory and reaction that's become ingrained."

"Steve and Talbot were going to check the torch and lanterns for fireworks." Derek's voice had been rising during his explanation. He paused, looking at me, not saying that the obvious place — the bonfire—was under my jurisdiction and shouldn't have needed checking. He continued in a lower voice. "If Talbot started that stupidity about the dole, and Steve heard some fireworks exploding from kid's play…" Derek glanced at me, as though we were thinking the same thing.

"I know," I said, standing up. "I wonder if Pedersen could have snapped, and Talbot had to kill him in self-defense."

Chapter 6

"Is that how you made sergeant grade?"

The question, though a joke, came from the sober lips of my friend, Margo Lynch. She was a constable, ten years my junior, and was learning from me as I was from Graham. Though I was certain Margo was getting shortchanged.

We sat on a bench outside the pub, half-filled glasses in our hands, expounding on the world in general and the murder case in particular. I shivered as I took a drink.

"Never mind the smart remarks," I said. "What happened to your rose-colored glasses? You're supposed to wear them when you look at me."

"I take them off at sunset."

"Great. I thought you wanted the benefit of my experience."

"I do, Bren! I marvel at you."

"You'll make sergeant quicker than I did, Margo, if you avoid my bruises and mimic my laurels."

"Will I know which is which?"

I glared at her, in no mood for humor. The hours were slipping away and I still had to talk with Graham before I slipped into my nightdress. I finished my beer before saying, "Why am I laying my theories before you, then?"

"So you'll hear them, find holes in them, and fix them before you recite them to Graham, who will, we both know, fillet you like a piece of cod and roast you for good measure if they aren't reasonable."

She stared at me, her dark eyes serious in the light from the pub's windows. She had a good figure and a good mind, and really had no need of my tutelage, but it was great to have a friend. Confiding in Margo was like writing in my diary.

Death of an Ordinary Guy

I sagged against the wall of the pub, a medieval relic that seemed to lean eastward. Probably to catch the first warmth of the rising sun, I thought, wondering how much colder the courtyard would be in January with the flagstones buried in snow and the roof gutters fringed in ice. The quadrant smelled of mold and dead leaves but I envisioned it in Christmas, perhaps enlivened with pine boughs and twittering birds. Now it was merely dark and dead, as though waiting for the winter solstice to resurrect it. I scuffed the toe of my shoe along the bench's base, barely aware of the cold stone at my back, deaf to the sounds around me as I mentally rehearsed my explanation. Margo drained her glass, set it down with a thud, and said, "Couple of the tourists want to leave. Can't say as I blame them. They're scared. Think it's some kind of strange village ritual, picking out a foreigner to sacrifice, or something. The Vic put a fast stop to that little idea. Probably scared them into staying."

I turned my head toward her, suddenly back in the present at the sound of Graham's nickname. 'The Vicar' or 'The Vic' had been born out of ridicule, as mine had been, but had now faded into our jargon, its reason and origin nearly forgotten. In spite of my unease at my upcoming chat with Graham, I smiled.

"I can believe that. He *is* forceful."

"Wonder what he was like in the pulpit?" Margo asked it like most women ask 'Wonder what he's like in bed?'

"Probably hasn't changed much. He's still Graham. Personalities don't change, even with a new set of clothes."

"He wasn't defrocked or anything, was he?"

I listened to a dog bark and watched a light go off in a house down the lane before I shrugged my shoulders.

"Well," Margo said, stretching, "it's a mess-up, this whole thing. Talked to the proprietors of the gift shop?"

I set down my glass and leaned forward, more out of habit than in trying to see across the car park. When I shook my head, Margo said, "They're nervous business will fall off."

"Because there's been a murder?"

"Sure. What do you want, Brenna — a dozen? Even one's bad for sales when the tourists get cold feet and leave. And I can't see a gift shop having that large of a profit margin. They have to sell a hell of a lot of post cards to pay the electric." She shook her head and stretched again. "Bad all around. So, what do you have for Graham?"

I told her, practicing the confident tone I didn't feel.

"And then, Talbot tried to cover up the killing by stringing up the body? Seems like a lot of trouble. Why not just plead self-defense?"

Margo's skeptical look didn't perturb me. I was glad to have something on which to work, a challenge on which to focus my brain. "So you think it's Talbot? When did he do it? And if not him, the killer?"

"Time schedule's pretty tight," I agreed. That was like saying Pedersen had stopped breathing. "We've got the Guy sitting out in plain sight from Thursday till time of the bonfire on Sunday. It sits there through the dole Friday, when villagers and tourists walked by it; it sits there through Mischief Night Saturday. Granted, the effigy isn't under lock and key or constant surveillance, but there are enough people strolling around the area during those three days to make a substitution difficult, in my opinion."

"But one was made," Margo gently reminded me.

"So, what do *you* think?" I said, challenging her.

"I think Graham will be happier with your success rate of zero firecrackers at the bonfire."

"Great."

"You can bring that up if things get a trifle warm. Remind him that the moronic element might have thought up something stupendous in the humor line, only your presence and vigilance —"

"Your words are a comfort in this time of trial, Margo."

" — prevented a greater mishap. After all, the moronic element never let an opportunity for a good joke pass. Especially if it causes alarm or disgust. You were saying?"

I stood up, smiled at her, and said, "To quote our Fearless Leader, '*Ora pro nobis.*' We who are about to die —"

"Don't give me that crap, Bren. You're too worried about what he'll think. Just go in and talk to him. He's not God, for Christ's sake!"

"Of *course* I'm worried! He's my superior officer!"

"You've been placed with him to support him and learn. So make a few mistakes and *learn!*"

She stood up, slung my bag over my shoulder, and pushed me toward the pub door before wandering off.

Graham and I sat in my room at The Broken Loaf, mulling over the possibilities already forming in this case. A combination art show/Christmas bazaar had eliminated the village hall's eligibility as a rural branch of the Derbyshire Constabulary. Exuberant displays

Death of an Ordinary Guy

from the area's talent smothered every interior inch of that hall. So, a space in the pub served as incident room. I was content. I got fed more regularly this way. And with any luck, we'd be out of here by the end of the week, and the publican could reclaim his territory. Murder inconveniences everyone.

I had relaxed considerably once we had started talking, but still struggled with unease at having Graham in my room. We observed the proprieties — he sitting in the chair and I on the bed. And even though we kept to the neutral subject of the murder, I couldn't help but wonder if I'd welcome or resist his advance if he chose to do so. I glanced at the bed, recalling times when I had wished for a romantic interlude with him, but now that he was so close, in such an intimate surrounding, I found my chest and throat tightening. I sought solace and protection in the murder. Angling the notebook toward the light, I said, "We've got the Guy Fawkes pre-bonfire festivities starting a bit before 7:00." I squinted at my handwriting. "Vamsyhe, Vanoyke..."

"Van Dyke?" Graham suggested. He never could bear any type of suffering. "Ramona Van Dyke?"

"That's the lady," I admitted, remembering she was Arthur's intended. "Thank you, sir. Usually I don't make such a mess of my notes."

Graham replied that normally my notes were the pride of B Division, and asked me to continue.

"As I said, the program starts a bit before 7:00. With Ramona Van Dyke doing the singing honors. Most of the village had gathered by that time. I think it's probably the same each year. Not much else to do at these village bonfires. We always told jokes at ours. Or worked up some sort of comedy routine. Not on the level of Eric and Ernie, of course, but it kept us entertained while the potatoes were roasting. Bonfires don't seem to be as good these days. Why is that, you reckon?"

"And Ramona's contribution to the evening's joy was over by...."

"7:10, or close enough to it. There was a rather embarrassing dance routine by a local girl —"

"Embarrassing? She fall into the bonfire?"

"No, sir. Suggestive attire." I remembered the scanty bikini. "More in keeping with August temps and the beach, I would have thought —"

Graham smiled, then asked me to go on. "Executed to music played on a portable cassette player. Following that, we have a poem read — written for the occasion, and a violin solo. That amounted to another five minutes or so. Then the vicar says his bit to the assembled mass, lights the torch, and hands it to Ramona."

"Who promptly reveals the effigy is in actuality a corpse, and faints."

"Easy and succinct."

"Wonder if everyone was where he or she should've been?"

"Meaning?"

"Meaning," Graham replied, "if this village drama is as old as everyone says, and it varies hardly a millimeter from year to year, and all of a sudden Talbot, say, wasn't next to the vicar to hand him the wooden torch —"

"I see what you mean. Kind of obvious, though. Wouldn't the murderer have more brains than that? Wouldn't he have thought that out and been where he should be?"

"Speaking of being in places, why don't you question Talbot, if he hasn't sought the refuge of eiderdown? And while you're breaking down his flimsy alibi, I'll see what our illustrious landlord has to offer."

"If it's beer," I said on my way out the door, "save me a pint."

TALBOT'S COTTAGE LAY in a thick pocket of the woods, at the end of an earthen track driven clean of grass through hundreds of trips. Tree branches and leaves littered the edges of the lane, barely allowing room for my passage. Once I had to stop mid-point, the engine of my Corsa idling in the quiet as I got out to drag a large tree limb from the road. There was a rustling in the undergrowth to my left, as though I had disturbed some animal's midnight foraging. But no eyes glared at me, no angry retort came. I heaved the limb into the woods, the leaves — crisp from frost —crunching under my feet. I wiped my hands on my trousers and glanced at the sky. Stars seemed to balance high overhead on bare branches, as tips of fairy wands. I got back into the car and turned up the heat, the scene seeming suddenly desolate. Minutes later, Talbot's house emerged from the gloom.

It was a gray stone cottage, half submerged in Virginia Creeper and half hidden by elderly oaks. A kind of witch's house from Hansel and Gretel, with a large wood pile leaning against the southern side to protect it from winter's blast. A curl of smoke seeped from the stone chimney that sat in the middle of the slate roof. Two windows, like giant eyes, stared into the woods from either side of the front door. Below the windows was the remnant of a small flower garden, its wizened stalks and leaves barely visible above the forest's castoffs. The door glistened bright yellow in the glare from the car's headlights. A beacon on dark nights?

I found Talbot, as expected, there. He looked to be in his sixties, and was as thin and gray as the weathered wood he handled for the annual bonfire. Nearly indiscernible dark eyes wedged between a craggy forehead and hollow, sunken cheeks in a long, gaunt face, producing a living likeness to a Grimm fairy tale goblin. He stood in the open doorway, a patch of moonlight catching his facial hollows. He cautiously eyed me before begrudgingly letting me inside. I took the indicated chair, aware that he still leaned against the closed door. He remained there for a minute or more, as though deciding something. When he finally crossed the warped wooden floor, his shoes clattered into the stillness.

Talbot came to a halt in front of a well-used chair, the back of his legs touching the knobby-textured fabric. His eyes fixed on me while his hand sought one of the chair's upholstered arms. Lowering himself into the lifeless cushion, he asked what I wanted, adding, "Kind of late to be rousin' folks, isn't it?"

"Sorry if I roused you, but the light was on, and you opened the door readily enough." I surveyed the room, not so much as to prove Talbot had indeed been awake, but as to set the man in his environment and help me understand him.

It was a small room, as all rooms probably were in the small house, serving as a catch-all lounge and dining room. A plate complete with dinner remnants sat on the end table, a heap of newspapers served as a place mat. Well-worn, solid furniture ringed the room's perimeter like American football linebackers. A low wattage light bulb from a floor lamp did its best to illuminate a corner. I could just discern a few books in the over-all gloom. The electric fire was on the lowest setting — barely glowing or disseminating warmth. I rubbed my arms.

Talbot noted the dinner plate, my observation, and the work clothes he still wore. Useless to pretend, Matey, I thought.

"Just talkin' general, Sergeant. Now, what's it you want? Suppose it's about the killin'. Can't think of why else you'd be here."

I felt more than saw Talbot's eyes drilling into mine. Like a vulture tracking a wounded mouse. I watched a brief flash of light skate across the dark hollow that hid Talbot's eyes. Unnerving. I pushed the discomforting comparison from my mind, and settled in for the routine of gathering information. Perhaps he'll thaw a bit once we're underway. "I understand you built the bonfire."

Talbot fidgeted and shifted his emaciated body, his veined hands gripping the arms of the chair. Moments passed before Talbot's head nodded, the thin gray hair slipping in and out of the lamplight like gossamer strands of a spider web undulating in a faint breeze.

"Near twelve, fifteen feet high, it was. I take my time with the buildin' of it." He settled back into his chair, his eyes buried even deeper in the shadow cast by the chair's high back. "Unlike most villages where they just let anyone throw on whatever. I take my time to see it's all set up proper. That means a solid base of the bigger stuff, then taperin' up to the smaller. Mind you, Sergeant, I can't always hold strictly to that 'cause sometimes people bring me old furniture or wood or whatever after I've got beyond the base. But I do with what I have, and do the best with what I have. And so far, there's been no complaints. Or mishaps from crumblin' wood."

"And probably won't ever be. You seem to have an excellent grasp of engineering. How many years have you been constructing the fires?"

"Since 1964," he said, screwing his eyes shut as though it was an effort to remember. It hadn't taken him long. I suspected Talbot knew readily enough; he just wanted to emphasize his importance in village life. Took it over from Mr. Brains when he left for study in America. The Polytech weren't good enough for him, it seems."

"Would that be Derek Halford?" I ignored the man's opinion.

"Same one and all. He takes himself off, spends four years in university and comes home with his degree. He built the fires before he left — *threw* them together would be the word. Didn't build them careful like I do."

"So he left in 1964 for his university courses, and you have been in charge of the bonfires ever since."

"You got it, Ma'am. Sergeant. Miss," he added, wondering about my title.

"He ever give you a hand with it? I just thought he'd miss the fun of it. They don't do this sort of thing in America, I understand." I thought of my discussion with Graham earlier that evening about necktie parties, and sighed.

"Indeed they don't. It's purely British, and I can't see it ever crossin' the Atlantic like so many other things of ours has done. And no, Derek's never had a hand with the fires since he come back. Don't know if he's too high and mighty for manual labor now that he

Death of an Ordinary Guy

has that university degree, or what. Seems it was fine for me as a thirty-one-year-old man with no education to do, but too common for a twenty-one-year-old educated one. And he's never so much as hinted he'd like to reclaim the buildin' duty, neither."

"Maybe he has other commitments," I suggested. "Marriage seems to take a lot of some men's time."

"Don't get started with that line of thinkin'," Talbot insisted, pounding his forefinger against his thigh. "Derek didn't bring back a wife when he returned from his studies abroad. Wasn't even courtin' Kris. Don't know why he wasn't interested in the Guy Fawkes celebration. Never asked him. Anyway, I'm happy with things as they are. I enjoy buildin' the fire — and I *don't want to give it up to Mr. Educated Halford!*"

I hoped the blast hadn't damaged my hearing. "You all seem to have your talents in this village, Mr. Tanner. You have the fire to see to; Ramona — "

"Ramona gets the dummy together," Talbot said, a grin slowly consuming his weathered face. "I'd say it suits her fine, seein' as how she's courtn' the village's biggest dummy!" He rolled back his head and laughed in one loud bark. "Her official part in all this is to ask at the homes hereabouts for any castoffs. But as she and Mr. Lord-of-it-All Catchpool are keepin' steady company and will probably be married in not too many months, that could change. Arthur's a bit jealous when it comes to Ramona. Can't see him lettin' her run about, beggin' for clothes from the men. But she's a willful lady. Rather enjoys it, and if I know Ramona, she'll keep on with it even when she's enthroned as Lady of the Manor."

"So it's more than keeping up an image, then."

"Can't see her givin' up that little bit of work when she gets that ring on her finger. There's nothin' to most of this work, is there? What's so damned hard about findin' old clothes?" Talbot's eyes stared out from the darkness beneath his eyebrows, daring me to contradict him.

"Nice that you have so devoted and caring a group in your village. Many places aren't so lucky."

Talbot sniffed, wiping the back of his hand across his nose. "Like I said, it's not all that bad. There's nothin' to most of it. It's a one-shot thing."

"Not like being church choir master, for instance?"

Talbot nodded and said no one would ever corner him into doing something on-going. "I've got my own things to worry about.

But it's not too much to build that fire. Only takes a few hours from my year. I just content myself with that and no more. The Big Three can bask in the limelight all they want. I like my dark corner."

"The Big Three...." I looked up from my notebook and searched Talbot's face for meaning. "Would that be Arthur Catchpool, Derek Halford, and Ramona Van Dyke?"

"Missed the brass ring, Sergeant," Talbot whooped, slapping his knee. "Though Ramona will be movin' into that slot soon enough after she's married. Can't be too soon for her, either, from what I hear. She'll certainly welcome Arthur's bank account. About run through her own, she has. Wants the Lord of the Manor to increase his B-and-B portion to take in more payin' guests and shore up Arthur's bank account, but I can't see him destroyin' any more of his precious rooms to give over to tourists."

I said it would be a shame, from what I had seen of the Manor, for Arthur to destroy more rooms to harbor en suite facilities.

"Got too many antiques, anyway. What would he do with 'em if he does over a dozen more rooms, say? Sure wouldn't pile them on the fire come next November! But as to the Big Three, now, no. Number Three of the Trio is Byron MacKinnon, Arthur's indispensable secretary and convenient shoulder to Mrs. Halford, should she ever need it. And many's the time she does. That's the high and mighty trinity that rule this village, our lives, and allow us to do what they like. That's the bloody group." Talbot's voice strengthened and soared to a dangerous high. "They've all cheated me out of my legal money, sought to cheat me out of *everything* due me ever since I told 'em who I really am. Ever since —" Talbot stood up and glared down at me. "But maybe you need to go now. Gettin' late. I need to get to bed. Should think you'd want to, too. You've been here all day. I saw you, down at the green. Nosin' about the fire. What for?"

I explained my original assignment, stressing that I had merely been there to prevent fireworks trouble. Talbot grunted. "Pure waste of time. We never had trouble with fireworks in this village. We don't go in for that. Hangin' out for *that!* Waste of money."

I wasn't certain if he meant the fireworks were a waste of money or if my assignment was. The ill-lit room did nothing to help me penetrate the darkness thrown over the man's face and read the emotions in his eyes.

Talbot bent forward, his hand supporting his thin frame as it dug deeper into the chair. I heard the metal spring contracting beneath the compressed chair fabric. "Government's into everybody's lives. Don't let a man breathe, go about his own business. What we need is a democratic government, individual rights, where a man ain't beholdin' to no lord —"

Somewhere in the darkness outside, a dog howled. A long, slow, frustrating howl. Give me another minute, Dog, and I'll join you. "That's probably true," I said, glancing at Talbot's meager dinner remains, "but I need to establish a timetable for the day's events. It'd be very useful to our investigation if you could tell me when you recall —"

"If you want to do something *useful,* you look into this business of the dole. You look into the dealings of Arthur and Derek, and you find the money they've cheated me out of. You do that, Miss Detective-Sergeant," Talbot exploded, his knee pushing the heavy chair forward a bit. "You nose about a bit into that Terrible Trio's goings-on and you come back here and tell me I'm wrong!"

I mumbled something memorized and noncommittal, and left Talbot in the middle of his lounge. The lone, howling dog had induced others to join him and, to me, the yelping chorus sounded peaceful compared to Talbot's raving.

Chapter 7

I LEFT TALBOT'S bewitched woods and the cacophonous canine chorus, wondering if the man had assimilated to the setting, or vice versa. The night had settled in with a calmness that probably belied the agitation and grief gripping Ramona and the Halfords. Flashing past the blackness of the churchyard, I could see the brilliant openness of the village green where constabulary duties were still being done. A moment later I parked, last in a long line of police cars, at The Broken Loaf. Graham's red Insight hugged the curb opposite the front door — coincidence or right of rank?

Rectangles of light spilled from the pub's windows, washing the courtyard flagstones in liquid gold. An apt hue, I thought, recalling the region had been the haunt of highwaymen and criminals. The pub had catered both to them and honest clientele, storing chests of gold, silver plate and jewelry in its dim cellar. The medieval building still suggested its past through creaking floors and blackened timber, yet the publican had been careful to hide its modern appointments from the tourist eye. I paused in the courtyard, imagining a midnight call to the shutters, a clatter of horse hooves on stone. Now the air held only the familiar chatter of police business.

I turned to a noise behind me. Nothing moved in the darkness. At the farthest end of the yard, where the light did not reach, wrought iron tables and chairs huddled in great piles, waiting for winter storage. A fountain, waterless and looming like a nightmarish creature, squatted in the near corner. I caught an odor of wet stone as I passed.

The pub's main door had been braced open to allow for the myriad trips needed to start an investigation. I hesitated in the entrance, listening to a snatch of laughter from the public bar, unsure of where the lads were establishing the incident room. A SOCO

Death of an Ordinary Guy

nearly collided with me as he pushed open the door to the private bar. Blinking at me, he jerked his head and said, "In there. He's in a lovely mood," and hurried outside. Thanking him, I followed the sound of Graham's voice and walked inside.

Computers, boxes of paper and general office equipment sat on chairs, folding tables, stools and any available floor space. It looked more like a schoolroom at the end of term than it did a pub. I nearly tripped over a fax machine as I walked up to Graham.

Evan Greene, publican of The Broken Loaf, threw a damp towel onto a convenient table and joined us. The sweat on Evan's dark hair and beard told of his help in converting the room from bar to temporary police headquarters. He pushed up the sleeves of his black pullover and stood, hands on his hips, surveying the room.

The bar smelled of fried food and hot bread. In not too many more hours, it would also stink of smoked cigarettes and sweat — an unfortunate occupational hazard, for it was a nice room. A painting executed in somber oils by a heavy-handed artist consumed the wall above the fire's hearth, while at its feet an accent of yellow and gold mums complimented a brass cauldron. A telly — its screen nearly the size of a car — sat diagonally in a far corner, the room's one concession to Progress, while the traditional dart board hung below a large photo of a current Mid Eastern political leader. I was sure I could ascertain small holes in the picture, editorial comments on the state of the world. Even in the current clamor of carting in equipment, I could imagine the 'thwack' of the dart as its metal tip bit into the corkboard. The corner opposite the television sported a large sign proclaiming the meeting time of a local folksinging group. They would have to meet elsewhere tomorrow night. Not a bad room, but I felt like a fox in a hole. The dark curtains that smothered the pub's windows would have to be opened, for I already yearned for sunlight in this somber environment.

"Hard workers, your lads are," Evan said, watching Fordyce place a paper shredder on the settle near the fireplace. I wondered how much more weight it could hold, for it seemed already to be groaning under the accumulating equipment. "Never seen a group work so quick in all my life. Or so much equipment, for that fact. Guess I'm still back in Sherlock Holmes days. If I'd thought about it, I'd probably know you use all this. But a person tends to think of detective work as looking about on the ground with a magnifying lens, doesn't he? Must be a hard go keeping up with all this computer technology."

"It's not all that hard," Graham said, catching my eye. "We're given a choice each year of enrolling in open university for three months or sitting alongside some grade schooler for a week."

"That so? Well, the things kids know these days...." He shook his head in amazement as Graham smiled at me.

"I'd like to thank you for the use of your bar, Mr. Greene. It's more help than you can imagine, having a large, secluded place in which to work. Would you mind a few questions as long as you're here?" Graham gestured toward a table. "I know it's a hell of an hour, and you're probably dead-tired, but I'd like to get as much information as I can before we all collapse into our beds. Memories are so much fresher right after the event." He smiled broadly, evoking a genuine vivacity for life and his job, and a personal charm that very few people could resist. I had heard the talk; he had developed this quality while a minister. Just because he had switched careers was no reason to abandon the talent. Graham motioned again to the table, let Evan precede him, and waited until I had joined them before asking about the evening's schedule.

"I didn't have anything much to do with it," Evan replied, wiping his palms on his jeans. "Least ways, it's Arthur's show."

"Oh? I wouldn't have thought so. You supply the potatoes and the beer. Big enough contribution, I'd say — both in expense and time."

"I *like* doing it. And I can afford it, so it's no hardship."

"There are a lot of people who can afford to do things," Graham remarked, "yet choose *not* to. It's nice you help out. The villagers must be very grateful to you."

Evan mumbled that he supposed they were, but that wasn't why he did it. "I'm not out to prove anything, or to put myself above anyone. I like giving. Wouldn't be a proper bonfire night if we didn't have our potatoes and parkin, would it?"

I trembled at the thought of the oatmeal and treacle gingerbread. You either liked it or —

"Do you know when you delivered the potatoes to the fire area?" Graham asked.

"I must've unloaded the potatoes at quarter past six. Near enough."

"You didn't notice anything unusual about the fire area or the effigy, I take it."

Death of an Ordinary Guy

"Not likely to, am I? I'm not a bloody mind reader. We weren't expecting anything unusual, and I didn't see anything like that. It'd just gone sunset an hour before, so it was good and black out there."

"I'm surprised you didn't have an electric torch with you."

"Couldn't very well handle that plus the potatoes, could I?"

I explained to Graham that Evan had left the truck lights on.

"Parked near the circle since I came from the pub. So I was pointing away from it, toward the woods." His words rolled over my thanks. "I always park like that, parallel to the fire circle. I've been livin' here all my life, so I know the layout. Just need a hint of light so I don't step on some little feller crawlin' around!" He laughed, then said he hadn't seen anything he oughtn't to have seen.

Graham's low voice, smooth as silk, asked if anyone else had been at the green then.

"Kris Halford," Evan said, watching my pen skate across the notebook page. "She came over to watch the till here in the pub for a minute or two, and I trotted off with the potatoes."

"Came over from..."

"Her house. She lives just a minute or so away. That was after evening tea. Too early to put them on the fire to bake. Needed to be coals, didn't it? It'd just gone six, I think, when Kris got to the pub."

"Anyone else?"

"Few tourists. We get tourists all year long, but especially for the dole and bonfire nights. There are some in the village who count them more a nuisance, but I like having them here. Not only for the money they bring in, but 'cause I like folks."

"I bet you've encountered some interesting persons," Graham said. "Many unusual tales of where they've been, where they're going to. I should think you'd find that fascinating."

Evan nodded. "Lots of folks tell me their hopes for the future, where they'd like to live, what they'd like to do. We aren't so much different as the media tries to make us out to be. We all want a good job, nice nest egg to retire on.... But I will be glad when this bloody dole is over with and the village can return to normal, if you understand me. We've enough to worry us with the bonfire and mischief nights. Though it was comfortin' to see you, Sergeant, on duty, like. Ta."

I nodded while Graham replied that sometimes it did seem that the stars were at odds with human endeavors.

"But, about this other, now," Evan replied slowly, his anxiety vanishing as he warmed to his subject. He didn't add anything new to my timetable, but it was nice to hear his opinion of his fellow villagers.

"Right," Graham said suddenly, standing up. "I don't mean to keep you up till opening time tomorrow. I have the schedule now, thanks."

"Uh, Mr. Graham?" Evan strode up to Graham and inflated his chest as though he was trying to make himself taller. "Mr. Graham," he repeated when Graham nodded. "You find this lunatic. If you need my help, I'll gladly throw in with your lads. But you find him. Killing some bloke who only wanted to see his friends again, have a bit of fun on his holiday.... Gives the village a bad name, doesn't it? You catch him, Mr. Graham"

Graham, looking rather like a surprised fox, quickly said we would, and moved toward the door. "You're free to go to bed, if you wish, Mr. Greene. Only I'd be obliged if you'd leave the pub unlocked. I don't know if my men have quite finished setting up yet."

"Not to worry, Mr. Graham. I'll give you a key, and you can turn the latch when you're all ready. How's that?"

Graham thanked the publican and followed him to his office, leaving me to close my notebook.

IT WAS IN the dark of the night that it happened. Well, I don't know what the clock hands had designated, exactly, but that's how the mystery books phrase it. It was certainly dark, and it was certainly scary. Even now, long after it's over.

I had planned to rise at an early hour, full of determination to shine like the sun. On opening my eyes, I saw it.

A straw dummy — smaller but similar to the one Ramona had made for the bonfire — was hanging from the room's ceiling light fixture. My first thought was that I had effigies on the brain, that even in this short time I was overworked. But the sensation lasted a mere second as, fascinated and repulsed, I watched the revolving form. Morning sunlight, barely tinted yellow and above the eastern horizon, threw one side of the straw figure into relief while the opposite side hid in darkness. It rotated from a scrap of rope tied to the light fixture, the other end looped around the Guy's neck. The knot seemed drawn tighter than need be, for the fabric denoting its neck and face were gathered firmly, producing folds that hid the painted smile. Stray strands of straw littered my comforter and marked a trail to the door. As the mind sometimes does when

Death of an Ordinary Guy

presented with sudden shock or horror or grief, I wondered if I could discover the culprit by following the straw wisps down the hall.

But what pushed it past absurdity was the fact that my jacket was draped over the Guy's shoulders and my police badge was pinned to its shirt. Which also meant that someone had riffled my bag. I looked around the room for other signs of indignities. All was as I had left it on retiring to bed. After sitting there in fright for some time, my blanket pulled up under my chin, my eyes fixed on the slowly revolving dummy, I eased out of bed.

Normally I would have worn my jacket as a robe, but as it was on the Guy, I had no desire to touch it. Call it fright, call it instinct at preserving evidence, call it repugnance. I donned my shirt over my nightdress as I ran up the stairs.

"It's not so much the effigy, Margo," I said, my teeth still chattering as I sat cross-legged on her bed. "It's the idea that someone —" I couldn't say it.

"I know," Margo said, finishing my sentence and idea. "Someone got into your room. Also not so comforting to know he wanted you to understand he wished it was *you* hanging there."

"He could have killed me," I whispered, staring at the ceiling. It seemed barren without a Guy suspended there.

"Sure. But he didn't. He wanted to scare you. To warn you."

"Warn me about what? What've I done?"

"Nothing. Everything. You're a cop. Part of the investigation team that's poking around in everyone's lives. You might have heard something, seen something. Something supposedly insignificant, but immensely important. The Guy proves that. Anyway, this jerk means business, that's for dead cert. If it were just some kid out for a lark, he might just have put a goldfish in your bathroom glass. But hanging the Guy, now..." Margo forced me to take another sip of tea before asking, "Who've you been talking to? That might get us somewhere."

"Not many people so far. Evan —"

"He's got duplicate keys. He could let himself in and out easily enough. Who else?"

"Talbot."

"Old crazy brain? He's nutty enough to, but how would he get in?"

"Graham asked Evan to leave the pub unlocked last night so our chaps could finish setting up. Talbot could have sneaked in, I guess."

"Kind of thought that warms you all over and makes you glad you're part of the human race," Margo said, pushing the teacup up to my lips. "Ok. We've got a maniac hiding in the closet till you're all tucked in. Next."

"Graham and I talked to Arthur at the hall."

"The refined ones fool you. You think they've got too much class or breeding to kill, and they're the ones who turn out to be Jack the Ripper."

"He knew where we were staying," I confessed, hating to think a gentleman would resort to such a base act.

"That's in his favor."

"His *favor?*"

"As a suspect. I'm learning, too, you know. This will help my career immensely if I can solve this. Now. Anyone else you talk to?"

"Almost everyone *before* the murder — at the bonfire. Uncle Gilbert — oh! He wandered into the room as Graham and I were talking to Arthur. But he was awfully drunk."

"He's gotta sober up sometime. Could it be an act?"

"Talked to Derek, too. You don't suppose whoever this is got me confused with someone else, do you?"

"Who? You don't exactly look like Graham."

"I wasn't thinking of Graham," I said slowly, concentrating on her hair.

"Well, our hair's not the same color, if that's your suggestion. You're auburn; I'm brunette, or haven't you noticed."

"Perhaps my intruder didn't. It was dark."

"Well," Margo said, taking my empty cup from me, "it's unnerving but at least you're alive. Remember that. You going to tell Graham?"

"No."

"Wouldn't he consider that withholding evidence or something equally rank-busting? After all, this could be a clue to —"

"Pedersen?"

"Two Guys, two…uh, victims…."

She refrained from calling us 'corpses,' at least. I dug my fingers into the back of my stiff neck. Only one day into the case and it was already getting complicated. "You're probably right, Margo. But we can't spare the manpower for this. We're thin on the ground already." I wanted to add that that was the reason I'd been assigned Guy Fawkes duty, but thought discretion the better part of friendship. "Besides, it's pretty trivial when compared with Pedersen's murder."

Death of an Ordinary Guy

Margo stared at me. I knew she was thinking the same thing I was: it wouldn't be so trivial if I ended up like Pedersen.

Her voice picked up speed and raised in pitch as she said, "But if it's linked to Pedersen's case and it happens to contain the one lead element we need and you don't inform Graham and he finds out about it later and learns you're the culprit that had the clue —"

I wrinkled up my nose. Of course Margo was right, and I could have been busted back to constable. Or suspended, I guess. But this was personal. Two years ago during a case I'd asked for help with a personal matter. All that it had gained me was the scorn of my A.C. and the enmity of my colleagues. While outright name-calling had not been their forte, those who cared enough smirked or dropped hints as to my courage — personal as well as professional. Some even dropped classifieds. No, Margo. Once burnt.... I had learned, painful as it had been, not to air personal difficulties. Anyway, I was also reluctant to admit to a certain Male Presence that I ran with my tail between my legs at the first sign of trouble. So let Graham demote me, I thought, exhaling loudly. At least I'll go out fighting. Instead, I said, "No, Margo. And none of the lads' help, either."

"Too bad," she said, sighing heavily. "Here we've got a fingerprint chap who could dust for latents, a video team, a team of specialists who could set up a cunning little trap, and we can't use any of them. What a waste."

I nodded. "I guess Tolliver would notice if his camera went missing."

"From what you know about rigging up a trip wire and camera, with your luck you'd be broadcasting your nightly disrobing instead of filming the loony."

"Wouldn't be so bad if I looked like you," I said. In spite of the situation, we both laughed.

Margo got up and hugged me. "Please, Bren, don't worry. There are two of us, and we're gonna keep our eyes open. We're both trained, intelligent cops."

"Should strike terror in any perpetrator's heart."

"I can stand watch tonight, if you'd like."

I shook my head, thanking her, and mustered up a smile. "Feminine wiles have worked wonders before, haven't they?"

"Don't worry, Bren, we'll catch him."

I ran back to my bedroom, not at all sure I had Margo's confidence.

Chapter 8

DESPITE THE SHAKY start to my day, I dressed and forced the incident to the back of my mind. Margo was right — with two of us thinking about this, we could capture the joker without Graham's help.

The sun hinted at a clear day. A point in my favor, as Margo would say. After tangling with the Guy in my room, I didn't relish atmospheric fog as aid to the prankster. Taking a deep breath of cold air, I stepped outside.

A few sparrows were chirping, searching out their breakfast on the stone patio of the pub. I threw them my crumbled granola bar and watched from the doorway. One sparrow, larger than many in his group, grabbed a raisin and flew off quickly with his prize. I zipped my jacket, shoved my hands into my trousers pockets, and wandered down the road, curious to see the village. The chill of the previous night still hung in the air.

I had been walking for several minutes down a road of sleepy houses half surrounded by the deepness of woods and lingering darkness. Aromas of fried eggs and sausages, brewing coffee and hot toast drifted into the day. I was thinking of returning to the pub for my own breakfast when I heard voices. Pausing at the front drive of an ivy-smothered house, I noticed the residential name plate. Ivy Dell. Could also be named Buried Verdant, I thought, noting that the exterior needed a good hair cut. Or In the Thicket Things. I nearly laughed out loud, wishing Graham could hear my joke. Whatever its name, I knew it belonged to Ramona Van Dyke. Another early bird, I thought, wandering down the driveway to the back garden where the voices came from. May as well ask her about her part in last evening's fun, since we're both here....

Death of an Ordinary Guy

Talbot Tanner was straightening up from a wood-bundling chore to drag his shirtsleeve beneath his nose. He eyed the debris, then Ramona, a shapely blonde in her early 40s. She seemed to have recovered from last evening's shock, though her arm would take a bit longer to recover. It was held in a makeshift sling. The lilac print clashed with her teal blouse.

"Should've had this garden taken care of long ago, afore it got to be such a mess," Talbot was saying. The large rectangle of near-wild garden had indeed lost itself in the woods behind it. Vines, bracken and stinging nettles inched into cultivated territory. Ramona gazed at the invasive plants, shook her head, and apologized for being too busy to garden properly.

Muttering that people had their own priorities in life, Talbot tackled the litter contributed by the trees. He gestured impatiently toward the huge bundles of branches and sawn up limbs dotting the garden like trussed haystacks.

It was then that he saw me. Making some unpleasant remark about losing his breakfast, he showed me his backside as he stooped down to tie up some sticks. Ramona greeted me and asked who I was.

"A bleedin' copper," Talbot grunted before I could reply. "So ring up your solicitor, Ramona, afore she lifts you over her shoulder and throws you in jail!" His laugh disturbed the birds in the trees, for they flew up, chattering in annoyance and lighted in a grassy patch across the road.

When I finally explained the reason for my early call, Ramona asked if I could wait a minute while Talbot finished up. Just as happy to get Talbot out of my life, I told them to go ahead.

Talbot grumbled under his breath and applied himself to his chore. "If you call me afore you get so many castoffs," he said to Ramona, "it wouldn't take me so long."

We watched him make a final knot in the rope corralling a particularly large group of limbs. Ramona apologized. "Sneaked up on me, Talbot. I didn't realize how many branches were down until I started weeding the other day. Then, too, that rainstorm brought more down. Too bad we couldn't get to this before the fire. Could've used it last night."

"Might've if I'd had 'em earlier," he said, bending over a bundle. He opened his pocketknife, visually inspected the blade as though he could discern its sharpness, and began sawing through the rope. The rope gave a satisfying 'thwack' as the knife sliced through the remaining fibers. Talbot snapped the knife closed, dropped it into his trouser pocket, and slowly coiled up the unused portion of rope. "Have to come back for it all," he muttered, draping the rope over his shoulder. "When you said branches, I didn't know how much you were talkin' about. There's branches and then there's branches." He watched Ramona dig into her pocket and extract several pound coins. In greedy anticipation, his tongue leisurely ran across the roughened skin of his lips. He took the money without a word of thanks. "I'll be back for the lot. Can't say when, exactly. Have to see what I'm doin' the rest of the week." The coins clinked as he shoved them into his pocket. "Anything else you want? That tree'll need some lookin' after soon. Top her off so she won't have all those long branches beggin' to come down." Pointing toward a patriarchal oak, he added, "I can do it pretty cheap. Halfords want some work in their back garden, too. I can do it all on the same day. Save myself a trip and give you a good price, since I'll be right across the road."

"I'll have to see, Talbot," Ramona said, glancing from her watch to me. "I really have to get busy. I've a load of items to get through before I go to work. My half day," she explained.

Talbot tugged at the knot of the bundle, making certain of its strength. "Don't want no accidents," he said, tucking the rope's end into the tangle of branches. He ignored me as he passed, coiling the leftover rope around his left shoulder.

"I've had enough accidents, Lord knows," Ramona said, lifting her slinged arm as though she was a bird with a broken wing.

"Not painful, is it?"

"Not the way I'm doped up. God, first this, then that damned corpse. If I'm not taking codeine for the arm, I'm downing Mogadon for the jitters. Makes me sleep."

I thought she wouldn't be on the Mogadon for long. "Recent injury?"

"Sunday afternoon. Byron stumbled into me. I sprained my wrist in the fall."

I gave my condolences and asked if she had a few minutes for some questions about last night.

While Talbot leisurely backed his truck out of the driveway, I followed Ramona into her house. Could either of them have rigged up the effigy in my room? Talbot certainly could — he was already on my list of Prime Suspects. But Ramona was doubtful, with her sprained wrist. Still, people have moved grand pianos single-

Death of an Ordinary Guy

handedly in a time of stress. I put her on my list of Doubtfuls. Ten minutes later I was walking back to The Broken Loaf, having learned about her Sunday.

Even though my stomach prompted me to return to the pub for breakfast, I decided to question the Conways, owners of the village gift shop. It was next to the pub, but more importantly, I was determined to impress Graham with my initiative.

The shop looked more like a cube of scarlet Virginia Creeper and green ivy than a man-made building, for its gray limestone was disappearing beneath the foliage. Rhododendrons, decades old, fanned out from the foundation, while crimson chrysanthemums dotted the greenery at its base. A gray flagstone path, free of autumn's dregs, meandered from the road to the red door proclaiming 'Conway Gifts' overhead in white, Old English lettering.

Eleanor Conway was sweeping the front step as I walked up, calling out 'good morning' in a puff of white vapor. The sun had just touched the shop's tile roof, transforming the dew into sequins. A bullfinch perched on the gutter, alternately eyeing us and singing into the cool air. A nearby bush seemed to respond in kind. Love song or territorial war? The bird seemed undisturbed by either prospect, for he leisurely drank from the water in the bottom of the gutter.

I stopped, trying to discern if it was a female or male bullfinch. In the dim light I couldn't make out the coloring clearly, which would announce its sex to me. But I did know that quiet warble. What incredible luck! Bullfinch sightings were rare, a red alert posted for them. Their breeding pairs were down to 190,000 last time I had checked. Unlike the sparrows I'd seen earlier, which were upwards of seven million pairs. A pity, for this bird was beautiful, with its red chest and belly, black wings and cap, and white rump. Yet this bullfinch sat on a gift shop roof as though it was the most ordinary occurrence in the world.

Reluctantly I tore myself away from the bird, hoping I would sight it later.

Eleanor seemed less interested in the bird than in knowing who was at her shop so early. I introduced myself and explained my errand. She nodded, setting her broom aside, and opened the door.

It was a classic gift shop, offering the tourist the typical knitted apparel, jewelry, post cards, and mugs, and a small offering of emergency tourist essentials. It also offered the less typical pottery, watercolor paintings and embroidered place mats. A balance of predictable, indispensable and refinement.

"We haven't been here all that long," Eleanor said, exchanging her nylon jacket for a wool blazer. She was soft, pink and round like an overripe peach, her cheeks flushed from her custodial duty. We sat in the back room — a catchall for received shipments, returned items and pre-posted packages, and a dispensary for quick meals — the electric kettle heating water for our tea, a tabby cat rubbing against my legs. Eleanor paused at a small mirror hung near the sink and pulled a leaf from her hair. It was brassy orange, the product of a bad dye job. Satisfied with her primping, she cleared a space on the wooden table top, spread a checkered tablecloth on it, and pulled out two mugs proclaiming 'Buxton.' It threw me momentarily. I had quite expected something more general, such as Derbyshire. But Upper Kingsleigh people can be tourists, too. I eyed the biscuit tin on top of the small fridge, wishing she would offer them. Unfortunately, her mind wasn't on our stomachs.

"Mason's never here this early," she said when I complimented her on the shop. "I open up. Mason joins me around 9:00, then I take a break for an hour or so, depending on customer flow, then rejoin him when business usually picks up. We both work together until late afternoon, when I leave to get tea on. He locks up at 7:00."

"Nice arrangement."

"It is. Especially since he's an evening person and I'm an early riser."

"And it's just the two of you working?"

"We have help in the summer, when tourist trade is high. Doesn't pay to keep on a third person during off season."

"And you've been here...."

"Four years. We bought it when Mason was made redundant."

I accepted the hot tea, added two lumps of sugar, and said, "Oh? I'm sorry. It must have been hard for you. What was he in?"

"Accounting. All of a sudden they had too many accountants. They hadn't hired on new staff in *years*, but all of a sudden they had too many. No loss of clients, no deduction in business. Just too many accountants. Mason was the first out the door."

There was an awkward silence in which I could hear the electric kettle murmuring and the cat purring. I counted the seconds between purrs and the drip of water from the spigot. The droplets echoed as they hit the water in the saucepan. Domestic, safe sounds that comforted in an upsetting world. "We thought it was a safe venture," Eleanor said, as though reading my thoughts. "It's hard when you reach a certain age, Sergeant. Employers look at you, see

Death of an Ordinary Guy

only the wrinkles and age spots and broadening waistline. And then calculate the years till you'll retire. You, as a person with a brain, vanish. They forget you're just as capable as you were yesterday and the day before. Yet suddenly you're too stupid to do *anything*."

I felt self-conscious about my relative youth, and tried to hide my unblemished hands. After I made some inane remark about knowing a lot of people who were in that situation, Eleanor said, "We're not so old. We're just 59, for God's sake!"

I refrained from saying that was my parents' ages. There are times when consoling banter is out of place.

"Mason's a hard worker. He tried for months to get another job but after repeatedly hearing the same excuses, well.... We thought we'd go into business for ourselves. Might as well kill yourself working for your own benefit instead of for some ungrateful boss, as Mason puts it."

I agreed silently, though not putting Graham into that boss category. I'd had my fill of ungrateful bosses before I had joined the Force.

She sighed, staring into her tea. "It's worked out well so far."

Until this murder, I thought. And with the threat of Upper Kingsleigh losing more tourists, what would that do to their trade? And future?

"We were late to the bonfire," she said after I had asked her about Sunday evening. "We arrived just as the vicar was finishing his speech and handing over the torch. We try to miss the opening shenanigans — not because we don't like them or are anti-social. It's just that Mason gets uncomfortable around Talbot."

He's not the only one. I asked her if Mason always felt like that.

"No. Just around dole and bonfire time, when Talbot grouses about the dole money."

"He does tend to rabbit on about the subject, from what I understand."

"It's not so much the continuous complaining. It's Talbot's talk about the war. It reminds Mason of his own tough times. He was an orphan."

An emphatic ringing of the shop's overhead doorbell pulled Eleanor from her chair. "Now, who on earth...."

"Want me to see?" I asked.

"I'll scream if I need you. Early for a burglar, don't you think?"

I agreed, and stood up, looking around for a weapon. Two sets of not-so-stealthy footsteps approached and moments later Byron

MacKinnon and Mason Conway walked into the back room. Mason reminded me of the numbers he used to work with: round as a zero from hours of sitting at his books.

Eleanor looked relieved, and I sat down, releasing the paring knife. Greetings were exchanged. The men sat at the table while Eleanor refilled the kettle and turned it on.

"Didn't mean to interrupt," Byron said, giving me the once-over, "but Eleanor usually has the shop open by now and I normally stop by for a cuppa. If this is a bad time — if this is official business —"

"Not at all," I said, thinking I could check Byron and Mason off my interview list at the same time. "Tea and a chat — nice way to start the day." I bent over to pet the cat. He was entwining himself around my legs, as though he expected me to feed him. I hoped I would be able to make it to the door when I had to leave.

"You're starting the day early, dear." Eleanor gave her husband the mug with a chip on the rim.

"I was up—couldn't sleep well after…. I—I saw Byron coming, and thought I'd join him in a cuppa." His stare was subtler than Byron's. I decided to let them think this was purely social.

Byron took it as such, for in the brief silence he said, "Do you know what Arthur's done? Thanks, El." Byron accepted the cup of tea and poured a great deal of cream into it. He stirred it, clinking the spoon against the cup's sides. The clinking increased in volume and tempo as he explained. "Another couple wanted to leave this morning. Halfway into their stay and they want to leave. Of course, he rang up Graham to see if it was all right. Which it was! Just 'Keep me informed of your whereabouts' and off they went. Sorry." His clinking slowed briefly as he looked at me, only to return to tempo and volume when he continued. "They must be low on the suspect list if he lets them go."

I looked at the three of them, again mentally calculating if they could have rigged up the Guy, or even why they would have done it.

"Poor Arthur," Eleanor said. "Is he dispirited by all this?"

"He's not exactly dancing through daisies, but to look at him, he's fine. It wasn't his fault Pedersen was murdered."

"I better see Kris when I close up." She scribbled 'Kris' on the flap of a convenient cardboard box.

"You can go during the day if it's slow," Mason said. "Won't interfere with tea when Derek gets home."

Death of an Ordinary Guy

"The thing is," Byron said, the spoon falling onto the saucer. "The bloody thing is that Arthur refunded their money!" He waited for his statement to impact the Conways.

Blinking either at the volume or at the meaning, Eleanor said, "He always was a gentleman, Byron. You can tell breeding without a coat of arms painted on everything."

"Has he ever made refunds before," I asked.

"Oh, a few people have canceled a trip and have received their money back," he said, his voice back to a more normal volume, "but that's once or twice a year. And certainly not at the rate they're wanting to leave now."

"How many guests are at the manor?"

"We had booked nearly a dozen rooms — singles and doubles."

I agreed that the reservations would bring in a sizable chunk of cash.

"You're damned right about that! And with Arthur returning everything — even after expenses —"

"Hope he won't get burnt," Mason said. A silence settled on the group, now somber. Mason got up and poured his tea into the sink, muttering it wasn't to his liking. Byron shoved his cup from him with such violence that the remaining liquid in the cup sloshed into the saucer. Eleanor thought better of pursuing the biscuit tin and said, "I'm amazed people are leaving. People are such voyeurs these days. Court telly and tell-all talk shows, things on the news I never would have imagined seeing.... I would have thought this would induce the crowds instead of reducing them."

"Maybe it will," Byron agreed, his eyes brightening. He smiled as though he could see the reservations piling up. "But right now it's a repellant. When you're too close to it, when you've been in the fray, it's frightening. Especially if you think you're the next victim."

Mason said, "There are many types of victims. We may all end up as victims before this is over. How long you people planning on being here?" He leaned forward, coming close to me, as though challenging me to answer correctly.

I told him we wouldn't leave until we had secured an arrest of the guilty party.

"And how long's that?" His breath came across the table in one quick exhale.

"Mason," Eleanor said, her hand going to his shoulder, "what kind of question is that? The sergeant —"

"The sergeant knows what kind of question it is. One from a concerned citizen. One who doesn't want the police traipsing around, scaring away tourists. What the hell's wrong with that?"

I assured the Conways it was all right and that we were working as efficiently and swiftly as possible.

"I should damn well hope so. You can't expect tourists to hang about all week until you lot get out of their way. Blocking everything they've come to see...."

"They may come later," I said. "It's just like the curious to want to see Where It Was Done."

"And take away a piece of the scene?" Byron said.

Eleanor shuddered. "Gruesome souvenirs."

"Let's hope they still want less grisly ones," Mason muttered.

I asked Byron if he thought any more tourists would leave the manor.

"I haven't a feel for it yet. Last night I wouldn't have thought this would happen, but this morning...." He shrugged and grabbed his cup. Throwing his head back, he finished his tea. "Cold," he said, grimacing. "There may be a life line in this morass. This is one of our busiest times of the year. The three-day events are getting very popular. And we do an awful lot at Christmas — mummers and the Merrie Olde England bit with feasts in the manor's dining room, carols on authentic instruments. That sort of thing."

"Byron spares no detail to make it accurate," Eleanor said, patting his hand. "The hall and room are so lovely. Ropes of holly and ivy, candles everywhere, pine logs in the open fireplaces. Gives you the thought he's lived it before."

"And the boar's head?" I said, already feeling Elizabethan.

"Complete with apple in the mouth. Well, I've got Evan's books to balance." Byron got up and stretched.

"Time for the day to start already?" Eleanor glanced at the clock. "Seems like the sergeant just had her tea."

Yes, that's all I had. Just tea. I glanced again at the biscuit tin and stood up, thanking them for the information.

Eleanor walked us to the door. "Well, I am sorry for Arthur losing some of his business, but don't worry about what hasn't happened, Byron. I was just licking my own wounds before you arrived. It's natural for Arthur to play Good Samaritan. That's his character. But Arthur's got a beautiful establishment, and the village has a lot going for it. I just hope we can weather any storm that may blow up."

Death of an Ordinary Guy

I glanced around her shop again, noting the handmade sweaters and tams, the homemade biscuits and breads, the paintings and photographs of local scenes. A lot of local talent had their hopes and money tied up in the Conway Gift Shop. If it died it would take more than Eleanor and Mason with it.

"It can't drive *everyone* away," Eleanor said, forcing cheer into her voice. "There'll be tourists."

But tourists gawking at *what*, I wondered as I extracted myself from the cat's tail and left the shop.

Chapter 9

MONDAY MORNING'S DROWSINESS was punctured by a peal of church bells announcing the nine o'clock hour and nudging the idler into activity. Graham stood in the feeble sunlight, sipping a cup of coffee. I had just returned from my talk with Eleanor and wanted my breakfast, but he grabbed my arm, explained that it was a good time to see the village — the scenes of the crime, as he put it — and so we walked.

Upper Kingsleigh was laid out along three roads that comprised the letter "H." The cottage of Talbot Tanner snuggled near the top of the eastern road, his house nearly swallowed by the woods. Faint rustlings murmured from the underbrush while a chorus of chirps squawked overhead from the obscure gloom. The world was waking. A hill rose along the left side of the road, harboring church, churchyard, and residential cottages farther south of the church. The expected duck pond and village green sprawled along the southern side of the connecting road, an assortment of shops facing its verdant calm. A few hearty ducks dotted the pond's surface, plunging into the cold, gray water only to emerge in a chorus of quacking and flapping wings. On the right-hand western road, opposite Talbot's cottage in distance and station, the manor house consumed its acreage, its turrets and limestone proclaiming everything Talbot would never have. The village pub and post office faced each other at the intersection of the shorter cross street and this long, winding road. More cottages trickled down the western road until the woods finally reclaimed the land and melted into the craggy Derbyshire dales.

Now back at the pub, we dawdled over a later-than-usual breakfast while considering the sprouting bits of facts and follies that seemed to walk hand-in-glove with this deplorable case. And, from

Death of an Ordinary Guy

the slice of life we observed from our table, we hadn't been the only late-nighters last evening. Evan had taken our breakfast orders, eyes blinking owl-like in the sharp early light. He had asked me how I had slept, and I wondered if his words held more significance than the casual polite phrase. Outdoors the pale sun joined the attack on sloth, pulling villagers and the investigating police into the new day. Can't blame anyone for his languor, I thought, swallowing the last of my tea. Late night and shock make for slumberless bedfellows.

"You up to having a visitor, Mr. Graham?" Evan Greene alternately glanced over his shoulder, then to my superior. He twisted the signet ring on his left little finger. Coupled with the continued strain of the murder, this additional role of master of ceremonies was evidently too much for this bull of a man. "Vernon Wroe," Evan replied to Graham's question, then explained Wroe was a frequent visitor to Upper Kingsleigh. "Former Army. Near as thinks he's still in WWII. Caught up in the old days, but knows his current dates and such. He's not befuddled. Likes to be called 'Colonel,'" Evan added by way of smoothing the water.

"Let's hope he's more coherent than Uncle Gilbert," I said, then groaned at the thought of having to interview the drunk.

Graham threw down his napkin, smiling at the pub owner. "Likes the village or the excitement as much as that? Have him come over, by all means." Fortifying himself with the last of his coffee, Graham watched Wroe's confident approach.

He was immaculately dressed in tan trench coat, which when unbuttoned revealed his three-piece tan suit, tan shirt and tie. Removing his hat, he sat down quickly, as though he had no time to waste. He eyed me, probably wondering who I was and if he could get rid of me. Seeing I had settled in for the duration, he addressed Graham.

"You'll forgive my early intrusion into your day, Mr. Graham," Wroe declared after declining a cup of something. An enthusiastic gray and white mustache bracketed the corners of his thin lips, stopping just short of his jawline, as though it would fall earthward if it hadn't been attached to his skin. Pale blue eyes stared from an equally pale face. No color or obvious physical feature helped define his flesh, for Wroe was completely bald. Consequently, speaking with Wroe gave the observer the strange feeling of talking to a head of cauliflower. Perhaps it was this lack of physical coloring that tainted Wroe's personality, prodding him to strive too hard to be noticed or heard. He spoke with authority, his language peppered with Tommy Atkins jargon and stories. He sat down, as poker-backed as one of his privates standing at attention.

"You've done nothing of the kind, Colonel Wroe," Graham assured the man. "I was just finishing up my breakfast. A bit late for me, but I was up till all hours last night."

Not to mention up with the sun to check out the territory, I wanted to say. Not many could match Graham for stamina.

"Same things I ran into during my stint in the Service," the colonel replied, commenting on the shared problems in the two men's jobs. "Hurry up and wait, isn't it?"

"I understand you saw action during the war."

"Was in the Eighth. In Electronic Intelligence. Stationed in Sicily for a good part of the war, though we moved about. Anywhere I was needed. I tapped into the Germans' communications, came up with some interesting bits that happened to do some good for our side. Saved a few lives."

"You must have many fascinating stories, Colonel."

"Damned right. Best years of my life, Graham. Best years. Gave me a chance to prove myself. I went in as a captain, retired as a colonel. Where else can you get such advancement? We went through hell, and that's not the over-used expression you might think. It forged us, made us strong or we died. And through all that I got to know as good a group of lads as you'd ever hope to meet."

"Adversity does that," Graham said. "War, hostage situations, accidents —"

"God, I loved the camaraderie," the Colonel continued, as though Graham had never spoken. "Loved whipping Jerries' ass, too. We showed 'em they couldn't do that sort of thing to innocent people. Me and my mates gave it to 'em, and we're still mates fifty years later."

"Not many people can claim such long-lasting friendships," I said, venturing to respond even though Graham had been mowed down. Wroe looked at me, blinking as though he had just seen me. Smiling, he started to reach for my hand, apparently thought better of it, and laid his hand in his lap. "Exactly, Miss," he said, his voice now barely above a whisper. "You speak wise beyond your years, which — if I may say something personal and not meaning to be offensive — can't be many. Yes, Miss. Chums for life, many of us. Counted Talbot's dad as one of my mates till he died. Where else but in war can you develop and maintain that quality of friendship?" He turned back to Graham and examined him as though he were looking for something wrong with Graham's suit.

Probably wants to put him on report, I thought as Graham smiled contentedly back at the veteran. Or ask about his two years' National Service. If Graham doesn't maneuver this back to the dullness of a murder investigation, we'll be chatting about Super-Pro receivers and ground waves by teatime.

"I don't mean to hurry you along, Colonel," Graham said as though sensing my thoughts, "but I assume you didn't drop by just to chat me up. May I help you with something?"

"It's about that damned business at the fire last night," Wroe snapped. He leaned forward, jabbing a gnarled finger at the rumpled napkin lazily trailing across Graham's plate.

"Know something about that, sir?"

"Damned right I know something about it. I know a damned sight more than lot of folks would credit. I may be slow in getting around, but I still have eyes, ears and a brain."

Graham said that he would be glad to know what the Colonel had seen that everyone else had missed.

"It's my duty, Chief Inspector. I'm glad to help the police. Wish more people felt this way. Country'd be a lot better if more people felt this way. As it is, it's become every man for himself, and to hell with the other bloke. But I still believe in doing my duty. Was reared that way." His chest swelled slightly as he drew in a breath and seemed to hold it.

"I appreciate your loyalty, Colonel. Would you mind —"

"What? Oh, certainly. Last night, Inspector, at approximately 1630 hours, I observed Gilbert Catchpool loitering by the oak — that tree commandeered for hoisting the effigy."

"I see. And was Mr. Catchpool—how shall I put it— cognizant of his surroundings? Did he seem to know what he was doing, what was going on around him?"

"If you mean, Inspector, was Gilbert Catchpool in his usual addled, soused state, I cannot report that with any accuracy. I didn't get close enough to smell his breath, thank God. But he was at the tree, near the rope. I am aware of Gilbert Catchpools' 'state,' Mr. Graham. I am not unknown in the village, and he and I have met here many times previously."

"Was Gilbert actually doing anything to the rope, or fussing about with the Guy? Did he look as though he were trying to hide something, however nonchalantly he might have loitered?"

Colonel Wroe inflated his chest again, threw back his thin shoulders, and replied rather too loudly, "I am too much of a gentleman, Inspector, to reply to that impudent remark. I came here to offer my observation of Catchpool. I assumed, however unwisely, that since the deceased was found at the end of a rope and Gilbert Catchpool was at the other end of it, as it were, you might be interested. Other than that, you may investigate as you are moved. There are other ways, Inspector, of divining the enemy's movements than by infiltrating their stronghold. Use your electronic surveillance, man! Plant a bug on him. Run DNA testing. If he has the deceased's hair or flecks of skin on him, he's your man. You shouldn't have to be told."

Graham diplomatically thanked the colonel and stood up as the elder man left the table. "You certainly have a magnetic attraction for the Senior Citizen, Taylor. He would have talked your ear off, told you his life history."

"Perhaps a career as a biographer is more in my line."

"There's no denying, Taylor, you have a talent with the octogenarian age...."

I was hoping I'd get some genuine compliment instead of the banter he hurled at me, but he was concentrating on the case. "What a humble old thing he is," Graham said as we watched the man leave the room. "What's the older generation coming to, Taylor?"

"He was aching to tell us all about his valiant contribution."

"Damned if I wouldn't have asked if I had the time, in spite of my abhorrence of bravado and vanity."

"Then I commend you on your restraint," I said, smiling.

"And you need to atone for that load of rubbish you just dumped. Repent in church — it'll do you good."

THE VICAR OF St. Michael's church was evidently one of the few who had kept to his normal weekday schedule, for he waved—cheery and freshly scrubbed—when Graham called out his 'good morning' to the approaching figure. Lyle Jacoby was short, pudgy, and practically bald. More like a monk than English vicar, I thought, noting the fringe of pale hair that shone halo-like in the sun. Steady, clear eyes, devoid of the puffiness or redness that spoke of the few hours' grabbed sleep, gazed frankly back at Graham. Most likely stayed till the wee hours comforting the Halfords, I thought.

"I'd no idea when you'd be coming, Mr. Graham," Lyle sang out after Graham had introduced us. "I thought you would find me wherever I was, so I went about my usual offices. Though that could change abruptly."

"How are the Halfords?" I asked. "I assume you've been rather busy with them."

Lyle nodded slowly, supporting the unspoken acquiescence and his dejection at the same time. "They both reminded me last night of little children. So terribly sad, this tragedy. Such a shock. Reunited with their friend after thirty years of believing him dead, then to have him die like that, so quickly, so horribly —"

Only *this* time, I wanted to add, there is no wondering at Pedersen's disappearance. There would be no further reunions.

Lyle shook his head and turned to face the approximate direction of Halfords' house. Gesturing toward the west, the vicar said, "I don't know which of them is the more upset. Kris, now, I'd expect to grieve, being as how she was engaged to Mr. Pedersen. But Derek—well, not that men can't mourn. It's such a silly, self-destructive trait we've harnessed men with over the years, this machoism, being stoic and brave and keeping grief hidden. Asinine, if I am allowed any say in the matter. However," Lyle said, blushing slightly, "Derek had a healthy cry last night. Don't know who was holding up whom when I got there; they were so shocked and overcome. I let them talk. Seemed the best thing. You know — the shoulder and ear that only hear and don't judge. They needed that more than any phrases I could give them about resurrection and heaven."

"Sometimes," Graham said, his voice thickening, "sometimes it's best just to be present and listen. Nothing wrong with being a shoulder or ear for an evening." A commiserate heart and a servile ear, I thought, remembering the over-used phrase. An observant ear, I called it.

"It's therapeutic. Helps them get a grip on the tragedy," I ventured.

"I suppose so," Lyle went on, sounding uncertain it was all right. We'd been walking along the High Street, gravitating without conscious effort toward the church.

In the center of the early morning sky, the square tower of St. Michael's pushed its way out of the dimness, the rosy rays of sun tingeing the church's ancient limestone walls. The same limestone dotted the churchyard in tombstones and memorial crosses, their ages evident from weather-washed engraving or angle of leaning.

The same cross shape was reflected in the building itself, solid, unmovable, an anchor of centuries of hope. It seemed to rise from the very ground that supported its massive weight. Clumps of chrysanthemum, sage and bare-branched wintersweet decorated its foundation, mixing with cast-off pine needles and dried, fallen leaves. The dregs of summer, I thought, my fingers suddenly aching to rake up the floral debris and set the perennials and rhododendrons in order. As if on sentry duty, a flock of rooks suddenly rose from their perch on the church tower, screeching into the morning.

"You have a beautiful church, Vicar," I said, noting the sunlight capping the top of the gargoyle above the door. It was a perfect waterspout, its gapping mouth appearing ready to devour anyone wandering too close. All that stood that danger were the rooks that nested there.

"What? Oh yes, Sergeant. Thank you," Lyle said quickly, as though he had just seen the church. "Lovely pile, if I am permitted to agree without sounding boastful, though it was built before I ever arrived. Do you know religious architecture well? No? Ah, then, I must point out some of the nicer features to you. The core of the building undoubtedly is early medieval, though a magnificent rood and screen were added late in the 16th century. Probably by a wealthy merchant. Upper Kingsleigh and its environs benefited from various industries as they rose and fell. Wool trade, taking the waters, milling, coal mining. As the wealth accumulated in pockets, it slowly trickled into the church. But we've had the devil of a time of late reinstating the church to its proper condition. Honestly! What those Victorian architects destroyed when they 'restored' the altars and gallery! But we've got it put to rights now. You must see our parclose screen, Sergeant."

I murmured I would love to, but thought I'd not have the chance. Lyle bubbled on. "*Magnificent* carving! But here we are, now. Climb's getting a bit longer each morning. But that's old age for you. Now, then."

Lyle bent to remove a damp leaf from the top of his shoe before following us through the lychgate. Its squeak mingled with the shrieks of the retreating birds. It also startled me, for I snapped my head toward the sound, expecting another Guy magically dancing before my eyes.

Graham noticed my unease. His eyebrow raised in silent puzzlement before he refocused on Lyle's unceasing chatter. "It's a shame this has happened to them." Lyle lapsed into a recital of the

Death of an Ordinary Guy

couples' volunteer involvement in the village, then said, "There's time enough for a memorial if they'd like one. Or a hymn or prayer at service next week."

"I always thought *Blest Be the Dear Uniting Love* is an uplifting hymn," I said, afraid to look at Graham. I know I blushed, for I could feel my face growing warm. "Such a healing text."

"How right you are, Sergeant!" Lyle bubbled. His face beamed, now that he had a musical soul mate.

"Charles Wesley had a genius for expressing the sentiment succinctly."

"Taylor!" Graham's astonishment could no longer be contained. In spite of my resolve, I involuntarily looked at him and discovered a bemused expression on his face.

I mumbled, "But put to *Evan,* not *Tiverton.*"

Graham nearly choked. I smiled broadly, then said to Lyle, "I think Wesley's text fits the *Evan* tune better. I like the rhythm. It's comforting. Like a lullaby or cradle rocking. And in times of grief…"

"You are so astute, Sergeant, if I may say so. But I didn't know the Methodist hymnal carried the *Evan* tune."

I replied that I didn't believe it did, but that I had an American Methodist hymnal at home.

"Yes, yes," Lyle said. "They are different, aren't they?" He shook his head, as though versions of the same religion were regrettable. He had no such problem with his religion.

Graham's cough seemed to shake Lyle free of doctrine contemplation, though I took it as a comment on my religious knowledge and his surprise.

Lyle said, "But *you* are here, aren't you? You kindly asked about the Halfords, Sergeant, and I'm glad. So many people are in such a hurry these days, and forget the basics of good manners. Not that they don't care. But with jobs, after-work meetings, children's activities…." He shrugged as if to say it was providential people even had time for all that. "But that's not your case, is it? You're here because of Steve Pedersen, and you want to ask me something about it. That's right, isn't it?" He cocked his head, blinking as the sunlight fell across his face.

Reminds me of a pigeon. With those eyes, that wisp of hair looking like a ruffled, misplaced feather, and those pudgy cheeks undulating as he breathes.

75

"Unfortunately, yes," said Graham. "Wish we didn't have to, but we've got a few things we need to ask if you have several minutes."

"Can't say no, can I? Have to help the police whenever I can."

At least he's not militant about it, I thought.

"Is it secret? I mean, do we need to go inside, or would it be all right over here? So few nice autumn days left to us. I like to grab them as they come." Lyle indicated a secluded section of the churchyard and led the way when Graham agreed that area would do nicely.

Autumn had splashed its colors on the deciduous vegetation, giving the somber, solid graveyard a spark of life. Across the tombs, gold, yellow and bronze leaves, like offered coins, shone with the morning's dew. Like Derek's bag of gold, I found myself fantasizing. My shoe crushed a fallen twig of pine. I drew in a lungful of the sharp scent, wanting this time in the sun to last.

"I suppose," the vicar continued once we stopped at an ancient grave and Graham had asked his first question, "I shan't be able to forget this particular Bonfire Night, no matter how I try."

"That's the bane of any tragedy. It stays in our minds and picks at our souls for more years than we can imagine."

"One of the thousands of things that form us. Well, where do I begin? Talbot was there, as you know, Sergeant, guarding his stack of wood as much as he was adding to it."

I asked if there was trouble with pilfering.

"Hardly any trouble to speak of, Sergeant," the vicar said. "Though that was why you were here, no doubt. Keeping an eye out. Some villages have more than their share of idiots, if you'll excuse me for saying so. But honestly, if these people would only stop to think about what could so easily happen by their disregard for safety. So many small children about. Why there aren't more accidents from fireworks and such is beyond me. I pray each November fourth for a safe Bonfire Night, and so far God's blessed us. Perhaps our quota of idiots have taken residence in other villages."

I wanted to say that Upper Kingsleigh had two candidates for the role right now, but satisfied myself instead with a noncommittal safety statistic. At least it showed Graham I read the truck dished out by the Super.

"I don't know. I've given up trying to sort it out. Talbot, I'm sorry to say, was as upset this year over the graveside dole as he

Death of an Ordinary Guy

usually is. I'm afraid he latched on to poor Kris when she came up. Then he poured his anger onto Derek. Uncle Gilbert — he's Arthur's uncle, do you know? — maneuvered Talbot out of the way, and I did the same with the American couple who are staying up at the Manor. You know the Oldendorfs?"

Graham said he hadn't met them yet, but he'd probably get to them before the day was finished.

"Well," Lyle continued, leaning against a weathered tombstone, "I was thoroughly embarrassed by the entire scene. And it was a scene. Talbot carrying on like a right berk, confronting Kris and Derek as if they had anything to do with a ceremony instigated one century ago! And then the Oldendorfs had to witness Talbot's antics. I can not believe Talbot did that. If I've told him once, I've told him a thousand times that there's nothing the Halfords or Arthur can do without any proof from Talbot."

"If Talbot is so persistent about his claim, why hasn't he brought forward proof?"

"There's a small problem, Mr. Graham. You see, Talbot was born in 1934. He lived in Coventry."

Chapter 10

THE VICAR PAUSED to let the significance of the date settle into our brains. World War II — Coventry — bombing — city, pesky legal documents et al destroyed.

"Poor Talbot," Graham finally said. "His proof goes up in smoke."

"You may well say that," Lyle agreed. "I feel sorry for him — if he really is the lawful claimant, as he says.... Well, he could use the money, there's no question."

"So just why does Talbot think he's entitled?" I asked. "I understood the dole went to Derek because he's grandson to the original dole recipient. Hurt in the carriage accident. Crippled him for life."

"Men get crippled in all sorts of ways. If they're not crippled in the flesh, they're crippled in the spirit or mind. Or in the purse."

"Some," Graham added, "have the misfortune to be crippled all ways."

I nodded, knowing what Graham meant. I was still struggling from the effects of my tyrannical father. "He and Talbot aren't brothers, are they?"

Graham made a face at the thought of kinship among so unlikely a pair.

"That is doubtful, but..." Lyle looked at us, as if wondering how many village secrets to divulge. "This time of year, Talbot chatters on constantly about how he would be able to prove his claim if only Derek's dad were alive. He swears he was adopted. Yes, you may well look incredulous, Mr. Graham. Without the legal papers, presumably filed away in Coventry, anyone can venture a guess as to its validity. But he asserts the dole through rightful inheritance."

Death of an Ordinary Guy

I let out a low, slow whistle, all sorts of scenarios filling my mind.

Lyle nodded. "Now you can understand the intensity and duration of his row with Arthur and Derek."

"Do you think," I asked, "this row was serious enough for Pedersen to get involved in? Since he was a close friend of the Halfords...."

After several moments of careful consideration, Lyle denied the suggestion. His eyelids pulled back slightly at Graham's soft expletive, but he quickly explained his answer. "Talbot flares up like this for two or three days each year, then forgets all this foolishness about being included in the dole, and goes on with his routine as though he had never heard of the ceremony."

"But Pedersen, being a stranger," Graham persisted, his voice rather hard and sharp, "wouldn't know that it was normal for these brief temper displays. He'd assume it was serious, and he might interfere, thinking he was doing a noble thing by defending his friends against Talbot."

I can see it, strangely enough, the confrontation focusing in my mind, the heated exchange of words ringing in my ears. Just the sort of thing a former soldier would do, especially one who was still in the throes of bliss with rediscovering a cherished friendship.

"Perhaps," admitted the vicar reluctantly, as though not wanting to give any false hope or steer us to the wrong conclusion. "But unless Talbot can tell you, we won't know. Besides, I don't recall if Steve actually saw any confrontation. Dear me, my mind is becoming so hopeless lately. Advent, you know. There's so much to do in the next few weeks before it starts. But I do know that the Oldendorfs were spared one distasteful scene last night. Gilbert," Lyle nearly whispered, looking around the churchyard. "*Disgraceful!* The man was drunk. I won't mince words, Mr. Graham. He was drunk. Why Arthur can't keep him in check..."

Graham muttered that it was difficult to keep one's relatives or loved ones in line at times. I only knew from the gossip circulating in Buxton's police station that he was the victim of a broken engagement. Some say he never got over it.

From my vantage point slightly behind him, I gazed at Graham, envisioning his fiancée, the dates they had gone on. Had it been after a concert that she had ended their relationship? Or perhaps over an intimate dinner Graham had prepared, his flat warm and glowing from candlelight, when he had suggested they part. Had it been problems with their careers, religion or personalities that couldn't be rectified? Graham could be stubborn, I knew, but would that have prodded her into calling it all off? Had he tried to keep her in line for some reason? If so, why? Had she been a druggie that he was trying to reform and failed? Was it tough love that had ended it all? I stared at him, looking past his handsome features to the man within. Granted, I had only worked with him for a month, but police investigations — especially murder — showed personalities more quickly than in ordinary 9-to-5 settings. And I couldn't accept an obstinate Graham. He would have needed some flexibility as a minister. Or would he? I wondered, suddenly remembering that he had left the clergy under some cloud. I looked at him again, trying to paint his character in this revelation, then gave it up. I needed more information before I conjectured about his past. I shook off the mental fiancée, shoved her whining voice into the background, and concentrated on my note taking.

"I understand," Graham said, "Pedersen checked the bonfire earlier for firecrackers, and that Talbot helped him."

"Must have been before I arrived on duty," I said. "I never saw him."

Lyle said, "I can only repeat that Talbot is the person you need to interrogate on that subject. I don't know what went on between the two men — if anything went on at all. I wasn't there. I hadn't any idea until you said something. But personally, I find it rather far-fetched that Talbot would kill this American — temper tantrum or no. He didn't know the man. What motive did he have?"

That, I silently agreed, is what we're trying to ascertain.

"No," Lyle said. "Talbot may be a bit funny about this dole business, but he's not violent. I bet he's just as saddened over this man's death as are the Halfords. As are we all," he quickly amended. "Derek loved Steve Pedersen as a brother."

Good God! I thought, my mind pulling up the recent photograph Derek had shown me. Loved as a brother, no doubt, but the two men certainly looked like brothers, too.

Death of an Ordinary Guy

Chapter 11

As is usual on the 'day after,' the village's bonfire circle lay in disorder and inelegance. Graham stood at the edge of the brutal scene, visually taking in dozens of burnt, untasted potatoes among the cold, charred wood and ashes. Merry-making and death, laughter and fear shoved together, the lightness of one relinquishing its segment of the evening for the petrifying horror of the latter. His eyes turned to the table on which the glasses sat glazed in lingering frost until thawed by the emaciated sun, everything neatly corralled within the confining circle of plastic police tape.

"There's something offensive about it, Taylor," Graham said, shaking his head over the waste — time, effort, money, and human life. "The innocence of a homely scene like this dragged into a murder investigation. The scarring Lyle mentioned will break open for many of Upper Kingleigh's folk next Bonfire Night. Perhaps for me, too."

"Sir?" His declaration caught me off guard.

Before he could explain, a decidedly American couple wandered up to the fire area, their steps slowing as they approached us. Her white hair was carefully combed and she had added a touch of lipstick to her pale, wrinkled face. Her eyes were red and swollen. A night of crying?

"Morning," uttered the man, pushing his low-slung camera out of his way and blowing on his hand before offering it. He spoke with a slight southern accent. Like his wife, he was in his sixties, yet he wore a look of harder living than she did. The wool jacket he wore reeked of newness and nearly matched the cotton baseball cap angled back on his head. A tuft of hair poked out of the area above the cap's adjustable strap. The Oldendorfs. I recalled seeing them at the green Sunday with Byron and Steve. "Saw you talking with the priest a few minutes ago. Didn't want to intrude, but we guessed you're from the police. I'm Tom Oldendorf, by the way. This is my wife, Carla."

Graham shook hands, introduced us, and added that we appreciated Tom's thoughtfulness.

"Thought we might as well save you a trip. You'll want to question us, I expect."

"You knew him, then?"

I unobtrusively opened my notebook and sat on a bale of straw.

Tom managed to look embarrassed and inquisitive at the same time. "'Course we knew him. Used to be related to him. He was married to my sister."

Graham tried to recover his astonishment as gracefully as possible. "Divorce, might I ask?"

"She died." Tom's response rang through the still morning air with the sharpness of a rifle shot. After Graham's offering of sympathy, Tom said, "You can very easily say you're sorry, but it doesn't bring her back. No," he shrugged away Carla's restraining hands and phrases. "This officer might as well know. He'll find out anyway, and then how will we look if we didn't tell him?" He turned again to Graham, letting his voice match his anger. "Gail died four years ago, and it was *Steve's* fault. It *was*! I don't care what the doctor's report says. Steve's to blame."

"Accident?"

"Only accident was that damned idiot of a doctor. Gail had been sick for years, only Steve wouldn't believe her. She went to doctor after doctor, saw specialists, but Steve wouldn't believe anyone. He did, though, when she died." Tom seemed almost triumphant to prove everyone wrong.

"Tom, dear," Carla murmured, squeezing his hand. "You're getting all worked up again. Why don't you sit down over there? The officer can talk to you later if he needs to." Her smile held both sympathy and authority. Nodding, Tom stumbled off to the nearest bale of straw and sagged onto it. Carla watched him pull out a straw before she addressed Graham.

"Please excuse him, Inspector. He's still angry over his sister's death. They were very close."

"He was distrustful of the attending physician, I take it."

"Yes. Gail had been a hypochondriac practically from childhood. She had been plied with placebos to calm her fears and the family's nerves."

"Does take its toll," I agreed.

Death of an Ordinary Guy

"Yes. When she disclosed that the doctors had found stomach cancer.... Well, Steve said he felt worse than she ever did. Of course, if any of us had expected anything was really wrong with her...."

"Who's to know when the cry of 'wolf' is real?" Graham supplied.

Carla smiled weakly. "Anyway, it's the same story, unfortunately, as many others. Tom tries to forgive, but it's hard. Aside from blaming Steve, I think he secretly blames himself. He thinks he should have known something was really wrong with Gail. But of course that's not a rational man speaking. How can anyone divine another person's problems?"

"I'm amazed your husband consented to holiday with Pedersen, feeling as he does about the man."

"He didn't want to come at first. He was afraid he'd start some argument with Steve. Tom hates squabbles — only blows up when he's been provoked for a while. Usually he can swallow his anger, but he does have a temper. I won't say he doesn't. Aside from being connected by marriage, they really did like each other once. That's why I — we both thought this trip would be good for both of them. See if they could patch up the contention."

Contentions, I thought, are unfortunately part of relationships.

"And did they?"

Carla's cheeks flooded in her embarrassment. "I think they would have. We only just got here a few days ago. We — they didn't have much time to sort things out. Steve was intent on contacting his college friends and delivering a family heirloom to Kris. He got kind of wrapped up in that. Stayed with them until —" She broke off, her face reddening deeper. It took several moments before she could continue. "Tom was content to prowl about the village. He loves photography, so he didn't mind waiting for the real start of our vacation until Steve had finished with the Halfords. We were all pretty excited about seeing the Lake District."

In the silence, Tom got up, threw the chewed piece of straw to the ground, and rejoined us. "Can't believe it," he muttered as though we had been privy to his thoughts. "I mean, things don't happen like this to people you know. It's always strangers."

"Steve was so nice," Carla said before hurrying on to Steve's stellar qualities. "Just an ordinary guy. No one harms ordinary guys."

I wanted to tell her we investigate ordinary guys' deaths all the time.

"Just a shame. We talked about it last night. I mean, we couldn't sleep anyway with that terrible thing so recent. It was like a nightmare."

"I'm sorry you had the experience," Graham said. "I don't expect many people got much sleep last night."

"Police included?" Tom stated, his eyes on the taped-off fire area.

"Police included," Graham echoed. "Unfortunately that comes with the job many times."

"How did Steve seem?" I asked. "Nervous, agitated?"

"No different from usual," Tom returned. "What should he seem like? Just glad to be here and happy he found his friends."

"He was kind of worried, though," Carla said. "You know he was, Tom. Don't gloss over it."

"Yes?" prompted Graham. "Why was that?"

Carla shrugged. "Sunday he heard about the Guy Fawkes celebration, about there possibly being firecrackers planted in the fire. He was afraid of sudden, loud noises, afraid they would trigger memories of the war. He got flashbacks quite often. Triggered from ordinary, everyday things — planes, helicopters, car backfires. That sort of thing."

"I can understand that," I said, remembering similar stories from veterans. "Must be a nightmare to live with."

"We searched Sunday morning," Carla said. "I met up with him in the bar. *Pub.* Sorry. Takes a while to get my tongue and brain coordinated with your English. We didn't find anything, but I think he felt better that we looked. Moral support. Everybody here kept telling him there wouldn't be anything like fireworks, but he wanted to make sure. Then you came on duty, Sergeant. I saw you and told Steve."

Tom cleared his throat. "I strolled around the area late afternoon. I wanted one final check, in case some kid had crammed something into the torch. There was nothing obvious."

There wouldn't have been, I wanted to shout, or I would've seen it.

"And when," Graham said, "did you and he part? Were you with him until tea, or until he returned to the Halfords?"

"I didn't look at my watch, if that's what you're after."

"An idea would be helpful."

Death of an Ordinary Guy

"Before tea time. I don't know where Steve headed. I expected to see him at the fire, but I really didn't think anything strange about it when he didn't show up. Must have had second thoughts about it. Probably thought it would be safer not to come, just in case."

"I suppose *someone* saw him after 4:00," Graham said.

"Not just his killer?"

"Hopefully not. So you didn't see him after that."

Tom picked up a rock and looked at it carefully before saying, "Bunch of people were here. I didn't really think so many would show up in this small a village, but they do say it's a famous three-day event here. Steve could have been here and we missed seeing him. Maybe the vicar saw him. He got around a lot. He was down here before the fire started. Took Carla and me on a tour of his church, as a matter of fact. Nice guy. Not at all what I expected. You aren't either, if you don't mind my saying so."

Graham let the obvious question pass. The response might embarrass more than Tom.

"The man from the pub was here, too," Carla reminded us.

"Well, I won't keep you any longer. And my condolences again on your relative's death."

"Hell of a way for a marriage to end," Tom said, throwing the rock at a tree.

As if nervous about Tom's response, Carla waved hesitantly, calling out, "Have a nice day."

God, I shuddered. They really do use that abominable expression. It's not just a telly invention.

I bid the Americans good morning, glancing at Graham to see if my initiative was acceptable. He didn't seem to hear a thing, the tree evidently fascinating him. I stood there, alternately watching him and glancing about, embarrassed that he stood mutely, dazed, wondering what I should do. I could wander back to the incident room, leaving him to his thoughts, but would I hear about it later? I could interrupt his thoughts, but I might put him off an important theory he was considering. So I, too, stood, feeling foolish and impatient and inept. If I had worked with him longer I would have known what to do; if I was of equal rank I would have had no qualms about disturbing him. But now, as a newly-promoted sergeant paired with a new partner.... I counted different bird songs, watched a dog run across the green, and counted to 100 before I finally took a deep breath, prayed to a saint, and asked him if we should be heading back to the pub.

"Sorry, Ray?" He emerged from his world with a startled look, his brown eyes wide and hazy as if roused from sleep.

"It's Taylor, sir."

"Yes?"

"You called me Ray, just now. I'm Taylor." I shifted my eyes to his tree, wanting to avoid embarrassing him further.

"Did I?" he said, blinking quickly. When I nodded, he rubbed his hand over his eyes and sighed. "You don't look like Ray."

I was going to ask if that was a compliment to me or Ray, when he apologized again. "Oldendorf's statement."

"Which one, sir? About —"

"Hell of a way for a marriage to end," he said, slowly repeating it verbatim. The words, so filled with anger when Tom had uttered them, now sounded heartbreaking and regretful, as though he had experienced the pain of the tragedy. When he again looked at me, he said, "That talk about the wife's death.... It bothered me more than I realized. Sorry." The corners of his mouth lifted slightly, as though he was forcing a smile.

I mumbled I understood — which I didn't — and wondered why Tom's simple statement had evoked such an intense reaction in Graham. Office rumors were rife with hints at his failed engagement, but nothing was whispered about a wife. Did she occupy an earlier corner of his life, one that was still raw with his loss?

Graham glanced at his watch and swore. I was spared making a response as dear Colonel Wroe and Talbot converged near us at the fire circle. Either not noticing us or thinking we couldn't hear, Wroe hailed Talbot, chattered about the pleasant morning and hideous previous evening almost as though he were describing a slightly-botched military campaign.

Seems like he's ready for one, I thought, taking in Wroe's emphatic wrist watch, sunglasses and sturdy shoes. So where are we off to, then?

Graham, sensing the meeting could be important, motioned me to accompany him back to the pub. "If Wroe can use subterfuge, so can we humble cops. Where's your disguise kit when we need it?" Before I could reply, he signaled to Margo, who was standing in the pub's doorway. I glanced back at the fire area. If Graham wanted Margo to stroll around and eavesdrop, she might be the perfect candidate. She hadn't had much to do with the villagers yet. And she looked innocent. Like a tourist.

Death of an Ordinary Guy

She wandered off, zigzagging toward the circle, nonchalantly consulting a guidebook and searching her bag. We watched her perch on a bale of straw within several yards of Talbot and Wroe before we went inside.

Quarter of an hour later, the men had separated and Margo was reading to us from her shorthand notes. They were scribbled, I noted with amusement, inside her guidebook.

Talbot: "What the hell you want now?"

Wroe: "Should've got you into the army. Straight to the point, no time for the fal de rol peppering most communications."

Talbot: "I got things to do."

Wroe: "Well, here you are, then. Just wanted to do my boy a favor, Tal, that's all. Just a bit of a favor. How'd you like a bit of help catching the lovely Ramona?"

Talbot: "What are you on about, then?"

Wroe: "Shouldn't have thought it needed any clarifying, but if needs must. I'm worried about your future, Tal. You don't look too well off to me. Could do with a bit of help in the money department, I don't doubt. Ramona's got plenty of her own, never mind her shaky alliance with the village's High-and-Mighty. Now's the time, Tal. Strike now before she marries that milk toast Catchpool. If there's one thing I've learned in my years of serving my country, it's the value of offense. Catch the enemy unprepared and unexpecting. Worked in the war. It'll work with a certain lady, too."

Margo looked up from her notes as a telephone rang. A constable grabbed it, held his hand over the receiver, and looked hopefully at us. I mouthed 'Who is it?' When the constable pointed heavenward, I grimaced. It was Detective Superintendent Simcock. Probably checking up on Graham's progress. I shook my head and held up my hand, fingers spread. The constable nodded and returned to the phone. Margo, who had witnessed this pantomime, said, "Couldn't quite hear what Talbot answered, Mr. Graham. He turned away from me. All I really heard was a belch."

"In keeping with his character, at any rate," Graham said.

"Then Wroe said something that I also couldn't catch, being as he turned in the same direction as Talbot. Some agitated conversation ensued, during which Talbot sniffed, wiped his nose with his shirtsleeve, and crammed the cigarette he was smoking back into his mouth. He gestured toward Ramona's house, which caused him to turn again in my direction. I could easily hear them again. Talbot said, "Why should *you* worry about *my* future? You've never done much for me in the past, only comin' 'round to see me every few years. 'Sides, it's all taken care of. I've already seen to my future security — past the plannin' stage, even — and through no help of yours, *Dad*." In a more conversational tone, Margo said, "Talbot was very emphatic about calling Wroe 'dad.' And Wroe seemed happy. He smiled."

"About what," Graham asked. "The 'dad' part or Talbot's information?"

"That's open to interpretation, sir. After that, Talbot said his partner has already seen to his part, then he walked off. I'll type up these notes for you, sir."

"Thank you, Lynch. So what was that about," asked Graham as we watched Margo settle herself at a computer. "Talbot and Wroe related?"

"I thought Talbot was related to Derek."

"I'd hate to see his family tree."

"Branches kind of intertwined and tangled," I said.

"They're both a little squirrelly, but who will turn out to be the nut?"

"I'd rather be the nut off the tree than the poor sap." Graham grimaced and I quickly said, "Just how successful were we in all this? What have we really learned?"

"Aside from us not being Tom's idea of English police detectives, you mean?"

"What's he want? Deerstalker hat, or monocle and manservant?"

"Most likely a crossword sticking out of one jacket pocket, and a bottle of Samuel Smith jammed into the other. You may ask him if you feel so inclined. Only, I'd wait a bit. He's had a nasty eighteen hours, what with the murder, us and Upper Kingsleigh's dear vicar tarnishing his images."

"What's wrong with the vicar, then?"

"Suffers from the same malaise as we do. Uncooperative costume or personality, or something like that."

I muttered that Tom should leave his prejudices and preconceived notions behind, and maybe he'd not only learn something but also have a better time on holiday.

"I think he'd have had a better time if he hadn't gone on holiday with Steve Pedersen. Don't think his first taste of Old Blighty is exactly his cup of tea."

"The Super rang up just now," I told him.

Death of an Ordinary Guy

"What's he want? No, don't tell me. A miracle. Right."

He reached for the phone and I excused myself, disappeared for a few minutes and returned with two mugs of tea. "Everything all right?"

"Heavenly," Graham said, hanging up the phone. "Just asked if we'd had any luck with tracing the jacket found on Pedersen."

"Speaking of which, Ramona was in charge of the effigy's clothing. She got the cast-offs this year from Arthur. Do anything for you?"

"Convenient, keeping it in the family like that."

"Sir?"

"She snags Arthur and gets a suit of clothes for the effigy all in one transaction."

"Yes, sir. Conserves energy. Anyway, Ramona wasn't at Friday's dole. She was still in Buxton, doing her weekly grocery."

"Small world, TC."

"She works in the Crescent — at the visitor's center."

Graham nudged the handle of his mug, rotating it three hundred sixty degrees before replying absent-mindedly, "Probably seen her a hundred times, and I don't even know her."

"Quite a striking woman. Blonde, figure reminiscent of the 1950s. Curves," I answered in response to Graham's confusion. "Very nice figure, if that doesn't make me sound envious." I sucked in my stomach, and thought again that I should lose 15 pounds.

"I think you can safely voice your opinion of the lady without my spreading gossip."

I announced my gratitude. "In her early 40s, I'd judge. Widow. Local gossip has it she's after Arthur for his money."

"And all this before our walk this morning? You have been busy, TC. Who else have you been talking to? I'd bet my undernourished pay packet the desirable widow didn't tell you all that."

"No, sir. Well, I *have* been walking about a bit this morning, listening. Did you know Kris Halford's the product of an English father and American mother? One of the few British-American marriages to have endured over here, I'll warrant. What is it — our climate, food, culture differences? Why do most mixed marriages fizzle?"

"I'll leave that to psychologists," Graham said. "You are a wonder of eclectic information."

"Also talked to Eleanor Conway, owner of the gift shop." I related my conversation, trying to keep the pride out of my voice, hoping he would realize I hadn't been assigned the duty.

Graham said, "I repeat, TC, with all awe — you *have* been busy."

I shrugged, trying to keep my pleasure from showing. "I guess they don't mind talking to a woman."

"The motherly attitude? You don't in the least look matronly, TC."

"Thank you, sir. Must be my face, then."

"Either that, or you're a born gossip. You're a gem, TC. Glad you're with us and not the *Sun*."

I muttered that I'd probably be paid better by the publication.

"Then let's applaud your devotion to detection, and distaste for wealth. We'll file that with the rest of the pertinent info."

"Our Ramona remembers Tom and Carla in Buxton's visitor's center. She recommended Catchpool Manor. Even phoned the reservation through for them."

"We could assume she was feathering her fiancé's nest, but I'd like to believe she's more honest than that would indicate. Nothing wrong with suggesting the manor house. It's handy to the festivities, grand, and probably just what the Americans were looking for. Don't they have this thing about staying in castles and such?"

"Catchpool Manor's quite popular. Even Chesterfield and such places give it a good push to their tourists."

"It *is* in the books. Well," Graham sighed, stretching. "Ramona likes to dabble in straw and old clothes, does she? Probably likes amateur theatrics, too. Does she actually make and hang the effigy?"

"I think," I said slowly, flipping through my notebook to the desired information, "Arthur did that. Yes. Here it is." I rattled off the facts. "Arthur volunteered to make it this year. Normally she does it. Arthur usually drops the clothes at her house, and she then lets her artistic juices flow and creates the Guy. It's probably not so hard to get it over to the fire circle when it's finished," I concluded, mentally judging the weight and length of the dummy. "And there's really no lifting involved. Just tie the rope around its waist, run it up the back beneath the jacket, loop it around the neck to simulate a noose, and Bob's your uncle."

"Then she hoists it to keep it off the damp ground and free from creepy-crawlies," Graham said, throwing his pen at the mug. "Only this year, of all years, Arthur makes it. Tell me, Taylor, could Arthur have dressed Pedersen up in place of Mr. Guy Fawkes?"

"A very stimulating idea."

Chapter 12

GRAHAM'S FINGERS DRUMMED on the outside of his mug. I could imagine he was good at playing his keyboard instrument. His fingers moved quickly and easily. I wanted to hear him, wanted us to be in his flat, having tea, talking music, playing duets. I tried to recall something my brother had told me of the Baroque musicians, something that would impress Graham so he would see me as something human instead of a police badge. But all I could remember was the tidbit of Bach and his 20 children. So I sat, feeling another chance of developing a friendship had passed, hating myself for my stupidity.

After many moments, Graham said, "Wonder how we can find out if Arthur had opportunity. Did Pedersen disappear some time close to the dummy's delivery?"

The crisp flip of pages soared over the incessant tapping, like a descant to a bass continuo. My pen jabbed at the note page. "No where close, sir. The dummy was originally delivered and hung Thursday morning around ten o'clock. Arthur — perhaps to impress his girl friend with the size of his muscles — lugged it out of the car himself, and brought it to the fire circle. And Pedersen —"

"And Pedersen was still walking around very un-effigy-like until tea time on Sunday. Damn." Graham muttered the oath rather than hurling it at someone specific. "Hate to waste great theories. Damn." He repeated the word, more as a feeling of loss than of anger.

I gave him time to sip his tea. "It's a bad case. I mean, here Kris sees her ex-fiancé after thirty years, and then, in the next minute you might say, she sees him hanging there in front of her. Not a pleasant thing to remember. Almost make her wish he's stayed in America,

Death of an Ordinary Guy

and spared her and Derek any brief pleasure they might have had with their reunion."

"I wonder, Taylor, if Kris married Derek because the two men looked alike. Well, there is a similar appearance about them. Like relatives."

"You mean like being proposed to on the rebound? Wouldn't be quite the same as true love."

"It wouldn't. Still, if you have a fixation about someone, and that person's out of reach, you *might* grab at the available person because there's a resemblance."

"And you think Derek offered that option to Kris?" I tried remembering the faces of the two men.

"Yes, but it was probably not a conscious thing on her part. Wish I had a photo of the three of them in their rowdy university days. I just bring this supposition to you now because it struck me that there is marked sameness to the men. Same height, give or take an inch, same hair color and build. Could the one have been mistaken for the other?"

"But why would Arthur try to kill Derek?" I said, jumping in on Graham's idea. "That's what you're leading up to, isn't it? Asking about Arthur making the dummy and such. If it is mistaken identity, there's the problem of motive. And I, for one, would think it obvious. I mean, wouldn't the finger point to Arthur as substituting the corpse for the effigy if he's the one who made the effigy? And he can't have needed the money that badly, if you're thinking along the lines of him stopping the yearly dole. Three hundred pounds is a lot of money to the average person, which Derek certainly is, and Arthur certainly isn't. Why kill someone just to put an end to that payment? After all, Arthur's lord of the manor." Motives are such a nuisance, probing into each suspect's personality and past.

Graham smiled. "I've known country squires, landed gentry who weren't as well off as the title and house would imply. Besides, what's Derek good for — another thirty or forty years? That's thirty years of dishing out £300. Arthur could do a lot with £9,000."

I mumbled that most people could, then ventured, "Maybe his fiancée nagged him into it. I don't mean she came right out and told Arthur to kill Derek. In a roundabout way. You know, when Arthur and Ramona were discussing their marriage, say. She sighs prettily and says she sure wishes they could replace the draperies in the drawing room, or wouldn't it be fun to have matching pink Jaguars and mink driving gloves."

"A woman's point of view, Taylor. Well, that's a nice little job of work for you. Find out the financial status of those involved."

"Yes, sir," I muttered, knowing what I was in for. Maybe I could pawn it off on one of the constables.

The noises of the incident room had quieted to a background rumble of ringing phone, beeping fax and conversational buzz. The door banged as someone left; a metal chair scraped across the floor. Someone was complaining about the weather forecast and wishing he had warmer socks. Graham leaned back in his chair and stretched. The morning was nearly bumping into afternoon and, if I knew him, he would be feeling we weren't progressing very quickly.

"So, Taylor, what did you think of our Colonel Vernon Wroe?"

"He of HRH George VI's Armed Forces?" I said. "Besides my vote for family nut?"

"Retired," Graham reminded me.

"He's still an *active* nut. Do you think," I asked, attempting to believe the scenario, "Wroe, priding himself on being a vigilant officer, would lie about seeing Uncle Gilbert?"

"He may not have lied, but he could have misinterpreted what he saw."

"Hardly speaks well of a former colonel in Intelligence. I thought those chaps were highly trained. Always saw their man, as it were."

"Anyone can assume, and it was dark — way past sunset. And don't confuse the Mounties with Wroe." Graham pushed the mug across the table. "I don't recall the Intelligence branch, or any branch, having a monopoly on expertise. Lord knows we haven't."

"Still, being so highly trained...." I paused to consider Wroe's dubious talents. He may have had lightning-sharp skills during the war, but would they still be as honed fifty years later? Did they stay with a soldier so that he lashed out in instinct? "Sounds like he reveled in what he did during the Great Conflict."

"He *loved* it." This time there was no mistaking Graham's bitterness. "You heard him. He was absolutely dripping with emotion about the good ole days. I'm all for patriotism and defending the home soil, but our dear colonel bordered on fanaticism. I got the distinct impression that he was sorry when the war ended."

I stated that there was no accounting for some folks' tastes. "Ardor aside, do you think he could be right in what he saw? You think he's a reliable witness?"

"That's a very difficult question to answer. Short of staging one of those witness exercises we had to suffer through in our police courses...."

"At least he's trying to help. Makes a nice change of pace."

Graham smiled. "You always try to see both sides of a situation. It's wonderful to have such law-abiding citizens, yes. They'll point out a possible murderer but they won't actually lower themselves to slander by saying he's drunk."

"What *is* this world coming to?"

"You have asked The Question. So what've we got, then?"

We bent over our notebooks, conferring and sorting through possible motives until I insisted on lunch.

UNCLE GILBERT HAD forsaken the whiskey bottle Monday morning for his lithium salts, I discovered when I tried to interview him after lunch. It was his normal antidote for the attacks of manic-depression that cyclically claimed him. He was not altogether good at remembering to take his medicine. And right now he was not good at remembering much about the previous evening. He sat on the edge of his bed, his feet dangling over the side, his body still in rumpled pajamas, and half-listened to his nephew. It was obviously still too early to think. Besides it probably hurt his head.

"You bleeding berk!" Arthur yelled. "You're looking at a murder charge!"

Gilbert blinked stupidly at Arthur, hearing the words and the wrath behind them, yet not comprehending what he had done to warrant such an outburst. He asked again whom he had murdered.

"That American tourist," Arthur snapped, forgetting I hovered in the open doorway just behind him.

Uncle Gilbert sagged against the pockmarked headboard, the pillow puffing out on each side of him like whipped cream oozing from a cream puff. His eyes tried to determine from his nephew's face what his ears couldn't, for he stared at Arthur. "Don't yell at me, Laddie. I'm under a lot of stress. I'll forget to take my medicine." He didn't have to enumerate what that might cause. Evidently they both knew.

"*You're* under stress?" scoffed Arthur. "Hell, what about *me*? What about this nose-above-water establishment? If many more guests check out and the business should fold —"

Gilbert groaned and pulled the sheet up to his neck. His fingers gripped the fabric as though he needed the tactile assurance that he and Arthur weren't players in one of his alcoholic nightmares. He squinted at Arthur, who was pacing the floor and coaxing all types of groans and creaks from the wooden floorboards. Yet there was something surreal about the scene, something Max Ernst might paint.

Arthur stopped his pacing and turned to me. "Honestly, Sergeant, the man's more of a nuisance than he's worth at times. But what can I do? He's family and I love him."

I said I'd known many similar situations.

Arthur glared again at his uncle, evidently short on sympathy. "Where were you last night? The Sergeant wants to know. And so do I. I didn't see you all afternoon, and you weren't at evening tea. Byron said you were at the bonfire. Where'd you go afterwards? I didn't hear you come in."

Gilbert pulled the sheet tighter, shielding himself from Arthur's verbal battery. "Art, why all the questions? Slow down, slow down! Where was I, when did I come home.... What's so important? Who's that behind you?" he said, seeing me for the first time. "Ramona? Come in, Dear. Such a bold one you are, coming into my bedroom."

"That's not Ramona," Arthur yelled. "That's Sergeant Taylor. Police! *C.I.D.* And what's so important is that Steve Pedersen was *murdered*." He tried conveying the problem by loudness where logic failed. "You made an ass of yourself last night, confessing you had killed Pedersen. The Sergeant, here, heard you. Now she wants to question you."

Either volume or repetition finally won over. Gilbert sat up, letting the sheet fall from his chest, and stared open-mouthed. He screwed up his eyes, as though willing his mind to sort through the confusion. "The fire. Yes. I remember. There was Talbot and the vicar, and a tall, trim man taking tea. Right?" Arthur swore. Gilbert took that as encouragement and went on. "Were we talking over your wedding, Art? That'd explain the vicar. But that tall chap — He an antiques dealer? But there's something about the woods, isn't there? Did I kill someone in the woods?" Gilbert rubbed his eyes, opening them to look at Arthur's bright crimson face. A hint of saliva ebbed from a corner of Gilbert's mouth as he squeaked out his disbelief.

"Can't remember?" Arthur asked. He strode up to the bed, grabbed Gilbert's pajama shirt, and shook him till the mattress springs squealed. "I'm not surprised, considering the whiskey and brandy you put away earlier yesterday. It's another typical day, isn't it, with you not recalling a thing. Is this sergeant going to accept that? Will she overlook your convenient faulty memory, whisper consoling things about your mental illness, or figure it's all an inept attempt at an alibi — that you really did kill that man?" He had finished his speech in a fury of sound, and pushed his uncle back against the headboard. He paid no attention to Gilbert's wailing of innocence; the slam of the door behind us punctuated his opinion.

Chapter 13

AFTER MY SOJOURN at the manor house, I wandered down the road, enjoying the autumn afternoon and trying to make sense of the scene I'd just witnessed. Not that there probably was much, considering Uncle Gilbert's condition. But it was something to think on.

I met Margo as she emerged from the gift shop. No doubt interviewing Mason Conway, I thought, noting the time. I waved at her and we walked to the pub.

"At least I didn't have to put on one of those space suits you and Graham had on last night," Margo said, referring to her eavesdropping of Wroe and Talbot. "God, if there's anything that camouflages my figure —"

"Margo," I said, interrupting her tirade on fashion, "have you ever taken any acting classes?"

She stopped to throw the last bit of her sandwich at a group of sparrows, watching them peck at the bread and ham while she said, "No. At least no RADA stuff. Strictly amateur in the church hall. Charades and things. Why?"

"I don't suppose someone could put on an act every time you see him, pretending to be inebriated."

"Why? Who's pretending?"

"Uncle Gilbert. Gilbert Catchpool," I explained as she straightened up from watching the feeding frenzy.

"Don't blame me, blame the booze and my genes?"

I found myself looking at her, wishing I had her genes. Even ten years ago, the age Margo is now, I didn't look that good. I never had a great figure. It was lying somewhere beneath the two stone of baby fat I euphemistically called my weight problem. And my shorter stature tended to make me look dumpy in a way Margo never would experience. I ran my fingers through my short-cropped hair. That was one of my good features. It was copper-blonde and glowed like a new penny. I was proud of my blue eyes, too. At least genes had handed me something nice.

"Bren?" Margo called me from my contemplation. "Did you hear me? Why would he pretend to be drunk?"

"Only thing I can think of is he doesn't want to be questioned about something. He's using it as a shield."

"Are you getting any information from him?"

I shook my head and showed her a blank notebook page.

"Works damned well, I'd say."

"And Sir Lancelot only had a shield of heavy metal."

I returned to the pub's private barroom. A few of the constables were back from their early afternoon investigations and entered computer data or made the myriad of telephone calls needed in a murder inquiry. Graham was at a computer, conferring with Constable Fordyce, obviously pleased. He equated the hum of efficient work with progress. And he hated to think that a killer would get away with murder.

"Suppose it's too early for anything medical from Ahrens," he said to no one in particular. He consulted his watch. "I'd like to know what he's found, if it differs from last night's cursory report. Oh, hello, Taylor. How'd it go with our favorite relative?"

I told him he didn't want to know, and slumped into a chair. "So, nothing from Ahrens, I take it."

"We must maintain the constabulary rule of patience right now."

"Along with the Force's attitude of courtesy, compassion and understanding? Tall order."

"Obviously they didn't tell you in school you'd have to be so stoic. Were you ill that day?"

"If they had told us, many of us wouldn't have continued."

"So, what we've got so far.... Doesn't matter now if Pedersen was bludgeoned or hanged. For the moment, let's abandon the line assuming Pedersen is the intended victim and concentrate on the mistaken identity theme. Makes more sense to focus on a local, anyway. There are all those years of village living that give your neighbor reason to wish you dead."

"And opportunities to do it," I volunteered.

"If you're agreeable to my little suggestion, Taylor.... Who'd want to kill Derek? You may consider the dole or not, as you wish. Let your imagination soar."

"Well, I'd say most likely it's Talbot."

"Even if he can't substantiate his claim, aren't there any friends, old-age pensioners who would've known him, someone who could prove his family line? Never mind Coventry's disaster. Someone must be able to speak for him. What is he?"

"Sixty-two. Not so very old these days."

"Wroe's eighty. If he knew Talbot, he's got eighteen years on him. He could have known Talbot when Talbot was growing up."

"Either one could have baby-sat the other," I said, thinking they were both infantile.

"But who'd watch the baby sitter?"

"Some older relative would certainly help Talbot's case. Family photo album ought to be somewhere. They didn't all live in Coventry, did they?"

"Since you've turned the mere act of gossiping into a higher art, Taylor, would you mind seeing if you can ferret out something along that line?"

"Now?" I asked, gazing rather fondly at Graham's coffee mug.

"I know you just returned from battle, but if you wouldn't mind. Strike while the day has light."

"Yes, sir." I stood up, then paused for a question. "I'm not betting either way on anyone. But as much as Talbot screams 'real motive' to me, I've got to ask if a sixty-two-year-old man isn't a bit old for this sort of game."

"You mean murder? If he did kill —"

"No, sir," I interrupted. "Proving he was adopted. That was fifty-five years ago!"

"Some people are never too old for greed, Taylor."

The computer printer at the next table began spitting out paper and Graham walked over to it. "Might be Ahrens' report. Hold on, Taylor."

In response to Graham's inquiry, Fordyce looked up from the huge monitor before him. "Nothing from Buxton — or Ripley, sir," he said, referring to Constabulary headquarters. "But I've finished entering all the names. And the current notes from the other constables. I'll type up yours and Sergeant Taylor's if you'd like."

Graham sighed. "Thank you, Fordyce. You're up to the task, I shouldn't wonder."

Fordyce nodded, thanked his superior, then sympathetically uttered that some cases were worse than others.

"A truer statement, Fordyce," Graham said. "Any time you want to show off your questioning technique, you can have a go at Uncle Gilbert. Or Talbot."

Fordyce shook his head, punching a computer key before stating, "I've seen him. Heard him. I'd hate to be up against Talbot on a bad day."

Graham, his eyes still fixed on the page before him, casually asked why.

Surprised, Fordyce stammered, "Oh, sorry, sir. Thought you'd read all the notes on the Pedersen case."

A slow blush crept over Graham's face. He gulped, explaining that he'd had a late night and had only returned from questioning some people and conferring with me.

"Well, sir," the constable offered, "Talbot Tanner almost killed a man twenty-two years ago."

Chapter 14

FORDYCE AVERTED HIS eyes from Graham's astonished face. God, I thought as Graham threw his notebook onto the table top. The man's either going to have a stroke or have Fordyce's guts for garters. Fordyce raised his eyes from the computer monitor as the room grew quieter. The other constables had abandoned any semblance of work to stare at Graham. It wasn't often he did a cock-up of anything.

"*Killed* a man?" exclaimed Graham after he found his voice. "Are you certain?"

"Yes, sir. In 1973. I can print it out for you."

Graham thanked the constable, but said he would read it in detail later. "Who got into a dust-up with Talbot? Don't tell me Derek. I don't think I could take that just now."

"No, sir," Fordyce returned quickly. "Byron MacKinnon."

"Arthur Catchpool's secretary?" I said.

Fordyce nodded. "The only thing that saved Byron, evidently, was the vicar."

A hurried 'thank you' just squeaked out of Graham's mouth before he tossed me my jacket and we left the pub.

Luckily for Graham's blood pressure, Lyle was at the church, bending over a letter he was laboriously composing in his crowded, small office. The vicar looked up as we entered, smiled at the postponement of his disagreeable task and the companionship our visit offered, yet managed to conceal his surprise at seeing us so soon after that morning's meeting. Perhaps police work is more like parish work than I imagined. Whenever someone needs us, we're there. I'll have to ask Graham sometime.

Death of an Ordinary Guy

Lyle indicated two chairs, realized they were impossible to get to, and mumbled his apologies. He rose from his desk, picked up the stack of books that hid one chair seat, and told me to sit.

"I'm delighted you dropped by," the clergyman said, turning slightly, trying to find a depository for his armful.

"Hope we haven't come at an inconvenient time," Graham returned, taking the books from the man and setting them gently on the floor. He cleared his own chair, winking at me.

"No, no," Lyle hurriedly assured him, reclaiming his chair behind the desk, looking relieved that the books had found a temporary home and that his composition chore was delayed. "Nothing that can't wait. I find these letters difficult to compose. What can one say after the first sentence expressing sorrow for a death?"

"You're writing to the Halfords?"

The vicar nodded, sighing loudly and pushing the pen away from the paper. "I was with them last night, of course, but I always think it nice to follow up with a note expressing my understanding of their grief. I try to offer comfort, you know — remind them of our Lord's love and the certainty that Mr. Pedersen's in heaven — but sometimes...." Lyle shrugged his shoulders, indicating the difficulty of such an epistle. "It's my duty, as it is with every caring human being, don't you think? Where would we be if we didn't care for each other?"

Graham refrained from saying the obvious. In a way, ours was a strange job, combining the extremes of uncaring and caring. Uncaring, self-centered people broke laws — robbed, assaulted, killed. Caring, respectful people became witnesses, comforted the victims. We dealt with both. And Graham had too, as a minister. He had merely changed clothes and rules.

Graham coughed and remarked instead that it was very kind of Lyle to give his support.

"Only doing what I want to do. I need to help."

"Well," Graham said, "perhaps you can help us for a moment. I was told you know something of a tiff involving Talbot and Byron MacKinnon a few years back. 1973, I believe it was."

I did some hasty mental arithmetic, eyed the pudgy, short man, and wondered how he could have stopped a fight involving that leviathan. Even now, the handyman wasn't exactly in his dotage. Like David confronting Goliath — without the slingshot. "Case of attempted murder," I said, nudging Lyle's memory. "Assault with a hammer."

"You referring to Talbot's little trouble?" The vicar rubbed a pudgy hand across his chin. "Yes, I remember it, though I must confess I'd nearly forgotten. Haven't dredged that up in ages. What do you want to know about?"

"Any particulars you may remember. Reason, outcome — that sort of thing."

"I don't suppose I'd be doing anything unethical in relaying the story." He eyed Graham as though judging the man's honesty.

"I shouldn't think it's anything like revealing a confession," Graham replied. "I'm conducting a murder investigation, sir, and one of the usual dull bits of routine is the sorting out of pertinent and irrelevant facts. This may or may not have anything to do with Pedersen's murder, and if it hasn't, I'll forget it. But if there's a link between Talbot's rash behavior with Byron, and anything with Pedersen... If one of the men told you something in confidence, you may leave that out. I'm not asking for a baring of the soul. I just want the bones of the fight. Who started it, how it was resolved...."

"Yes." The vicar, now released from guilt, readily gave the information. "If you say it was 1973, it was 1973. I'll accept that. I'm not much good on dates. But I do remember the altercation. It was, amazingly enough, this same time of year. Is that what brought it into the open?"

"May I venture a guess, and ask if the Catchpool dole sparked it?"

"Yes, Mr. Graham, that blasted dole. I swear I don't know if it's more of a blessing or a curse. The money helps the Halfords, I'm certain, but the discomfort that comes with it —" He shook his head, no doubt recalling previous trouble with Talbot. "Not only for the Halfords when Talbot's in one of his moods, but also for the poor man himself. He can't be a happy person if he's always so agitated over this dole business. But you asked about the fight. I'm afraid I'm inclined to ramble.

"Anyway, Talbot was going on and on about his rightful fortune, and Byron called Talbot a liar, I'm afraid. Nasty scene. That was bad enough, but then Byron suggested Talbot leave the village because no one liked him, which wasn't true. I do! Byron said Talbot had no real job, just the few odd ones he got from Arthur, me, or some of the villagers who felt sorry for him and had a few pence to spare. We've been remarkably successful. It's kept Talbot here ever since he arrived in the '50s. Anyway, Byron got angrier and angrier at Talbot, finally boasted that when he — Byron — married Kris Alton — oh, that's Kris Halford's maiden name, by the way. Byron bragged that when he married Kris, Talbot had better not be poking around the manor house."

"Implying Talbot shouldn't be expecting any odd jobs from that direction," I asked. "Did Byron oversee such things?"

Lyle nodded, his eyes blinking again like a pigeon. "Yes. Byron had the key to the till, as it were. Powerful man, Byron MacKinnon, in his way. Controls the running of a good portion of the estate. Though what right he had to say that to Talbot —"

"Can't read any other meaning into it at the moment," I said, marveling at the vicar's memory.

"Exactly. Well, Talbot, who has always liked Kris and made no secret about it, snapped. First he had heard of Kris' engagement, I suppose. Talbot was holding a hammer and swung it at Byron's head. He succeeded in knocking him to the ground, whereby he kicked him in the ribs, still trying for his head with that hammer. *Nasty* scene!"

"Where was all this?"

"Just outside. In the churchyard. Talbot had just finished with some chores I'd given him, and Byron came strolling up the walk to talk to me. Byron had innocently asked where I was and Talbot asked why he wanted to know. Byron, of course, said it was none of his business, and it worsened from there."

"That's why no one else was around to help you stop the fight," Graham said. "And why he had the hammer. Unfortunate."

"I tell you, I don't know how I got the two men separated. 'Course, I wasn't yet into my fifties." He shook his head.

"Maybe Divine intervention?" Graham offered.

Lyle nodded, and said quite truthfully, "You're amazing, Mr. Graham. Yes."

"Did Byron marry Kris? I know she's married to Derek now, but with divorce so prevalent —"

"No. They got as far as the engagement and that was it. Probably some pre-wedding tiff about child rearing or mothers-in-law. All too common, these fall-outs. But isn't it better to get that all sorted out before you need it? Of course, you'll want to ask Byron or Kris the reasons. I don't reveal more than the obvious. Or what is common village knowledge."

Which constantly surprises me, I wanted to say.

Graham thanked the vicar and we left to see if Byron's intended was awake and ready for a game of 'Do You Remember?'

SOUNDS OF EVERYDAY life washed over the village as Graham and I drove to the Halfords'. Not for the first time I thought how odd life was: we were investigating a murder, yet wet laundry flapped from clothes lines, women shopped at the butcher's for tonight's mince or lamb or chicken, the baker's shop displayed fruit flans and iced buns in its window. Farmers from the outlying farms stopped at the pub for a quick pint before heading home. Children playing in the school yard laughed and played at football or tag. People unconcerned about the murder, cocooned in their world and ignoring us as long as we didn't intrude on their comfort zones.

Kris Halford had been one of these people. Now, cradled in a blue duvet, she was lying on the living room sofa when we entered the Halford home. Her night of sorrow was etched into her face as though a sculptor had cast it in stone. The dark eyes stared at me from beneath reddened, swollen eyelids, and a box of tissues near the sofa suggested her interminable crying. She pushed a coil of limp brunette hair behind her ear, making a semblance of caring. Graham took a chair opposite her while I sat on the end of the sofa.

"Yes, I suppose I am better," Kris murmured, dabbing at a tear with the damp tissue. "If you can call a numbed head and a confused mind better. All I see is Steve. Him sitting here, so happy to be with us. Him at the pub where we had dinner Saturday night. Him in that chair."

Just as well Derek shelved Pedersen's photograph for a while, I thought, noticing its absence from the tabletop. She remembers readily enough without that visual aid.

"I won't apologize," she said, her voice stronger after her cry. "I'm going through hell, and if anyone can't see that and sympathize with me —"

"I'm neither impatient nor condemning you, Mrs. Halford. Unfortunately, I have to ask questions concerning Pedersen's death, and *you*, also unfortunately, are part of the tragedy. If you'd rather we return at some later time...."

Kris waved her hand, stopping his rising from the chair. "Please. I'm just lying here. Please stay. I'm all right. Derek's at the office. I couldn't see him staying home for me. Besides, either Arthur, Byron or Lyle stop by every few hours to see how I am, warm up some soup. You know."

Death of an Ordinary Guy

I said it would be hard to beat help like that.

Kris nodded. "Besides, I wasn't good for anything except having a lie in and a cry. Silly of him to take a day off for that. If you want to talk to him again, he won't be home till six or so."

Graham assured her that he could catch up with Derek later, but that right now he wanted to ask her a few questions if she was up to it.

"Haven't done a thing all day. I'm living on hot chocolate and tea. Plenty of nutrition there."

I gazed at the array of mugs littering the tables, their interiors circled with dried chocolate froth or bits of tea leaves.

Kris, following my gaze, asked if we would like tea or coffee. "I can do a no-brainer like that."

I looked at Graham, who shook his head. I declined, also, but said, "If you'd like a cup —"

"Thanks, Sergeant, but I'm full to the gills. I'm either experiencing a caffeine buzz, or your surgeon's pills still have a hold of me. Mogadon, I think," she replied in answer to Graham's raised eyebrow. "Yes. Great sleeping pill. I'm out in twenty minutes. Sleep like the dead."

I averted my eyes as she reddened. In the silence I heard a cat outside. Kris' or Eleanor Conway's wandering moggy?

"I must admit," Kris said, regaining her composure, "I rather enjoy the hot chocolate. I haven't had any in ages, but Derek insisted last night. Said it'd make me sleep. Something about hot milk..." Her hand fell suddenly, limply to her lap and she laughed. "God, as if I needed hot milk to top off the pill. Funny. While we're working we say we'd love a day of just doing nothing. And here I am, doing nothing, only it's not the relaxation we dream of. Do people really know what it's like, how hellishly boring doing nothing is?" Her eyes sought Graham's for a gesture of understanding, asking no response. "Why *Steve,* of all people? Can you tell me that, Mr. Graham?" She held the empty mug, almost like a caress.

"Sure I can't get you anything?" Graham asked. "I'm quite handy in the kitchen. Been known to make soufflés, even."

"You've got my husband beat." Kris grabbed a tissue and dabbed at her nose. "He knows his way around the tinned soups and such. Even makes the occasional sandwich or cooks a banger. But you and the Sergeant don't want to know about our domestic bliss."

"I understand Talbot, Evan and Lyle were at the bonfire. But we don't know about Pedersen's involvement. I know this is painful,

Mrs. Halford, but do you know if he changed his mind about attending the event? It would help us in our investigation if you could talk about it."

"My husband and I didn't see Steve after tea. We had it early, around half three, I should think. I wanted to help Evan in the pub. He needed to get down to the green while it was still early. Steve —" She broke off, fighting down a sob. "Steve left after the meal. He said he wanted to check the torch and lanterns for fireworks. Derek and I were surprised we didn't see him at the fire, though after a while we assumed he was somewhere in the crowd watching the foolery, or else he had figured there would be fireworks after all so he felt safer skipping the fire."

"I understand that the reason Pedersen came to Upper Kingsleigh, apart from renewing his friendships with you and your husband, was to bring you a family heirloom."

"Gran's ring," Kris said, waving her hand at Graham so the opal winked with fiery colors. "Grandma Warren. It's one of those family jokes that you don't quite expect to mature. Gran promised me this ring, then before she got around to giving it to me, it got mislaid. I thought that was the end of that. But Mom wrote to tell me she'd discovered it quite by accident one day when she was going through some of Gran's things, and would see I'd get it. Mom lives in the States."

"Must be wonderful to have it," I said.

"Yes. I assumed it would come with my Christmas parcel. I never dreamed it would be hand delivered. And by Steve."

"More trustworthy than the mail," Graham said. "How did Steve get the honor? He knew your mother, I take it."

"He had looked her up when he got discharged from hospital. After he returned from Viet Nam. He was trying to find me, so he contacted her. That's when he found out I had returned to England on our graduation from university. And that I had married Derek. Mom gave him my address."

"And his arrival was a surprise?" I asked.

"That's like Jonah saying 'What fish?'. After I got over the shock, I was elated. Steve came laden with other family mementos besides the ring — Dad's scouting paraphernalia, Gran's favorite doll, some duplicate photos that Mom had even assembled into an album and labeled for me. Some from my university days, family snaps of holidays and such. God, it brings back the memories. Birthdays, Thanksgiving, Fourth of July...."

Death of an Ordinary Guy

"Fourth of July. Of course. Their holiday with fireworks. Is it usual for Upper Kingsleigh to use fireworks during Guy Fawkes Night? I thought they were generally outlawed these days." He looked at me as though wondering why headquarters had assigned me bonfire duty. Was he finally noticing my potential?

"If you're trying to get the names of any criminals, I can't tell you. And I mean 'can't,' not 'won't.' We've never had them, but Steve had no way of knowing that. There's always the odd chance that some child might think it funny to poke a firecracker into the tower of wood — even with your constables on guard. They do use them on Mischief Night, however."

"Yet in all your years living here...." Graham suggested.

"Nothing. We follow the speed limits, adhere as closely as we can to the Ten Commandments, stand patiently in queue at the post office window. We're a law-abiding village, on the whole. Except when it comes to murder." She banged the mug onto the table, her eyes glaring at him, not because she held him responsible for her friend's death, but because he was handy.

Graham said nothing, and I wondered if we should leave. Before I could suggest it, Graham asked if her marriage to Derek was her first.

Kris' knuckles grew white as she twisted the edge of her duvet. "It's none of your business, Chief Inspector, as far as I can see. I shouldn't be surprised if you ask me next to see my bank statement."

"I apologize if I've offended you. But there's a good reason behind all my apparent poking and sniffing about. I was informed today that you'd been engaged to Byron MacKinnon in 1973."

Kris' eyes shone through her tears with an intensity that startled me. It was as though she glowed with the rage fueling her grief. "It's true. I'm sorry. I shouldn't have gone off like that. It's just that, well... It's not as buried as I thought, is it? That's what makes it hard, losing Steve like that. After I'd lost him to the war, as we supposed, and then Byron walked out on me.... Well, Derek was my last chance for happiness. I wasn't getting any younger. What a moronic phrase, but it's true! If Derek hadn't come along, offering love and security, ignoring the faults of my aging body and personality... Sounds like I accepted him for something other than love, and that's absurd. I'm clinging to Derek with every fiber in my body. If anything ever happens to him, if he's ever taken from me...

The narrative had cost her. She leaned her head against the back of the sofa, shut her eyes, and choked down a deep sob. "You've found your niche in the C.I.D., Mr. Graham. You've done a first-rate job of ferreting out the little dramatic bits of village life. The sordid or just plain embarrassing secrets most of us have and most of us pray will be forgotten."

"If you think I'm impertinent or being just plain nosy, I'm sorry. I assure you I'm just gathering facts at the moment. I don't go to bed and gloat over people's misfortunes or think about methods of blackmail. That's not as flippant as it may sound. I've been accused of both, unfortunately. I only ask because it may give me an insight into Byron's or Talbot's behavior or emotional stability. It may come in handy, it may not. And if it doesn't —" He shrugged.

"In one ear and out the other?"

"Precisely. I can't be bothered remembering trivial bits. Cases get too complicated too quickly for me to retain such pieces of remarkably exciting information such as what Talbot has for breakfast."

Kris laughed suddenly and released her hold of the comforter. "I wouldn't dream of asking you. But I don't think I can tell you details of Byron's and my engagement. You must ask him. He ended it. Tell him I sent you, if you need to break down his reluctance."

We uttered our thanks for her help and let ourselves out while Graham echoed Kris' general opinion that Upper Kingsleigh was a respectable village except for murder and greed.

Death of an Ordinary Guy

Chapter 15

FORTIFIED WITH AFTERNOON tea, I parked my car at Catchpool Manor. I leaned against the open car door, mesmerized by the magnificence of the house. The late afternoon sun shone halo-like behind it, casting blue shadows into the eastern woods. I recalled the brochure's text, and mentally checked its accuracy against what I had seen. 'Catchpool Manor, predominant and well-positioned in the picturesque Derbyshire village of Upper Kingsleigh. En suite facilities, exposed oak beams, gourmet meals, peaceful flower gardens.' But there was more than this simple declaration. A curving, tree-framed driveway from the main road from the village eventually led to an immense lawn, which lay like a green table cloth under the building's limestone grandeur. That same green color accented the northern side of the house with its walled rose garden and head-high boxwood maze. A confusion of oriel windows, strapwork, and sharply-pointed gables welcomed callers to their own slice of England. Sunlight and shadow played against the far western window, re-enforcing many speculations that perhaps ghosts did walk the corridors after midnight. This November afternoon, however, the ancient walls harbored only a handful of tourists eager to explore the halls and surrounding hills.

My minute of recreation over, I once again sat in Arthur's study, my notebook on my knees. I wondered if Uncle Gilbert would stagger in, if he had sobered up.

"I assumed you or the inspector would be around for this story," Arthur said, cradling his teacup on his lap. "Talbot seems to attract attention, whatever the year or circumstance. Even if it is ancient history, I suppose you must delve into it. We can't keep much private in a village. Not that anyone cares about Talbot's claim. It's just an annoyance at times, the way he goes on and on about it. Still, it's the type of thing that could yield so much to an investigation, isn't it?"

"Depends, sir, on how the investigation proceeds. If there's nothing to it, we forget it and get on with another line."

"Wouldn't that be a waste of time?"

"Both the chief inspector and I have wasted a good deal of time through our careers. I wouldn't let that worry you."

"I won't. Just intrigued with the policeman's job. Err, woman's," he said.

I figured he was confused about being politically correct. I let it pass. "It has its moments."

Angling farther back into the chair, Arthur nodded. "Well, Talbot was born in 1934, survived the air raid on Coventry in '40, though the bombing demolished his house. Fortunately, he was living with an aunt at the time."

"Parents killed in the war?"

"Parents were killed in '38. This aunt took Talbot in, gave him a home and such until he was adopted. Was a bit of a long process. There was no thought of adoption when Talbot first came to his aunt, of course. She was all for doing her duty by her brother's child — some sort of misplaced family loyalty — but she couldn't quite handle the financial end of it. Plus, I don't think the two of them exactly hit it off."

"Bit of an odd man out, was he?" Uncaring homelife, lack of understanding, and associations with hooligans tainted many a teenager. Nice that Talbot had straightened out.

"Probably, knowing Talbot. He's a screw loose, at any rate. Can't see him fitting in with most normal households. That's assuming this aunt had a normal household."

"There's no accounting for some folks' life styles."

"No, there isn't. And I wonder how some of them survive in society. Well, all I know is that Talbot was living with his aunt from '38 until he was adopted. 1951, I think, though I'm not certain."

"Dare say we can look it up if we need to."

"That's the problem. Coventry got it pretty badly, didn't it? Talbot's family belongings, including his adoption papers, were destroyed."

"Pose any difficulties for him later on?"

"Every year. His aunt was confirmed dead years ago. I checked. Thought I'd help out the fellow, at least put a stop to his annual whine. But I can't prove his adoption, though privately I believe it happened."

"Would you happen to know the name of Talbot's alleged adoptive parents?" I looked up from my notetaking, holding my breath.

"Certainly. He made no secret about it. Flaunted it, in fact. Only trouble, as I said, he couldn't prove a thing. Talbot always swore that his adoptive father was Peter Halford, Derek's father."

I asked if anyone else knew of the supposed relationship.

"Should think anyone older than forty would. No secret at all. Peter Halford always called Talbot 'son', but then he called all the boys in the village 'son'. Derek insists it was just an affectionate nickname his dad used for all the lads, Talbot included. The older Halford was keen on children. I always thought it a shame he only had one. But it does seem reasonable that Halford would adopt Talbot. He and Talbot's dad were chums as lads. I've often heard Derek's dad talk of Talbot's parents."

"I suppose Peter Halford —"

"Dead, I'm afraid, yes. Died in 1973. No, no. That was Kris' dad. 1970. Heart attack. Doesn't help with this adoption puzzle, does it?"

Nothing would help, I thought, except the official paper from the adoption service. "So, from 1951, say, Talbot became fixed on this legal son-and-heir bit. That is when he first began spouting off about it, or do I have it wrong?"

"If only they would've let Tal alone. If only people would let others just live. Tal's not a bad chap, really. He does good work, doesn't ask for much out of life."

"Just every November third at dole time he goes crackers."

Arthur nodded. "And him being older than Derek.... Well, you see why it's important. If he was legally adopted, he'd be the older son and entitled to the dole."

"So there's no proof to Talbot's claim. None that anyone has ever found to date, at least."

"I'm hoping to set up something for him without his knowing of it. A bit of annual income."

"How will he receive that without being suspicious of a handout?"

"That's my legal team's worry. But I've talked it over with Ramona, and she's in favor of it."

I thought that was democratic, including the fiancée in the financial arrangements. I asked how Ramona was getting on with her wrist.

"Of course, she's limited in what she can do, but it's the pain that's the problem at the moment. Byron and I have been going over, seeing to her meals and necessities. I've been insisting she be faithful in taking her pills. You don't know Ramona, Sergeant. She can be very stubborn."

"Even when it comes to medication?"

"If the problem's painful enough, she'll take it. I was there Sunday evening, when your police surgeon tucked her in. And Byron or I will go down tonight with dinner. I tried to get her to move into one of the guest rooms for a few days..." He trailed off. I knew he was thinking of the vacated rooms from the tourists.

"That would be a help," I agreed.

"She won't have it. Says it would look bad."

"Nice to see someone still worries about proprieties," I said. "Well, thank you, sir." I took my leave, wondering if the adoption mess would ever get sorted out.

"I TELL YOU, sir," I said as Graham and I compared notes in the incident room. My half pint momentarily forgotten, I tried to put sense to the mountain of growing information. "I'm amazed at these villagers. If I lived here and had to put up with Talbot's constant whining, I don't know if I wouldn't be moved to do something about it."

Graham paused with his half pint to his lips. He set the glass down. "That's a bit thick, TC. You, of all people, talking like that. Where's that famous detachment?"

"Stretched thin, I'm afraid."

"Well, it's a good thing you don't live here, if that's how you feel."

"Probably is. Anyway, I found out Kris Alton Halford's dad died in 1973, if that's of any interest to you."

"Popular year. Also the year of the quick engagement and subsequent breaking of same between her and Byron MacKinnon."

"You think the two incidents are connected?"

"I don't know. It's tempting to put too much weight on it. 1973... What month did Mr. Alton die?"

Death of an Ordinary Guy

"December. I checked it through the computer. Just to substantiate Arthur's story. I like to be thorough. It was a wintry road accident."

"Bad way to go." Graham closed his eyes, then rubbed them. "Life for our two love birds was certainly fine in November. That's when the perpetual row came up and Talbot got the news of the forthcoming wedding."

"So what happened to break it off, then?"

"Couldn't get a clue from Kris. Shall we try the unlucky groom?"

"Might as well. You haven't talked to him yet."

"We must rectify that, Taylor. He'll feel left out."

"So how many rooms, then, you think?"

Graham came to such an abrupt halt outside Byron's office that I bumped into him. He held his finger to his lips and inclined his head toward the door. It was nearly closed, yet left ajar an inch for the skilled listener to sidle up to and listen. Which is what we did, I stooping somewhat to accommodate Graham's tall frame. His chest was against my back and I could feel his warmth. We must have looked ridiculous, but I loved it. I had never been so close to him.

"I'll know more when we get the plan finalized."

"And when'll that be?"

There was a scraping of a chair, as though one of the talkers was getting to his feet. I recognized the voices — Talbot and Byron. Seemed like strange bedfellows, but perhaps not. We had yet to deduce the topic of their conversation.

Byron said something that I couldn't hear. He had moved away, possibly turned his back to us. Graham leaned closer to the door. I could feel his breath on the back of my neck.

Talbot said, "Fine. Just so as you keep me up to date. I don't like surprises."

"You sound as though you don't trust me. Is that a way for partners to start out?"

Talbot's verbal reply was inaudible, but I did hear his belch. Seconds later he said, "And converting it will take —"

"Now you sound like a ruddy banker."

"Well, when there's this much at stake—"

"You leave it to me, Talbot."

"That's just what I have to do for the moment, don't I? I'll feel better when I can actually get my hands into it."

Another verbal exchange that was muffled by a moved chair followed this, then two sets of footsteps growing louder. Evidently coming toward the door. Graham and I stood up. He motioned me to the opposite side while he then took a large step backwards. I raised my fist as though about to knock. It was not the first time I wished I had some Royal Academy dramatic classes under my belt. When Byron opened the door he saw what appeared to be two police officers just walking up to his office.

"I'll see you later, Talbot," Byron said after recovering from his initial jolt.

Talbot mumbled something just audible about never knowing what will turn up on your doorstep and being careful what you step into. He sniffed as though there was a putrid aroma somewhere, and left. Byron then held open the door for us.

Looking like a patient who's been given bad news by his doctor, Byron took us into his office and asked us to excuse the mess. It consisted of the expected letters, books and brochures of a tourist-oriented business, yet harbored more papers than I had expected. Either business is so good he can't keep up with his paperwork or the man's heart's not in his work. He belongs to the landscape and the breed of nature-linked ancient Scot, I thought on seeing him again, taking in his ginger colored hair and mustache. Remarkably like over-grown patches of heather on a craggy mound.

"I'm afraid you've caught me at a rather bad moment," Byron said, clearing a space on his desk.

I could believe that. Did he suspect we had overheard his conversation or was he referring to his work?

He quickly jammed his personal cheque book into a drawer, crumpled up a paper nearly black with mathematical calculations, and tossed it at a full waste bin. The sheet glanced off the edge of the bin and rolled beneath the desk. "Sorting through my accounts," he explained.

"If we've come at an inopportune time," Graham began, only to be waved off by Byron, who said it was all right.

"No time's *really* good when it's got to do with murder."

"Murder does seem to take up a bit of everyone's time," I agreed. "Far reaching effects, if that's not too trite a statement."

Graham asked about the car crash involving Kris' dad.

Byron seemed mesmerized by my pen. "I, uh — oh, December 1973? I can't remember. Sorry, but there you are. If you give me a day or so, I might remember…" He played with his watchstrap, then rushed on as Graham coughed. "Ah. Yes. Well, uh, it was a hell of a winter, even at that early stage, wasn't it? George Alton and I had been debating about the trip to Edinburgh. But since he had cleared his calendar and sort of made up his mind... Well, I used to do a lot of driving for Mr. Alton. I wasn't his 'driver,' or anything like that. He wasn't that well off! It's just that I was in my thirties then, needed a bit of extra cash, and had the time."

"I understand Kris had gone briefly to America in the mid-sixties. When did she return?"

"Oh, must have been 1971. Yes. I started driving Mr. Alton about, quite sporadically at first. He and his wife had gone over to America just before Kris' graduation. Something about seeing where her mum had grown up. Illinois, I think. They made quite a holiday of it — several months. Well, you would, wouldn't you, going all that way?"

"Was Mr. Alton banned from driving?" I said, wondering about the circumstances that warranted a chauffeur.

"You mean had he any restrictions on his license? No. He simply didn't like making long trips or driving at night. I didn't mind, so I ended up with the job. We liked each other well enough. I liked Kris, too. Well, to this day I don't know what went wrong. I was driving, must have hit a patch of ice. The car skidded. I couldn't control it, no matter how I steered it. God, I *still* hear it, the brakes squealing, the crash against the stone wall, the screams. Anyway, I couldn't go through with the marriage after I had killed her dad, could I?" He asked the question as though he were challenging our morals.

"But it wasn't deliberate," Graham said.

"No. And Kris knew that, but I couldn't have her look at me each day and be reminded of the accident, or her dad. So I broke it off. Walked out of her life. Literally. I left the village."

Uncomfortable with Byron's emotions, I looked at Graham, mouthing my request to leave. Shaking his head, Graham asked quietly, "When and why did you come back, Mr. MacKinnon?"

The secretary's hand dropped to his lap. He raised his head, squinting at Graham and looking as though he had just awakened and was bothered by the light. "1975. When I heard she had married Derek. I knew it was safe for me, for us. I still love her, though."

It was then that Graham nodded and we quietly left the room.

Jo A. Hiestand

We interrupted our return from the manor house to pause beside the burnt-out bonfire. The police tape still fluttered in the breeze, the dregs of Guy Fawkes Night still sat mutely where they had been left. The dole and Guy Fawkes — two ceremonies dealing with long-ago deaths. The first ceremony honored a death, reverently recalling personal passions of a loved family member. The second ceremony ridiculed a death, transforming an ancient tragedy into a mocking entertainment and social festivity. Amazing, I thought, staring at the charred potatoes, their blackened skins barely discernible in the ebony mess of the fire and the fading afternoon light. Two events two days apart, illustrating the two sides of human nature.

A gust of wind whipped up a handful of ashes and dust, mixing them into an eddy that peppered the air. "Dust to dust, ashes to ashes," Graham said. He rubbed his nose. The aroma was not pleasant. It stank of spent wood, old ashes and dry earth. "How many hundreds of fires, Taylor, have been enjoyed without any tragedies?"

I thought he wanted an answer, but he kicked at a potato, just tinged gray from the fire. "Burnt potatoes and burnt chestnuts," Graham sniffed. "Burnt offerings to Revelry and in merry memory of Mr. Fawkes. Burnt offerings, sacrifices that are ignored or go to no avail. The broken hearts are still there, for all the efforts. Remember, remember the 5th of November. *Damn.*"

Graham picked up the potato, flicked off an annoying ant, and threw it at the gallows tree. There was a satisfying splat as the potato hit its mark. He turned and hurried down the road, his shadow momentarily obliterating the few potatoes scattered in the grass.

I TOOK THE scenic route back to the pub. Not that it was difficult to do, for any walk in the village was proving a picture post card vista.

Taking the eastern road, I walked past Talbot's house, entered the woods, then turned toward Arthur's castle. The climb had been steady, yet not tiring, and I emerged from the woods into the open greenery. Rather like a woman gone mad with cosmetics, sunset splashed its lavenders, blues and vermilions across the leaden sky. A hint of crimson glowed along the western horizon where the sun hovered, its base nestled firmly on the hazy hill. On the summit of Ashmoor Pike the trees stretched like black lace across the lowest edge of the mottled sky.

I paused to pick a crocus — the *Crocus sativus* of saffron fame — astonished to find the fragile purple flower still in bloom. Yet, it was

Death of an Ordinary Guy

sheltered somewhat from the cold, northern wind. So I picked it, thinking I would admire it more in my room tonight than anyone else would do in passing along the road. Twirling it slowly against my thumb and index finger, I could feel the stiffness of the stem. I peered into the cup, looking at the small stamen. I decided to sketch it as a last offering of autumnal joy before winter swept all delicate beauty from the land. I should have left it alone, then perhaps I wouldn't have been so preoccupied with my find.

I might have seen him. But I didn't. On turning toward the village, I heard "Hey! Top Cop!" It was the ridiculous, taunting nickname he had created for me in police class. I had colored when he had whined it — anything to demean or make it arduous on me, the sole woman. It had been born of my determination to succeed as a police officer. Mark had laughed at his cleverness in inventing the nickname. By now, though, 'The Top Cop' had disintegrated into 'The Cop' or 'TC,' and most of my colleagues had forgotten the story.

I know I blushed. He always unnerved me. I hated myself for it. Of course I couldn't pretend not to have heard or seen him. I held my flower in front of me, as though it was a banner leading me into battle, and smiled.

"Hello, Mark. You having a busy day?"

A foot taller than I, he towered above me, which added to my anguish, for I was forever looking up at him. His muscles were obvious and contributed to part of his cockiness. The other ingredient was his premature gray hair, which he wore down to his collar. It was thick and curled becomingly, I had to admit. Complimented his gray eyes.

"Not as busy as some," he said, noticing that I had been intent on his face. He flashed his white, even teeth at me. "Even got your walk in this morning before dashing about with The Vic."

I colored, upset he had been watching me, despising his use of Graham's nickname. The way Mark said it gave the name an indecent, offensive quality.

"That all you could find, one lone pansy?" He reached out and I clutched it closer. His laughter held a mocking that reminded me of class. "Still learning about the birds and the bees? Is that why you're still single, Darling? Don't know about the finer points of marriage — or life? Any time you want to learn under my tutelage instead of Graham's —"

"You're certainly working hard," I said, wanting to change the subject.

"I like to work up a good sweat — I feel like I've earned my pay. But you, Babe; you're up earlier than I was. Find any two-toed toads?"

I kept silent and smiled, hoping it would give me some courage. I didn't even try to whistle.

"No. Not toads. Lily-livered *grahamisum dunghillium* is more your style, eh, Cop?"

"Haven't you got anything better to do, Mark? We're investigating a murder, or don't you remember?"

"Some of us have time for pansies, I see. Does The Vic know about your passion?"

"What's it got to do with Graham?" I felt my heart rate increasing and my jaw muscle tensing. "I'm not taking time off. I'm going to the incident room, if you have to know. To make my report —"

"Ooh. Talk cop-talk some more! Impress me, now that you're up with the rest of the boys in rank."

"If you'd apply the same energy to your work —"

"Hey, you don't have to explain anything to me, Brenna Darling. I'm a sergeant, just like you. Equals. Just don't work so hard in the woods that you can't get your beauty sleep tonight — not, that you have to worry about that. And if you don't feel like sleeping — well, Darling, you know where to find me."

He smiled, touched the crocus and walked down the lane, but not before calling out his room number.

I stood there for some time, trying to control my temper. Mark Salt was a good cop — had been near the top of our class — but he was at the bottom in emotional development.

After he'd had a five-minute head start, I tucked the crocus into my jacket and walked back to the pub.

"HE WAS JUST being his usual berk self," Margo said when I had found her at the pub. I was looking for Graham, but he was out somewhere. Margo was at a computer, typing faster than I thought human fingers were able. She seemed to be drowning in a sea of papers and sticky notes. I refrained from looking at the table Graham and I usually occupied, afraid I'd find messages from Simcock or notes from Graham telling me to take another statement from Talbot. Or work with Mark on something. I shuddered, thinking I'd rather endure a root canal procedure without novocaine. "You're letting him get to you, which is what he wants," Margo said when I finished telling her about my encounter with Mark. Luckily, he wasn't in the room. She looked up from the monitor. "Doesn't mean a thing, Bren. He's flexing his muscles."

"He didn't lay a hand on me, Margo."

"His badgering muscles. Follow the conversation, Girl."

"Wish I could believe you. I saw him talking to Evan this afternoon."

"So? I talked to Evan. Does that condemn me to having hung the Guy in your room?"

"No, but he could have got the key to my room from Evan, said he needed it for the investigation."

Margo shook her head. "Evan would've sent him to Graham for a key. He's not dumb, Bren."

"You don't know how much the average person fears the police, Margo. They're even afraid to talk to us. If we say something, they believe us. They obey us. We have an incredible amount of power."

"It's the uniform."

"*What* uniform? We're plain clothes cops."

"See? We need sweats. They evoke friendliness."

I groaned, rolling my eyes heavenward. "Big help. I still think it's Mark. He's devious. He can wheedle."

"He never tries to wheedle me. Wish he would. Don't you think he's handsome?"

"He thinks he's handsome."

"You're afraid to admit it, Bren. You know, men don't joke with women they don't like."

"You know the difference between joking and harassment, Margo?"

"Why don't you turn the tables and instigate something? You might get a date."

"I might get sick. Oh. Got to run. There's Graham."

I could hear Margo's whispered 'Give The Vic my love' as I headed for the incident room.

Chapter 16

GRAHAM AND I had no trouble finding a table that Monday evening at The Broken Loaf. And evidently Evan had no trouble in the kitchen, for he returned with our dinner orders just as Graham was draining the last of his beer.

"You'll be wanting the other half of that drink?" Evan nodded at Graham's empty pint.

I gave my glass to the publican, but Graham said he'd wait a bit.

"I know you're not much of a drinker, sir," I said when Evan had left, "but you usually have another with your meal. Feeling all right?"

"Not suffering from a gyppy tummy, if that's what you're hinting at. Glad to see we're not the only happy diners tonight. Murder hasn't put them off." He leaned back, chewing a forkful of ham, and looked around the room.

The public bar area was in keeping with the décor of the private bar, where we had set up the incident room. Photos of village events, framed articles from the local newspaper, and children's drawings covered the emerald green flocked wallpaper. Mahogany tables and chairs sat on a well-washed flagstone floor. An open fireplace large enough to roast an ox consumed a good portion of the wall opposite the bar, while someone's collection of royal and political commemorative china plates commandeered the wall before us. Staring at the names and pictures was a great time killer while waiting for your meal.

Derek sat at a nearby table, his voice low as he talked to Ramona. This time there was no door to hide behind or constable who could sit unobtrusively by to take shorthand notes. We chalked it up to the failure that occurs periodically. Besides, I thought, they wouldn't be talking about their part in the murder with us so close.

Death of an Ordinary Guy

But I glanced at them periodically, as though that would heighten my auditory senses. They both looked as though they had come directly from their jobs, for they were dressed in dark suits. Derek occasionally stroked his tie, a brightly colored conglomeration of fish, and glanced around the room. Was he afraid to be seen with Ramona, or just anxious to get home to Kris?

We finished our meal in silence before Graham gestured toward Tom Oldendorf, who was walking around the room, stopping periodically to examine something. "Must want a lot of memories of Upper Kingsleigh, the way he's using film in here." Another flash from his camera illuminated the room.

"Probably has shares in Kodak," I noted.

"What a suspicious person you are. What's he saying? Did you catch it? Don't be obvious about it, Taylor."

Graham, angling his thin frame in his chair so he could stretch out his long legs without entangling them in the maze of table and chair legs, appeared not only to be disinterested in his surroundings but also having a bit of a kip. If he'd had a hat, it would've been pulled over his eyes. But even without it, he looked completely off duty and relaxed, his arms folded across his chest, his chin nestled in the collar of his shirt. It was an attitude he employed often, and it usually helped glean startling bits of information. This time, the noise of too many conversations and the distance between tables prevented him from hearing anything.

Derek, meanwhile, got up, threw several pound coins on the table, and finished the last of his beer. Ramona grabbed the tail of his tie and pulled him down so their faces nearly touched, leaning in our direction as she tried to make herself heard above the din.

"Dear, you want to get home, put your feet up and watch the telly. I've never seen you like this."

Derek shook off her grasp and straightened up, running his hand through his hair. The graying brunet strands stood away from his pale skin, giving him the air of a hedgehog. He said something in reply but I couldn't catch it.

Obviously Ramona could, for she said, "Think nothing of it. You trot along home like the good husband you are. And I'll guard my tongue, so that worry's ended. After all, if I haven't said anything in all these years, your secrets are safe, darling. You and Byron have a good evening."

I watched Ramona's smile broaden as he left the pub.

"Hear that?" Graham asked, watching Ramona join the Oldendorfs at another table.

"Yes, sir. What's the little secret Derek's afraid of, do you suppose?"

"It's a secret, Taylor."

I nodded and wondered how many secrets Upper Kingsleigh's residents harbored. Minutes later, Graham pulled in his legs, threw his napkin on the table, and stood up. He glanced down at me. "I think we'll do the Public Servant bit and help Tom with his holiday budget."

I murmured it seemed the friendly thing to do.

Tom had just finished preserving This Moment on photographic film when Graham walked up to him. Tom was seated with several tourists from the B-&-B, none of whom was his wife. I looked for a vacant chair that indicated she was momentarily away from the table. There was one, pushed slightly away from the group to give the others more elbowroom. I hadn't remembered seeing her when we came in. Graham nodded to everyone, then asked Tom how the holiday was going.

"Great," the man said, depressing the spool-release button on his camera. "Carla's had it, though. What with Steve's — Well, we've done a bit too much today, so we're calling it an early night. Going back now, in fact, and crash. She left a while ago. You just missed her." Then, perhaps thinking he had been too personal with police officers, said, "You anywhere closer to solving the murder, or don't you let on?"

"I don't think you'd be happy with anything other than the name of the murderer, would you?" Graham smiled pleasantly. "Things are developing, let's just say."

Tom sat down abruptly, cradling the camera on his lap. The back of the camera gave a satisfying 'pop' as Tom released the catch. He opened the body and pulled out the film cassette. Graham, unusually interested in Tom's procedure, said, "You take other photos than this group tonight? I remember you had your camera when we met at the bonfire."

Tom dropped the cassette into the plastic film case and snapped on the lid. "Sure. It's one of my hobbies. I'm partial to architecture and landscape — church, gravestones, Haddon Hall. Though I take shots of people, too. Why? Have I done something wrong? If I've been a nuisance to someone...."

Death of an Ordinary Guy

"So you've been about the village and photographed parts of it, then?" Graham's voice remained calm, but I could see the faintest tensing of his jaw muscle.

Tom nodded, his attention torn between his film cassette, a polite Graham, and me.

"I know I'm a hell of a nuisance," Graham went on, "but would you mind telling me what you snapped of the village? It's an odd request, but I wouldn't be so insistent if it weren't important." He stood in front of Tom, non-threatening, his dark gray suit and cranberry-hued shirt as foreign to Tom's impression of a policeman as Graham's manner was.

Tom swallowed repeatedly. "Just been taking shots like any other tourist, I guess. A dozen or so during the bonfire, some during the dole ceremony, parts of the village, including a close-up of the church tower. Got it with my telephoto."

"Excuse me for asking what must appear to be an odd question, but did you take any of the effigy before Bonfire Night?"

"Yeah. Carla and I were down at the fire area that afternoon, and the pastor —"

"Would you mind terribly if I had the film developed, looked at your photos, and then returned them to you? Developing and printing on us, of course."

"Well, I —"

"Strange request, I know. But I have to keep my reason to myself."

Tom shrugged, probably figured he was getting a better bargain than most two-for-one deals, and dropped the film canister into Graham's outstretched hand. I already had the receipt written out and into Tom's hand before he said 'yes.' "You want the other roll, too?" He dug into his camera bag. Moments later the second exposed roll lay alongside the first. "Just these two. I had another roll, but I've sent that off already. It was finished before Carla and I got here." Nothing followed Tom's declaration but a sincere 'thank you' and the transferring of the film to Graham's pocket.

"Seems to have recovered from his brother-in-law's death quite rapidly," I observed as we paused in the vestibule connecting the two bar rooms. "Must have an iron constitution."

"He certainly displayed more anger than grief at the fire circle," Graham agreed.

"Maybe that's why he came on holiday with Pedersen. Wasn't particularly friendly or unfriendly with him, so he's not all that broken up over his death. Anyway, women show their emotions more easily."

Graham pulled the film from his pocket, threw me a canister, and wrapped his long fingers about the remaining roll. "This just might have something on it. I'm not going to let this slip past us. Even at my age I learn from past mistakes."

Your age. You're all of 41, I wanted to say. Trim, healthy, good looking, mentally and physically able to beat most of us in B Division. Don't talk utter rot!

Graham pushed open the door to the incident room, noted the startled looks of the constables who were clustered around a single computer, and walked briskly over to a table, where I joined in. There were two new messages from Simcock, received this evening 18 minutes apart, stuck to the front of the case folder. But were marked 'Urgent.' Both asked the same question: had we learned anything more about MacKinnon's 1973 road accident? Ignoring the notes, Graham idly rolled the canister along the table top, as though it were some bizarre rugby game. The canister crashed into the case folder — thick with typed notes, statements and photographs — and I picked up the film. I knew Graham had seen Simcock's messages, yet chose to ignore them for the moment. Which was fine with me; Graham was easier to work with when he wasn't reeling from the Super's impatience. I placed the canister gently by Graham's hand. Granted there's very little leeway for mistakes in murder cases, but he's too hard on himself. He's got to be perfect, solve it as fast as he can. Like he's trying to prove himself all over again, make up for those five years of demotion. I let the canister roll back and forth a few times before my hand slapped onto it, quieting it.

"Fordyce!" Graham's head jerked up from his concentration, and he looked around for the constable. An energetic 'Here, sir!' echoed off the walls. Chair legs scraped across flagstone, and the steady tempo of hard soles tapped out the path to his superior officer. There was a sharper tap as Fordyce came to a stop at Graham's side and snapped to attention. Then the room returned to that quiet that settles on a space when people are comfortable with each other and their duties. Graham scooped up the two rolls of film and handed them to the P.C. "I want you to take these to the station. Get them developed and printed, and have them back here tomorrow — *early."*

Fordyce's 'Yes, sir" cracked into the stillness as he accepted the film.

Death of an Ordinary Guy

"Two sizes of prints — our standard working size, and 4x5 for the film's owner. Got that? Oh, and if the pathology report's ready, bring that, too, please. And, the knife. *Don't* forget the knife, Fordyce. That should do it."

"Very good, sir." The door opened and closed quickly, and the constable was on his way to Buxton.

"That knife'll be dusted by now. I want to dangle it in front of a few people's eyes, see if anyone recognizes it. Not that anyone will," Graham sighed. We knew that most everyone — guilty or not — guarded himself during a police investigation. "Is there a universal motto I'm not aware of, TC?"

"Besides 'Mum's the word'?"

"Unless it's 'Perhaps this too will be a pleasure to look back on one day.'" Graham smiled and glanced at his watch. "You feel like putting in an hour or so before we catch a final pint?"

"A perfect evening, sir."

"Right."

We sat down, shoving the case folder and Simcock's messages farther down the table, pretending we didn't see them. Graham grabbed the notes still lying in the printer tray, a pen, and laid a blank sheet of paper in front of us. He seemed happier now that he had dealt with Simcock.

"The more we get into this thing," I said, tapping my notebook, "the more these people get all intermingled and show up in each other's stories."

"Like a massive Celtic knot. You thinking of our favorite year, then?"

"Not just 1973. The entire village. Byron nobly gave up Kris Halford — Alton, as she was then — but still loves her. Kris was engaged-to-be-married to Pedersen. Talbot was adopted, if you care to believe it, by Derek's father, only he can't prove it. And Arthur's great-grandfather runs over Derek's grandfather and starts this whole miserable dole and its consequences." I threw my pen at the computer. "We need more than a computer to sort all this out. We need a ruddy crystal ball."

"Could come in handy, but let's spare the Derbyshire taxpayers the additional expense and try our brains first."

I mumbled something about it being a definite disadvantage, but jotted down ideas readily enough when Graham started talking through things.

"You mentioned Pedersen and Talbot. Would your credibility extend to Talbot killing Pedersen by mistake — if strangling is his preferred or first attack?"

"I don't quite follow you, sir."

"Think back to that entertaining bit Fordyce put us onto, Taylor. If Talbot lunged at Byron, ready to strike and kick the life out of him years ago, would Talbot also just as easily have struck *Pedersen?* Damn, I wish we had the pathology report."

"It's obvious he didn't die from the knife wound. Hardly have to wash his clothes for all the blood that was on them. It might have been part of their tradition, using a knife to affix a note to the effigy, but it's a silly one."

"So, what's the motive, TC?"

"Told you we needed that crystal ball." The minutes ticked away as we considered our suspects and motives. Finally, almost apologizing for interrupting our contemplation, I said, "Could Byron have staged it, wanting to kill Derek?"

"For what gain? The only tango those two ever did, as far as we know, was for Derek to take over as Kris' fiancé. And that was certainly nothing personal. Derek stepped into the matrimonial picture after Kris' dad was killed in that car accident."

"People harbor grudges for ages."

"*What* grudge? *Byron* was driving. *He* lost out on marriage, not Derek."

"I agree it's logical, but if you're overcome by remorse or bitterness or jealousy, you aren't as likely to think straight. Maybe while he was in his self exile he got to thinking about what happened, what he was missing in marriage. He had a lot of months to let those emotions boil. Maybe that car accident years ago wasn't so much of an accident. Maybe it was a suicide that failed."

"And it's a damned stupid, risky thing to do," Graham said, his fingers nearly crushing his pen. "Could you be sure you'd die? No. Besides, why should he take Kris' dad with him? You're clutching at straws, Taylor. Give it up. Besides, the man came back and in twenty-two years hasn't killed himself."

"Maybe the depression's over. Maybe he got a good therapist."

"You make it sound like the man suffered through Viet Nam."

"There are a lot of traumas in life, a lot of reasons people wish other people dead."

"If anybody deserved to be dead, it should've been Derek. With him out of the way, Arthur could keep his money."

Death of an Ordinary Guy

"Arthur and Ramona would probably vote for that," I stated, then added that I meant that only as an economic measure, that the betrothed couple probably liked Derek a great deal and wouldn't mean him any personal harm.

"But *someone* might have," Graham reminded me, staring at his mess of mind-mapped notes, the arrows, cartoons and boxed-off words remarkably accurate in portraying the condition of our minds at the moment. He hummed a snatch of a Gilbert and Sullivan song, and grinned when I joined him.

I sighed heavily, evoking fond memories of the operetta. "One of my favorites, *Yeomen of the Guard*. I played Dame Carruthers." I smoothed the fabric on my trousers, hoping he wouldn't say something about matronly type casting. "I still remember it all."

Graham looked at me with a new admiration, I thought. "I didn't know you sang, Taylor. What a deep, secret pool of talents you hide."

"Yes, sir," I said, embarrassed now that I had mentioned it.

"And where was this? I would have come if I'd have known. Next time, let me know."

I could feel the heat flooding my cheeks. Hating myself for being so self-conscious, I said, "The church hall. Um, a few years ago, I think."

Graham grinned, squeezed my hand, and said, "I bet the tower was never kept in better tune than by you."

My voice shook as I thanked him. For some reason, I was hoping he would say something further, something more personal, mentioning my singing voice, but he had dropped the subject and was once again focused on murder. Fanning through my papers, I said, "You have the time table handy, sir? Can't seem to place my copy. Thanks. Was our Good Arthur alone long enough to slip down to the green and waylay Pedersen?"

"As you said that, Taylor, I had the queerest mental image of Arthur gaily bedecked in some mumming outfit, running stealthily from tree to tree, dodging moonlight and villagers."

"Mummers' plays aren't for another month or so. Besides, Arthur would stand out like a sore thumb in any such outfit."

"Well, if Arthur did traipse down to the village green for some nefarious purpose, mum's the word from him."

"Very appropriate for a mumming play."

"But we're not dealing in Christmas charades. We're dealing in deliberate death." Graham groaned as he closed his eyes briefly and stretched, the stress of the case and the long days catching up with him. "I don't know, TC. I think I've had it. Can't seem to think any more."

"You've been chasing the clock hands fairly steadily, sir. Pity the overtime pay's a thing of the past."

"Nothing more than a fond memory," he agreed, giving way to a yawn after he had given his opinion of the constabulary policy. "We ignore the clock and plug along. Well, I, for one, am having a damned hard go this evening. What say we give it another quarter hour before surrendering to our beds? Now..." He folded back the top page of his notebook. "Let's look long and hard at these flittings by our key personnel. Motive aside for the moment, it seems to all hang on opportunity."

I nodded, but thought of the Guy that had been hanging in my bedroom. Who had had the opportunity to fix up that?

"Very little time to accomplish anything," Graham continued after he had closed his eyes. "We've got the vicar, Talbot, and the American couple at the bonfire area at quarter past six or so, with the place literally crawling with people from then on."

"Had to have been done earlier. Of course, there were snatches of quarter and half hours throughout the day when someone could have switched the effigy for Pedersen's body. Wouldn't take long if he had Pedersen all dressed for the occasion. But the American wasn't missing till after tea Sunday. Cuts down on the available time."

"I know you were wandering about, TC. Heaven knows you couldn't stare constantly at a pile of wood and remain alert. And I'm not criticizing your effort, believe me, but if you remember anything unusual as you walked your beat..."

I shook my head, feeling like a failure, feeling I should've seen something, wishing I could provide the "Ah ha!" he wanted.

"So," he continued, without any judgment or exasperation in his voice. "In those quarters of an hour or so when you were not all-eyes on the stack of wood, we've a bunch of tourists and villagers alone and at loose ends, waiting for the bonfire to begin, probably quite available to commit the crime."

"Alone," I echoed, turning the word and the meaning around in my mind. "I know our time constraint is bloody awful, but do you suppose our murderer could have had an accomplice?"

Death of an Ordinary Guy

"Nothing would surprise me, TC. God, what I wouldn't give right now for a stone-chiseled tablet of everyone's whereabouts. Where's Moses when we need him?"

Chapter 17

"So, anything happen last night?" Margo asked on coming into my room Tuesday morning. She looked at my ceiling fixture, expecting to see the Guy still hanging there. I didn't tell her, but it had taken all my nerve to touch it to take it down.

"What do you consider 'happen'?" I busied myself with brushing my hair, and avoided her eyes.

Margo laid both hands on my shoulders and turned me to face her. My resolve, so steady earlier, dissolved on the confrontation, and I felt tears forming in my eyes. "More importantly," she said, her eyes drilling into mine as though she was Mesmer, "what do you consider it? Anything gross and indecent?" She started toward the bathroom, seeing nothing obvious in the room itself. I pulled her back.

"It's not in there."

"So something *did* happen," she said with the suggestion of a smile. "Note? Phone call?"

"That I could deal with." I grabbed a tissue. Even now, eight hours after I had discovered it, I was still angry.

"For God's sake, Bren, what happened?"

I walked to the waste bin, reached in and removed the pristine pages I had torn from my notebook, then held the can so Margo could see the dead bird inside. A string secured a wilted chrysanthemum to the bird's chest. For once Margo had nothing to say. I placed the bin on the floor and slowly tossed in the papers.

I looked around, aware of the flowered curtains and coverlet, the fireplace and over-sized cushions and rocker, yet searching for some clue to the intruder.

Death of an Ordinary Guy

In the silence I could hear the sounds of the pub waking. The creaks of the wooden floor, the phone in the bar area ringing, the scratchings of a wind-tossed tree branch at my window. It wasn't until I heard a bird singing outside the window that I cried.

"Bren, dear, it's all right." Margo came over, smothered me in a hug that spoke of her anger and concern and sorrow. We stood like that for several minutes, my head on her shoulder, dampening her blouse with my tears, and her voice floating in my ear.

When I finally lifted my head, I said, "It's not me, Margo. I swear I'm not crying for me. It's the sparrow. Why anyone would harm such a defenseless creature who never did anything —"

Margo held me at arm's length, searching my eyes for some hint to my emotional stability. "It's not the bird, Bren." I must have looked astonished, because she hurried on. "Listen to me. Think like a cop, Bren. You're letting your emotions get in the way. And that's just what this berk wants. You're not using your brain, Bren. You're forgetting everything you ever learned of police work."

"But how does he know about me and birds?"

"Maybe he doesn't. Maybe it's just a coincidence. It's not the bird — I'm trying to get through to you. It's the message."

I gazed at the cloudy sky, at the patchwork of sun and shadow sweeping the land, before I could find my words. "He wants me dead? Like the bird?"

"Either that, or he's trying to scare you off this case."

We sat on the bed while Margo rattled off suppositions. They were probably good bits of wisdom, though I can't recall any; I was too emotional over the sparrow.

"So how is he getting in here?"

Margo's foot tapped the waste bin. "I'm not half so concerned about that as I am about his messages. This was left in your bathroom sometime yesterday, then, and you found it —"

"Around 11:00, when I was getting ready for bed."

We heard Graham's door open and close. She waited for his footsteps to fade before asking, "Does he know? Have you told him?"

"If I haven't said anything about the Guy in my room, you think I'm going to mention a dead bird? I told you —"

"I *know* what you told me," Margo said, gazing at the door. "But this thing's not just about a dummy anymore, Bren. It's escalating. And, in a frightening way. I think you should at least tell one of the lads."

Jo A. Hiestand

I must have grabbed Margo's hand rather tightly, for she yelled and asked what was the matter. I apologized and reminded her about Mark Salt.

"You can't suspect him, Bren. Really?"

I nodded. "Just the sort of thing he'd do. Birds, flowers, nature. Use my passions, as he calls it, to make me nervous."

"And hopefully propel you into his arms."

"Or his bed," I added.

"Just like him, the berk. 'I'm scared, Mark. Help me!' Men!" She exhaled loudly and stood up, her eyes hardened. "Well, whoever is getting in here at least isn't harming *you* — remember that. He's had opportunity."

"You don't think it's more of a practical joke, do you, Margo, instead of the warning off the case?"

"Now that could definitely be Mister Detective God's-Gift-to-Women Mark Salt."

I suddenly felt better thinking along that line. It would be just like Mark to first use a piece from the case, then something personally associated with me, as a big joke. Perhaps he even wanted me to confide in him. What had he said yesterday?

"Well," Margo said, her hand on the doorknob, "it's a damned shame we can't use some of our equipment to catch Mister Funny Man. What a waste. Come on," she said, opening the door and stepping into the hall. "You'll feel better after breakfast."

"Not necessarily," I said, then indicated Talbot at the end of the hall. The handyman had a large canister, into which he was dumping rubbish from people's rooms. I thought about ducking back into my room before he saw me, but then reasoned I'd have a face-to-face confrontation when he tapped on the room to get my waste bin. I stepped into the hall and quietly shut the door.

Fortune was not smiling on me that morning. Perhaps it couldn't break through the clouds. Talbot turned to knock at the next door in his procession, saw me, and called out, "Leave yer door open, will ya? I know you've got somethin' ya wanna get rid of." He shuffled down the hall, his eyes fixed on me rather like a snake staring down a rabbit. I stepped aside as he approached and opened the door. As he passed I could smell the cigarette odor of his clothes and breath. I turned my head to avoid the aroma.

When he had tipped the waste bin contents into his canister, he shoved the waste bin into my hand. "You're lookin' at me like I was gonna steal it. Here. Now you've got it again you can sleep safe."

Death of an Ordinary Guy

He bent over, butt angled toward me, conveniently picking up something off the carpet so he could show his opinion of me.

Margo called impatiently from the top of the landing, wondering what was taking me so long.

I put the bin back and shut the door. I tucked the key into the zipped section of my purse. In turning to go, I rattled the doorknob once more. It was locked.

"Go and fill yer belly, then," Talbot said on straightening up. "We can't have you fainting from hunger. Might hit yer head and get concussed. And then you'd be in hospital. What would we do then?" He ambled down the hall, rapping on the next door. Getting no response, he moved to the next. I noticed, on the door opening, that he could talk civilly when he wanted to.

TEA HAD JUST been poured the second time that morning when Fordyce dashed into the incident room. Thinking he wanted a hot drink after his drive up from Buxton, I held out a mug. He shook his head, and looked around for Graham. Seeing him at the far end of the room, he walked over, waving a folder that looked very much like Ahrens' pathology report.

The morning was well advanced. Shops were open, the Royal Mail van was on its rounds, and motorists were pumping petrol at the service station. The baker's shop discharged a handful of customers, all of whom hurried away with bags or boxes. I imagined the glass cases with their array of bread and biscuits, and wished for a pastry or a plate of digestives. Something nice for our mid-morning break. Instead, we had a tin of stale pretzels. Graham put down his cup, his attention peeled from the pathology report to Fordyce's impish face.

Opening his clenched fingers to reveal a roll of film, the constable watched Graham's confusion as he glanced from the metal roll to the processed photographs. The computerized report fell haphazardly to the table, momentarily forgotten. "No, sir," Fordyce said, handing the photos to Graham. "I didn't overlook it. I just received it from Mrs. Oldendorf."

"*Mrs.* Oldendorf? How'd —"

"Nice bit of timing, actually, I was coming, she was going." Then as though thinking he had better put it in officialese for his superior, Fordyce reiterated, "Upon proceeding toward the village from my duties in Buxton, I observed the aforementioned subject traveling at a speed I considered in excess of the speed limit.

Needing to reprimand her for the speed violation, I detained her. To make certain, as it were."

"Yes. Right." Graham's thumb and forefinger dented the edge of the photographs. "What, exactly, was Carla Oldendorf doing on the road with this film? Can you tell me in twenty-five words or less?"

"Yes, sir. Taking the film to Buxton to be developed. That was her story, anyway."

"You didn't believe her?" I said, enjoying the verbal tennis game.

"She didn't give me any particular reason not to," replied Fordyce, eyeing the pretzels. "Tom overlooked it yesterday when you asked for his film, Mr. Graham. He thought he'd given you all the rolls, but when she was hanging up her husband's jacket...."

"Behold the treasure trove." Graham tossed the photographs onto the table.

"Yes, sir. Also gave me another story. This one's about Colonel Wroe. As pertains to the murder. She wanted you to know that Wroe is an expert with knives. That kukri thing that the British troops used during the war. Probably doesn't make too much difference what type of knife. Just that he's good at handling such things." His message delivered, Fordyce remained at attention.

"Too bad it wasn't a kukri sticking out of Pedersen," I said. "We would have had our smoking gun."

"She would have told you herself," Fordyce said, "but to tell the truth, I think she's a bit frightened of you."

And the friendly village bobby offered more comfort during the investigative storm than Graham does, I deduced. There's a fine line between appearing Official and Stern. I had been frightened of him on our first meeting, seeing only the Stern. As we continued working together, I was seeing the three parts of him — there was also the man who liked to joke. I said to Fordyce, "Think she'd get more leniency from you? What's that say about us, sir?"

Graham slowly passed his long fingers over his mouth in order to hide his grin. He tapped his index finger against his lips, then slapped his hands onto the table top. The cushioning of the p.m. report muffled the crack. "Nothing particularly one way or the other, Taylor. Carla Oldendorf just grabbed opportunity when it knocked. So she thinks we should concentrate on Wroe, does she? Any other reason than her assumption Wroe could hit a gnat at one hundred metres with a knitting needle?"

Fordyce shrugged, relating that he only knew what he was told.

"She can't seriously believe we'd consider Wroe, can she?"

Pulling the imprisoned pathology report from beneath Graham's hands, I mumbled, "I don't fancy it myself, sir."

"Wroe had no motive as far as we've been able to discern. Didn't even know the American. And I can't see an eighty-year-old man strangling a healthy specimen like Steve Pedersen."

I nodded as I smoothed the wrinkles from the paper. "Seems like Carla's trying to save her husband's neck by accusing Wroe. Must be scared."

"She did seem that," Fordyce agreed. "But I put it down to her being apprehended and feeling the guilt of it."

"Maybe, but she's not above trying to take the spotlight off her husband. Kukri knives. Might as well blame everyone in the village who has a knife." Might as well extend it to Wroe's army mates, I thought, growing angrier by the woman's silly accusation. They could have sneaked into the area, helped with Wroe's reconnaissance of the area. It was something he might do.

"I don't think it's as bad as all that, Taylor," Graham said. "You're just jealous the lady beat you to the info. She gets around more than you do."

I replied that I would relinquish all information gathering if I ever stooped to anything so ridiculous. "Best to stick to facts. Like the pathologist's report and those photographs." I nodded toward the photos. "Then you make your case. Probably find something more pertinent in these snaps than we'd get by calling in the heavy gang to extract a confession from Wroe. All he'll be guilty of, when this is concluded, will be exaggeration."

"I'm inclined to agree," Graham said slowly. "But I'd also like to know why this wasn't with the lot bestowed on us yesterday."

"Couldn't be something on this roll that would prove she's right, could there?" Fordyce suggested. "But why she had to get this film developed right then, and why she was doing close to fifty —"

I said, "He could have shot it all today, I suppose."

"Then why not trot up to us with film in hand and tell us? Why sneak out of the village at such a break-neck pace? Whatever her devious scheme, let's hope you've thwarted her, Fordyce. Would you mind? Soon as you get your breath and a cuppa, back you go to Buxton. You do it so well." He thanked Fordyce, who muttered that it was his pleasure, and held out the tin of pretzels to him. Looking simultaneously astonished and pleased, Fordyce took a handful, thanked Graham, and left.

The pathologist's report was the one substantial element in the confusion facing us. Graham read the confirming details and smiled as he mentioned the high points. "Love it when we're right. Makes me feel like I'm earning my pay. It wasn't hanging that did in Pedersen. Death due to hemorrhaging, as if you need to be told, Taylor. Fractures of the skull...subdural hematoma...pupil dilated, indicating acute pressure on the injured side of the brain...numerous bruises to the left side of the body — waist, ribs, jaw and neck...cracked ribs, also on the left side..." Graham tossed me the report. "Weapon was your classic blunt instrument, though wider than Talbot's ancient hammer. Could be a rock, I suppose. Place is littered with them, with the creek so handy."

"This bruising on the left side of the torso...."

Graham eyed me, waiting for me to finish my thought. He leaned against the edge of the table, his arms folded across his chest, his eyes bright with interest. It was a common pose when he let me think things through. A teacher observing his pupil. I rambled on. "If Pedersen had merely fallen, as the bruises and cuts to the knees and palm indicate, I don't see how he could have sustained the bruising to the waist, ribs and jaw. Bruising there suggests a fight. How can anyone fall forward on his knees and come up with bruises on his left side?"

"And barring your personal demonstration, Taylor, which I'm sure you'd be eager to supply in the course of your work, I'm inclined to agree. What does the left side bruising suggest?"

I took a deep breath and swiftly ran through a short, mental prayer before I said, "He was involved in a fight before death."

"From a right-handed bloke standing in front of him. Or a left-handed bloke standing behind him, as Mr. Holmes might have said in his day. Do you think it odd that even a right-handed person wouldn't have landed a punch with his left hand on Pedersen's right side?"

I nodded slowly, the strenuous fight scene shimmering before my eyes quickly shifting into a different scenario. In a small voice, I said, "Attacked while he was down."

Graham nodded, his hand moving to his rib cage. "This area would be exposed if Pedersen lay on the ground from his fall. A couple of energetic kicks would produce the bruising and cracked ribs Ahrens found."

Death of an Ordinary Guy

I grimaced, not liking the image of the dirty fighting I conjured up. "And the bruises on the jaw and neck?"

"Fist fight, I should think." He made a fist and slowly, accurately aimed for the left side of my jaw, stopping so close that I could just feel his knuckles. Smiling, Graham dropped his arm and said, "Lights out. Pedersen down on his knees."

"Where does the rock come into it? Ahrens said a rock or something equally convex, hard and smooth fractured his skull."

"When Pedersen was trying to get up, perhaps. As good a time as any. Though our junior Muhammad Ali didn't really need it. From the depth of the bruises and the broken skin...." Graham stared at me, the humor gone now from his eyes. "What a lot of power he'd need to fracture Pedersen's skull."

And, I thought, not really seeing the photographs, the berk who had such free access to my room seemed to thrive on power. In my mind I could again see the Guy hung from the ceiling, the sparrow's limp head flopping as I picked it up from the bathroom basin. Someone's in love with the strength of his hands.

"All this bright, new information," Graham was saying when I refocused on his voice, "doesn't do much for us in terms of a solution. So Pedersen has a rocky start to his star performance as the effigy, then hoisted for the bonfire display. What's that get us?"

My eyes widened as he voiced what I had just envisioned. I blinked and said, "Nothing much. Easier to string up a victim if he's dead first, is the only thing I can think of. Anything on the knife?"

The knife, printed and analyzed to death by the police laboratory technicians, revealed blood on the shaft near the wooden handle and smears on the blade. It must've arrived safely, for I hadn't heard any swearing or threats of demotion from Graham. It also was now housed — for easier viewing — in a plastic bag, which Graham held up to the light.

"'The smiler with the knife under the cloak,' Taylor," Graham mused half aloud.

"Beg pardon, sir?" I said, wondering just what he had quoted and what he meant.

"Chaucer." He smoothed out a wrinkle in the plastic to see the knife edge better. It was four inches long and angled into the wooden handle when not in use. Graham tried to depress the latch at the upper edge of the handle. He struggled with the rusty mechanism, pushing on the blade to force it home. The blade resolutely refused to surrender its outward position. "This thing's as stiff as I feel some mornings."

"Scout knife, isn't it?"

"Old scout, to be sure. Probably dates back to my youthful days."

"Might have done, but not likely. Weren't the knives removed from sale for a bit in the late '60s or so — on account of all those accidents the lads were having with them?"

"So we've got a more current knife — is that what you're hinting at so subtly?"

"Or older, sir. Though there are other ways besides the flow of years that would rust a knife."

"Such as the flow of water. Careless sort of scout, leaving his equipment outside to be rained on. Well, it's a nice task for our energetic constables, then. See who's been a scout among the villagers. Should put a smile on their lips."

It would Margo, I thought. She would relish anything that would get her noticed by Graham. Promote her to an actual name.

"Speaking of smilers," Graham said, "do you think that's how it was done? Would have had to be a smiler — someone who wouldn't upset Pedersen, who could murder him without unduly warning him, don't you think? Otherwise there's the risk he would have given one hell of a fight."

"Scream his head off and alerted someone," I agreed. "Plus, there might be all those hard-to-explain scratches and bruises on the unlucky murderer's body."

"Came at him nonchalantly, all friendly."

"Who's more friendly, if it comes to that, and familiar to him than his former brother-in-law?"

"Carla Oldendorf, Derek Halford, Kris Halford." Graham turned the bag slowly, noting every inch of the knife. "Strange thing, this knife. Why use it?"

"You said yourself that it was just for dressing, that he was strangled and the knife used as part of their annual dramatics. But if you wanted a knife, you'd use a letter opener, say, or a carver. More common type of item."

"Or a Stanley knife," Graham said.

I nodded. Most households had one, just as they had a saw, hammer and stepladder.

"Well, we'll dangle it in front of a few eyes and see if we can cut through more than wood. Anything develop from those?" Graham set down the knife and gestured toward the packet of photographs developed from Tom's film.

"Nice, but not exactly startling. Nothing to hang a case on. Or a corpse. What were you hoping to find?"

"Something hinting to our murder," Graham said. "These don't prove a thing, damn it. Can't even prove the time when they were taken, let alone the day." He lowered his head, peering at the purple shadows that stretched across Tom's snippets of captured landscape. Mumbling in disgust, he waved the photographs at Constable Byrd. "Would you mind, Constable? Take these out to the corresponding areas in the village this afternoon and see if the shadows line up. Thanks." He waited until Byrd returned to his computer before saying, "I want to check up on the lay of the land as much as on Tom Oldendorf. Not that I don't doubt his veracity as a photographer or a tourist, but…. That lens of his, Taylor…."

"Telephoto."

"Maybe his roving eye caught some elusive detail of the crime scene before it got eradicated. If it did. We'll know with his weekend snaps."

Graham seemed to focus on the day outside — crisp, sunny and smelling of fallen leaves. Layers of clouds, gray tinged on their bellies, crawled across the sky from the west. The air held the scent of approaching rain. Inside the room it was quiet, some of the constables grabbing a bite to eat, others working at computers. I took a deep breath, pulled a folded piece of paper from my pocket, and spoke Graham's name. He looked at me, momentarily lost in his thoughts. I held the paper toward him and asked if he would like to see the chart of suspects and motives I had drawn up.

He gazed at it for several minutes, his pen making tic marks beside several of the columns, then looked at me. His eyes were brilliant and held no sign of mockery as he said, "I'm impressed, Taylor. When did you do this?"

"Uh, late last night." I refrained from mentioning it was because I couldn't sleep. I glanced at Mark, who had just entered the room. He caught my stare and pursed his lips in a kiss. I turned back to Graham, hoping I hadn't reddened.

"First class work. Really excellent. You have time to go over this?" He pulled out a chair for me and I sat beside him, not across the table as I usually did. We talked of Uncle Gilbert mistaking Pedersen for Derek. "To benefit from the extra money Arthur would get when the dole stopped," Graham read. We talked of Arthur mistaking Pedersen for Derek. "Same motive," Graham read, then smiled at my brief analysis. We talked of Ramona mistaking Pedersen for Derek. "Ditto," Graham read again, then laughed.

I hated the idea of a murderess. I hated it not because I thought Ramona such an outstanding woman as that I thought women above such emotions. They were the keepers of the hearth, the soul of the home, the giver of life. For a woman to taint that centuries-long gift was disgraceful. I knew women killed — there have been many famous murderers among the sex. But it still turned my stomach. And I couldn't see Ramona, independent as she was, murdering Pedersen.

As though reading my thoughts, Graham said, "I don't know, Taylor. No matter how liberated she is, I don't think she could kill him and get away without a scratch. She'd have to know jujitsu or something. Does she know jujitsu?"

"Do we know her sprained wrist is legitimate, sir?"

"Your idea being she's hiding a tell-tale scratch, received in her fight with Pedersen?"

I nodded.

Graham exhaled slowly, as he did when considering something he deemed important. He said, "Very well could do. I'm impressed you take nothing as obvious, Taylor. Could easily be window dressing, set up to fool us."

"I suppose there was an attending physician?"

"Why not find out, Taylor? Ask the populace. If no one recalls the stumble...."

"We unsling her arm. But is there any reason why Pedersen would be killed for his own sake?" I said, rather glad that Graham had seen the value in my suggestion about Ramona's sprain.

"What's your chart say?" He turned to it, not as a joke, but to see how I had reasoned it all out. He may have been impressed by the hours I had put into it, but I was impressed he was taking me seriously. Graham read aloud, "Derek. Although Kris was originally engaged to Pedersen, she seems earnestly in love with Derek, who also welcomed Pedersen." He looked up, supplying his own observation. "And if we're considering broken hearts as fuel, Taylor, Tom has had plenty of time to murder Pedersen. Why would he risk it in a locality he didn't know?"

"If his anger or hatred over his sister's death got the better of him, he'd lash out," I reminded my colleague.

Death of an Ordinary Guy

"What else?" He read my chart again. "What's this last column say? I can't make it out — Oh, Symbolism." This time his eyebrow was raised when he looked at me. I fought to keep from blushing. I knew at the time I wrote it that it would be questioned, but I had to put it down. A good cop, I had reminded myself last night, overlooks nothing.

"Yes, sir. Whoever killed Pedersen would be taking a huge chance by dressing him up as the Guy. Why not leave the body in the woods or wherever? It'd be a lot easier. All that time spent replacing the effigy with the body is just asking for discovery. There has to be a reason it was rigged up." I waited for what seemed a century for Graham to speak.

He had been focused again on life outside the pub window, watching the residents, tourists and police mingling and going about their own lives. Finally, he said in a barely audible voice, "All the world's a stage, TC, and we had a highly significant stage Sunday evening. But who was the intended audience?"

Chapter 18

GRAHAM ASKED ME that afternoon to interview a few of the suspects while he busied himself with hearing Tom's new story about the film. I needed my notebook and that was in my room. My bedroom door was locked, I noted on jiggling the knob. Good. One less thing to worry about. Besides, it was broad daylight. No need to fear ghosts or jokers lurking behind shower curtains. When I entered my room I found out just how wrong a girl can be.

My bed was strewn with photographs of me — me at the village pond, me walking to Arthur's, me standing at the pub door, me talking to Margo. I might have been merely annoyed if it weren't for the nooses. In each photo a noose was carefully drawn around my neck.

I don't know how long I stood there, unable to release my stare from the atrocity. I do remember my mouth had gone dry and my heart was beating as though I'd just run a marathon race up Mount Everest. I tried to put the outrage down but I couldn't control my fingers. My hand shook violently. The knock on the door restored what little sanity I had left. I stuffed the photographs under the pillow and yelled, "Come in." It was Mark.

I didn't know whether to laugh, cry, attack or hug him. I opted for asking what he wanted.

"Nothing more than the usual," he said, seating himself beside me on the bed. "Were you expecting me?" He smoothed out a wrinkle in the duvet and leaned back.

Angling my body against the pillow, I told him I had only come up to get my notebook, that Graham needed me. Which wasn't completely a lie, but I needed to get rid of Mark. I figured Graham's name would do it.

"What if I need you, Brenna?"

Death of an Ordinary Guy

"I know what you need, Mark, and it's a cold shower. Now, out."

"Is that any way to talk to a friend?"

"I didn't know you were one."

"A colleague, at least."

"There are all types of colleagues, Mark. Consider me a long-distance one. Now, out!"

"I just thought you'd have a minute or two. Saw you come upstairs."

"I didn't see you in the incident room," I said, feeling rather paranoid now that I knew someone was watching me. Whoever had taken those photos had a good quality camera. Those shots had to have been taken with a telephoto lens or else I would have seen the photographer.

"'Course not. I was in the public bar. Just walking out when I saw you on the stairs. Great timing, eh?"

Yeh, I thought, cursing my luck, stupendous timing. He was staring at my nightdress, which was thrown over the back of the chair. I grabbed it and stuffed it under the duvet. He laughed — one large roar that editorialized my prudishness.

"Can't you take a joke, Bren?"

I buried my fingers into the bedding, not knowing how to respond. Barely finding my voice, I stared at him. "Joke? You mean this whole thing —"

"I wouldn't force you. You could have my career for a charge of rape."

I exhaled, rather too loudly and quickly, for he added, "But a guy can always hope you'll come around. Would flowers do it?" He looked around for the lone crocus. "What do you like besides pansies? A dozen or two roses? Might be worth it if you'd come willingly." He patted the bedding before standing up. "Well, if Graham calls, you must obey. By the way, how much do you obey? Far into the night?"

I stood up, turning red. Shoving the chair into the dresser, I said, "You've got a mind like a cesspool. Been in the Porno Unit too long?"

"Round Two goes to Brenna Taylor," he said, flipping me a casual salute. "Never say I didn't try." He leaned against the doorjamb, his gray eyes traveling the length of my body. "You know, Bren, this is a compliment. A lot of women would love to be in your shoes. Or out of them," he added, staring at the bed.

I slammed the door, distrusting my voice.

But he was right. Margo would like to be asked, if not have the actual bed time. Well, I wasn't going to tell her about this.

The sun wandered over the village, peeking from rifts in the graying clouds, throwing the lower valley into gold, orange and ochre hues. The church spire of St. Michael's caught and held the light, the yellow rays nearly igniting the brass cross. I averted my eyes, not so much from the painful splendor as to keep my footing along the uneven cinder pathway. I walked slowly, quietly, as I imagined a native American walking, so as not to make a sound. I started out resolutely enough, but as I entered the shady path, my determination quavered. Partway up the path I turned suddenly, thinking someone lurked behind me. No one. Only waving tree branches and a frightened grey squirrel. A twig snapped and I froze. No one appeared. I walked as noiselessly as I could, determined to hear my prankster approach if he was following me. I emerged from the shady path, having met no one, and having succeeded in fraying my already tense nerves.

I found the vicar seated on a wooden bench, his black shirt silhouetted against the near-whiteness of the old tombstones. Lyle smiled at my approach and stood up. Assuring the clergyman that I was only there for a few minutes, I suggested he resume his seat.

"It's a peaceful time of day," Lyle observed, his eyes on the western horizon. "Lovely to take a breath and review where one's been. The Journey's rough at times, don't you think?" The vicar, speaking in ecclesiastical terms, took my affirmation of my cinder-strewn stroll as relating to something higher. "I assume you didn't climb this hill to listen to the sparrows, Sergeant. Although a police officer puts in as many and as unorthodox hours as a clergyman, you don't impress me as the sort who'd pause in a murder investigation to drink in the natural splendors. To what do I owe this visit?"

I explained that we needed a timetable of everyone's whereabouts from 3:30 to 6:00 on Sunday.

"Ah, the Fateful Day. I was in my study, doing a few odds and ends. Straightening my desk, dashing off a few letters. Nothing very interesting or that gives me an alibi. I assume that's what you meant. Do I need something public, something shared that proves where I was?" His cheeks bulged slightly as he grinned, the sunlight tinting the rosy flesh a pale yellow.

I nodded.

Death of an Ordinary Guy

"Thought so. Pity it wasn't Saturday, because I was with Ramona and Arthur. We could confirm each other's whereabouts. But you'll have to take my word about Sunday afternoon."

"And what were you and the betrothed couple doing?"

"Redressing the effigy." He spoke like an actor making his entrance and stating that the theater was on fire. "Though I overstate my role somewhat. In all honesty, I wasn't physically with them. I'd just walked down to the green. They were at the edge of the fire circle, back by Talbot's pile of wood. I only saw it from across the road. Is it important?"

I thanked the vicar and walked with as much dignity as I could down the lane.

Ramona hadn't much to add to the effigy-dressing narration. I'd found her on her day off, so was spared the drive into Buxton. I sat at her fireside, fortified with strong tea and a new felt-tip pen, adding notes to my growing collection, taking in the Victorian surroundings.

The front room of her vine-smothered cottage was itself nearly smothered. Plant cuttings in glass jars and mugs dotted window stills. Mementos of holidays, plays and concerts consumed every available space — miniature frying pans brightly inscribed with 'Crete' or 'Wales' or 'Gibraltar,' ceramic birds, salt and pepper sets, framed tea towels and calendar pages, a post card of a gilt-haired Lady Godiva, stacks of picture travel books, a black vase from Blackpool, a tartan-draped Highlander doll, several toy sheep, a too-yellow stuffed canary holding a limp ribboned 'Souvenir of the Canary Islands' from its beak, and a mirror elaborately bordered in painted flowers. No doubt to make the beholder assume she's still in the springtime of her life. The Antipodes were equally well represented with a wooden kiwi bird, a Maori tiki and mere of greenstone, a boomerang, an Indian pearl-handled knife, and a Chinese folding fan. Normally, I was Discretion itself. But the display demanded inspecting. And while not museum quality, it was certainly museum quantity. She needs Arthur's large manor for her display, I thought. The woman must spend half her life dusting this lot.

I abandoned my tussles with a fringed pillow on the sofa as Ramona asked if my tea was all right.

"Fine, thanks, but I wish you'd let me get it. How's the arm?"

She patted the sling and said, "More inconvenience than pain, now. But I'll survive."

I said I was glad to hear it. "You had it seen to professionally? I ask because those injuries can swell if not properly looked to, and cause no amount of pain and trouble later on."

"Local doctor saw to it, thanks. Evan phoned him up. I felt a right fool, all the fuss everyone made over me, but...." She shrugged and positioned her arm on a pillow. I repeated my joy at hearing it, then asked about the effigy.

"I normally make it. But Arthur volunteered this year although it wasn't the norm for him. He had a bit of extra straw from some landscaping he's doing at the manor. You know, from seeding the lawn. He said he'd do it, save me the expense and trip to get the straw."

"That was thoughtful of him. Lucky for you he was seeding."

Ramona nodded. "He feels an obligation — to the manor, to his father, bless his soul, and to his guests. Wants everything as posh as possible. Says it's worth the extra work if he gets the extra quid from it. I don't know about that, though. I must be thick as a plank. Spend money to make money.... Daft. Bit of a vicious circle, isn't it?

I agreed it was like treading water to keep solvent these days, then asked about the Guy's clothing.

"What Lyle saw us doing Saturday was exchanging jackets. I did it there at the fire circle so I wouldn't bring straw into my car or the house. It was a bit of a wrestle, but I did it."

"Anyone see you or help?"

"You're thinking of alibi, Sergeant?" She squinted at me, as though trying to discern if she was about to be carted off to the clink. "No one stood around and watched, if that's what you're suggesting. Arthur left. I suppose I can't ask why you're asking. Not even as girl to girl?"

"Did you have to rehang it yourself?"

"No. I was going to try to rig it up again, but I didn't want to fool with it. I left it, wanted to get home. I assume Talbot hung it since he's always down there fussing over his woodpile. When I got to the circle Sunday around bonfire time, I saw the rope around the thing's waist and neck. *Someone* restrung it, that's evident."

"Does it just lie there, until 7:00 or so when the program begins?"

"Talbot lets it down around lunchtime so we can raise it and torch it. You'll have to ask him exactly when. I only know it's down again for the hoisting. So, Sergeant, that's about it. Other than Arthur changing jackets because he'd given me the wrong one —"

"What jacket had he meant to give you?"

"That tan plaid thing it's wearing now. He'd originally given me a tweed, but had meant to give it to Oxfam, I think. It was still quite good, so he rescued it from the dummy. I didn't mind. Might as well give away the better clothing instead of watching it go to waste by the torch."

I thanked her and went to enlighten Graham.

As it turned out, Graham enlightened me. He had seen Tom Oldendorf but got nothing more than an earful of anger. "His point being," Graham said, "that he'd be an idiot to try killing Pedersen over here. He told me Scotland Yard has a 97% success rate solving their crimes."

"We don't do too badly either," I said, my pride of Derbyshire B Division rising.

"And Arthur gave us another date to consider."

"Lovely. I should have read mathematics at university."

Graham ignored me. "Talbot first appeared in the village in 1942, though he wasn't a permanent resident. At first he just came for the summers. On the invitation of Derek's dad. That was before the senior Halford had any children of his own. Four years later, Derek was born."

"Make any difference to anyone?"

"Not to hear Arthur tell it. Mr. Halford loved both boys equally, treated them the same. And Talbot needed a home when his aunt died, so Derek's dad took him in in 1951."

"Adopted him?"

"There's that awkward question again, Taylor. Anyway, Talbot didn't catch on to the dole business until some of the local lads explained it to him. He thought it was a bit of play-acting at first, like an outdoor pageant or charade."

"Three cheers for the local lads."

"Many people would echo your sentiments, I'm afraid. And how did you get on with *your* supply of thumb screws?"

I told him of my interviews with the vicar and Ramona, and we spent the rest of the day interviewing the other players, however minor in this game.

THAT EVENING, WE relinquished our usual late-night routine and went to bed early. It was just as well, for somewhat later my bedroom clock simultaneously announced the hour and the arrival of the rain. Midnight clattered in with a storm that threatened to peel the bark off the trees. Rain thundered along the pine-thick ridge, through the hills, down the dales. Along the pond's shoreline, wave and rain slapped the reed-wrapped rocks and cratered the smooth sand. Hat-holding blasts of wind scythed through the thickets, gleaning the pungency of moss and pine. Rain, heavier than chilled syrup, planed down plants. A cloud-splitting crack of thunder shook the pub, jolting me from my sleep.

Outside my window, the inn sign swung crazily in the wind, its screeching keeping time with an annoying banging shutter.

It was impossible to sleep. I sat up in bed, my knees drawn up to my chest, the skirt of my nightdress pulled down tightly. I stared into the darkness, cringing when lightning splintered the dark.

From the room next to mine a name, sharp as the thunder, jumped out of the silence. "Rachel." I listened, aware I was eavesdropping, but wondering if Graham was entertaining a woman. None of my business, of course. But if he was indeed sharing his bed, I was more than astonished. I was disappointed. Never mind I had secret desires to be in Rachel's place. Until I actually was there, I wanted him celibate, waiting for me — whether he knew it or not — because I was the love of his life. Of course it was ridiculous. But the emotions of love don't always allow clear thinking. I hugged my nightdress around me, remembering the ardor in his voice, and all of a sudden I wanted it to be my name instead of 'Rachel' on his lips.

I could hear the name again, more muffled this time, then several seconds of silence, followed by a chair scraping across the floor, and a book or something similarly heavy thudding, as if it had fallen off the bedside cabinet. I did not even attempt to visualize what Graham and Rachel were doing. When I heard another crash and an oath, I threw off the duvet, shrugged into my jacket, and opened the door.

The hallway was dark except for a feeble lamp at the end of the passage, marking the staircase landing. From the adjacent room, light streaked from beneath the ill-fitted door and across the floor. It was Graham's room.

I hesitated. The hall embraced the scents of wax and spent candles and winterberry. Comforting, ancestral fragrances. Had this been Graham's world, these aromas of altar trimmings and cleaning supplies? I inhaled deeply, and once again imagined him in his black robe. He had quit the pulpit, office tongues whispered, by as to

Death of an Ordinary Guy

why…. Shrugged shoulders answered my questions. Jokes and fabricated innuendoes stung my ears. Affair with a parishioner. Rudeness to the bishop. Struggle with his conscience over church doctrine. I could believe almost any reason, for I was learning how explosive Graham's temper was, how intolerant he was of bureaucracy and pedantic superiors. And for Graham, that was stifling.

A crack of thunder exploded overhead, and I ducked, thinking the building had exploded. There was no response from Graham's room.

I left my doorway. The floor, silent during the day, now groaned and popped with all the uproar of a 1930s American gangster turf war. Tiptoeing, though lessening the cacophony, increased the coldness biting into my bare feet. I paused just outside his door, wondering if he had fallen and needed help. It seemed plausible enough, for the sounds and following curses indicated a small clash within those four walls. Yet, I was hesitant to knock. I might embarrass him if he knew I could hear him. I also wondered at the protocol of a single woman, dressed in nightdress, entering a man's room. Maybe my concerns seem quaint or prudish, but Graham — no matter how long ago — remained a minister. And I didn't want to ruin my career over an indiscretion. Or confront Rachel.

Within his room it was as silent as the grave. I was about to return to my bed when a movement at the bottom of the stairs drew my attention. A whispered "Brenna" made me turn to the figure — it was Margo, cringing at the cracks of thunder. I went over to her, silently amused at her death grip on the staircase's newel post.

"Is this how you keep surveillance?"

"So it's not subtle," she said, ducking in the lightning flash. "At least I can see your room."

As much as I wanted to, I refrained from asking what Rachel looked like. Margo must have seen her enter Graham's room. Better not add fuel to office rumors by suggesting I was interested in Graham's private life. Instead, I said, "Why not hide under my bed?"

"My mum was frightened by a chamber pot. Let's go to your room." We ran down the hall, hoping the building would survive the attack. Once inside, I lit the dresser light. I should have left us sitting in the dark. The photos of me parading as the Guy sat on the dresser, and Margo immediately saw them.

After my brief explanation, Margo said, "This is beyond a joke, Bren. Anyone could be wandering about in the day, sure, but who would have a key to your room?"

"Take your choice. I don't think our suspect list has changed any since Monday morning. I thought it was Mark, but after talking with him today —"

"You talked to him again? When?"

I told her the bare bones of the afternoon's encounter, leaving out the gory details. "Now that you've got something to dream about, how about returning to your bed so I can get into mine?"

"Fine. Refuse my help. But I still say the key to all this is who has the key."

As I listened to Margo shut the door behind her, I wondered if we had a pick-pocket among us.

I emerged from my room the next morning looking as ragged and tired as if I had endured an all-night work session with Graham. I was used to lack of sleep, but every now and then I do like to augment my usual five hours to eight.

I clumped downstairs to the luring aromas of fried bacon, baked scones and warm cinnamon. Mark was just leaving the pub and hadn't seen me. Good. Better for my digestion. Graham, I was relieved to see, was alone, Rachel either slipping out at dawn or eating at another table. I looked around the room, trying to surmise which of the several single women might be Rachel. None of them fit my idea. Perhaps I was wrong about the entire incident. After all, wouldn't Margo have said something? Cheered by Graham's restoration to his pedestal, I walked noiselessly up to the table and chirped, "Praying for strength or guidance?"

His head jerked up, revealing eyes that might have stared at poker cards until the wee hours. He motioned to the vacant chair, groaned that I should know better than to do that, and said the coffee had certainly perked him right up.

Good thing I hadn't seen him half an hour ago. "I assume you've finished your porridge, bacon and eggs, and are now on to your second pot of coffee."

"Had everything but the porridge, bacon and eggs," he muttered, kneading his eyes. "Shall I make it a double order, then?" Graham looked up as Evan came up to our table. "Perfect timing. How about poached eggs and haddock, Taylor?"

"Haddock? You know *anything remotely* connected with the sea —"

"Cure all, Taylor. Evan —" He stopped as Evan's face lapsed into a sickly grimace.

"Sorry to bother you, Mr. Graham."

"Bother?"

"Telephone, sir. In my office. Byron says it sounds urgent." Stepping aside, he let Graham stand up before motioning toward the phone.

"Thank you, Evan. You might give the sergeant some tea, if you would. I'm afraid we didn't get much sleep last night."

I had barely drunk half my tea when Graham was back, extracting the car key from his pocket. "'Fraid we won't get that glorious breakfast after all, Taylor. It was Arthur Catchpool. He's at Ramona's. She's dead."

Chapter 19

GRAHAM RELATED THE skeletal facts during the drive to the cottage. His words came haltingly as he tried to concentrate on both the road and the death. Gravel splayed onto road-hugging plants, dusting the frosted vegetation a dull brown as he executed a sharp corner. It wasn't until he braked the car several meters from the cottage that I relinquished my life-preserving grip on the door's armrest. He was out of the car before I could unbuckle my seat belt.

We remained approximately 25 meters away from Ramona's body so as not to contaminate the scene, yet close enough to get a preliminary view. The paper suits we needed to wear to allow up close and personal contact with Ramona would arrive with the rest of the crime team. Until then, we would have to be content with examining from afar.

Graham paced back and forth on the driveway, trying for the best view.

Ramona lay on her back, her knees bent, her feet tucked beneath her. Her left arm was stretched out above her head as though she was in school, raising her hand. Her right elbow was bent, allowing her right hand to lay beneath the small of her back. She seemed more suited to the bedroom than to the wintry elements, for she was clothed in a matching turquoise négligé and nightdress.

Frozen, I thought, my eyes traveling over the frost-stiffened fabric. Frozen in time. As though mimicking a 1950s pinup photo. The negligee was open, the tie belt strung out and several feet from the body, having freed itself from the belt loops. She seemed to be barely wearing the garment, for the upper portion lay halfway down her arms, exposing her shoulders. The generous hemline of the nightdress fanned out and bunched up in one place to expose her right thigh. Like an absurd epaulet, a broken shoestring strap dangled over her right shoulder. She might have been provocative if it wasn't for the ghost-white, shocked face with its eyes staring at the sky.

She was also, I noted, very wet and very frost-covered.

"For God's sake, can't you cover her up?"

Arthur's voice pleaded behind us, yet we couldn't reply. It was a travesty, the body lying unprotected, the eyes moist, the eyelashes hoary and starched. I stared at the feathered mules encasing her feet, the turquoise feathers reduced to a sodden pulp. "Kind of inadequately dressed," I said to no one in particular.

"She obviously hadn't intended to stay out here," Graham muttered. He turned, gazing at the end of the driveway where Arthur stood, leaning against the fence. The man was hatless and gloveless. His heavy woolen jacket was unbuttoned, as though he had loosened the restraints to stoop over Ramona. Dampness had seeped into Arthur's shoes and edges of his jeans.

"Taylor," Graham called, gazing at his watch. "7:12. Fordyce, I assume, has created a sensation at the station. I told him to get everyone back out here."

"Should be here by 8:00 or so," I said.

"I don't suppose the scene will change much before Tolliver and his all-seeing video equipment arrive."

"Can't see it getting much warmer in three-quarters of an hour."

"Never hurts to be careful. So, just in case...." As well as distance permitted, he pointed out the details of the immediate area surrounding Ramona's body. "Someone's knelt next to her — Arthur, I assume. See the area there, where the grass is crushed and devoid of frost? And the same marks from the driveway?"

"Got out of his car, saw her and came over."

Graham indicated Ramona's right hand jammed behind her back. "Wish Karol was here. I'd love to know if that hand position's from death throes or if she was reaching for something."

"What would she be doing out here, dressed like this?"

Graham shrugged. "The back door's open. Barely, I grant you, but it's open. I only noticed it because it swung slightly in the breeze."

"Nothing wrong with that, sir. She was expecting to return."

"I should hope so, dressed like *that*...." Pointing to the broken nightdress strap, he said, "Might have done that in a tussle."

"If someone else was out here, why wouldn't she have on more clothes? Sexually assaulted?"

Graham shrugged, saying that was in Karol's realm of medical magic.

I pointed to the ground. "If another person was out here, wouldn't there be more evidence? Besides, this patch where someone — ok, probably Arthur — stooped can in no way be construed as a fight scene. There are less than a half dozen sole prints where he knelt and then got up again. His prints, too, go straight as an arrow back to the driveway."

In the quiet I could hear Arthur's incessant stammering as he poured out his heart to PC Byrd.

"Does he always come over for breakfast?" I asked. "He phoned you up at 7:00, for God's sake!"

"I don't know his habits."

"One thing's certain. He wasn't just leaving after a comfortable night out. The condition of the body screams that she's been out here for hours."

"Unless he left at midnight, say, and came back."

"Even if she kissed him good night —"

"I would have done that from the warmth of the house."

"Heart attack, you think?"

He shrugged. "Well.... I suppose we should talk to Arthur. You particularly keen on it?"

I said I may as well. It beat standing around slowly turning numb.

"Terrible thing," I said, walking up to Arthur. He nodded, staring at me, his red-circled eyes still moist from crying. "You found her like this?"

"Around 7:00. I got out of the car and was walking up to the house. I saw her — well, I saw something. I didn't know it was her. I didn't realize it was a person. At first I thought it was a bit of tarp or something. Something blown off the bundles of sticks." He turned his head, blowing his nose.

I waited, remembering the sage advise of never rushing your witness, letting him recall and report things as he could.

"Those are my footprints, Sergeant. I was walking up to the door when I saw her. I thought she'd just fallen, that I could help. When I found out — Well, I phoned the pub. I'm afraid Byron must think me an idiot. I started blubbering."

"No one can fault you for that. You have a key to her house?" We both knew what I meant, for there were no signs of his footprints leading from the body to her house.

Death of an Ordinary Guy

"No. We aren't — We aren't as modern as that. Or as immoral, however you prefer to classify it. You won't find my footprints leading to the door. I knew you were at the pub, so I used my car phone. Saved time."

"You didn't check to see if the door was open, then? I would have thought that would be a natural thing to do, assume the door was open — seeing how she was dressed — and phone from the house."

"Is the door unlocked? I didn't look. One doesn't think clearly in a crisis, does one? Car phone's a natural reaction for me."

"So, why did you come over at such an early hour?"

Arthur made a sound somewhere between a cough and a gag. "This is going to sound awfully inane."

"Don't let that bother you, sir."

"I had a few things that needed to go to the cleaner's. Ramona did too, only with her arm in a sling, she couldn't handle all the items, so I came over to get them."

I jotted down a note to check his car for the presence of the clothing.

"We talked about it over dinner last night, joked about her atrocious memory."

"Did you see anything out of the ordinary this morning? No strange car parked near the cottage, for instance?"

"Of course not. We never have any trouble in the village."

Except for a spot of murder for Guy Fawkes Day. "You didn't phone for a doctor or ambulance?"

"There was no need."

"Really? I would have thought that would be the first call you'd make."

"I — it was obvious she was dead." He colored instantly, darkly. It was the first time he had used the word. "It was the way she was, you see. I knew just from looking at her. She was all white, her body and clothes stiff. You could tell from the frost. Frozen stiff. There was no need for a doctor. Not when she was like that."

"And when did you leave her last night?"

"How the hell should I know?" Arthur threw his car keys at a nearby tree. "Sorry. Eleven, I think. Near enough. I think Byron heard me return last night. You can ask him."

I echoed the information noncommittally, making a note of it. "Excuse me for a moment." I walked to his car, picked up and searched through the bundle of clothes on the back seat, and returned. "Very good, sir. I must ask you to remain here for a while, until Mr. Graham can see you."

Mumbling he had nothing else to do, Arthur slowly picked up his keys and walked to his car, pausing just long enough to glance at the first police contingent arriving from Buxton.

"So, we're at it again." Karol Mattox nodded to us as she walked up to Graham. Since there was no suggestion of foul play, Karol had been called in. Otherwise, it would have been Ahrens again. "You got here bright and early."

"So did you," Graham replied, glancing at his watch. "Simcock coming?" We noted Harry Tolliver removing his video equipment from the car.

Karol shook her head. "It's your baby."

"Can't even share the blame on this one." He indicated the corpse. "Well, *she's* all yours. Hargreaves!"

Hargreaves came up slowly, noting the footprints and the condition of the area. He greeted us and began to suit up.

"You want to join the throng?" I asked.

Graham shook his head. "We've got a good team. They can handle it. I can view the video. But if you...."

"I'll watch here, from the sidelines, if it's all right, sir."

Margo, I was pleased to see, had been assigned an active role and was stringing up the police tape to confine the scene. DC Fordyce was placing the trail of milk crates up to the body and laid down a larger covering so Karol and Hargreaves could work there without damaging anything on the ground. Fordyce came back slowly and disappeared around the corner of the house. Karol and another officer finished suiting up and walked over to the body. Graham gave them three minutes by his watch before calling, "Well?"

"There's no way I can get an estimate of death from body temperature," Karol said. "And rigor mortis is largely discounted, too, for the same reason. Though I usually don't put too much weight on it. Too many variables, such as activity at the time of death, temperature of the environment." She paused, looking at the frosted grass and icy tree branches as though that upheld her argument. Graham said something about being thankful for frost instead of knee-high snow. I agreed and hugged my down-filled jacket closer to me. There was usually something unpleasant about every scene that had to be processed outdoors. At least this one was easy to work and in daylight.

Death of an Ordinary Guy

Karol lightly pressed her fingertips into Ramona's exposed thigh and called out, "No blanching. Blood's clotted. Fixed lividity won't help us any."

"You really expected to find that?" Graham said, his surprise evident. He watched a SOCO measuring distance of body from the driveway. Fordyce returned with a heavy paper sack and stood just outside the scene. The sack, I assumed, would receive Ramona's slippers.

"No. It's obvious she's been here over night. Just being thorough."

"If the storm began around midnight, and she was already dead at that time...."

Hargreaves nodded, scooting in a bit closer to the body. "She was rained on, judging by the condition of her négligé. You wouldn't get this frosty without a good prior wetting." He poked gingerly at an edge of the garment. It made a cracking noise as it bent against the spikes of silvered grass. "See? It's like it's cemented to the ground. More icy than frosty. Like I said. She fell and lay in the rain. Then the temperature dropped and the moisture frosted over."

"That makes it about seven hours, then," Graham calculated. "I'll have to find out if someone knows when the rain stopped. I don't think it lasted long, for all its punch."

"So even if she came out toward the end...."

"Fits with the lack of blanching," Karol said. "Which normally occurs six to eight hours after death. But of course the full body rigidity that one would expect to find after twelve hours doesn't mean a thing. Everything out here is frozen." She poked the gown as if to underline her statement.

"We've got such an accommodating refrigerator out here," Hargreaves grunted. "Good as a slab in the morgue any day."

"You probably can't see it from there, Mr. Graham, but there's whiteness around the lips."

Graham turned to me, frowning. "Did Ramona look like that yesterday?"

I shook my head.

"Then whatever caused this..." Louder, he called to Karol, who replied, "If I have to make a snap decision — which I hate to do — I'd say it's not from the cold. More likely the result of something chemical. Classic conditions of skin death."

"If it's chemical, would you find anything in her after all this time in the cold?"

"I should think so. The cold won't have affected it."

"I'm particularly wondering if she's lying on something."

Hargreaves stood up. "We'll find out when we shift her. I'll just go and set up." He turned and walked toward the police car.

Minutes went by, during which Karol continued her examination, Hargreaves set up his lights, Harry Tolliver busied himself with the video, and Graham directed the constables to their various assignments. He wasn't too keen on Arthur's tale of the purported trip to the cleaner's, but the crumpled suits in Arthur's car seemed to testify on his behalf. Or else he's a damned smart murderer.

Mark Salt and several other officers had just finished setting up the tent to confine Ramona and any possible evidence when Karol walked over to us. She peeled off her gloves and rubbed her hands. "I think it's colder than the other night, Brenna."

I nodded, recalling the chill of Sunday night, the great puffs of our condensed breath like a steam railway yard.

"This is all unofficial, you know," Karol said as Graham nodded. "The only thing that bothers me right now is how much I'll be able to substantiate when I get her back to the morgue. Cold is fine for some things, but if it will have destroyed anything vital...."

"Well," Graham said. "I know you'll do your usual first rate job."

"Did I ever tell you I hope you make Super?" She shared our opinion of Superintendent Simcock's bellowing technique.

"Not lately."

"Sir!" Margo called to Graham. "Sir, I'm having Harry video the hemline of Ramona's nightdress so you can see it later."

"Fine, Lynch, but what's unusual about it?"

"Puckers in the gown. Looks like she caught it on something."

"There anything out here that would have caused that?" He moved over a few feet so he could see the cottage's back door. "We'll get the lads to do a thorough going-over. Damn that storm. It might have wiped out more than we know. All right, carry on."

Karol returned to her preliminary examination of the body and Graham nodded to Custody Officer Peter Kelly. They walked over to Arthur, who was leaning against his car. I could hear his yelp of indignation as Graham requested his shoes. After a brief argument, Arthur shoved them at Peter, who put them into a paper sack, folded and sellotaped it closed. Arthur slid into his car seat, talking to Graham and gesturing toward the house. A SOCO was measuring

Death of an Ordinary Guy

and photographing Arthur's footprints that lead to Ramona's body. The photos, I knew, would be black-and-white and to scale. Another SOCO was taking samples of the grass from the print depressions. Another SOCO was taking samples of the grass from the print depressions. When he had collected samples from several areas in the garden, he sealed them in paper sacks. The mortuary van attendants, bored and yawning, stood at the end of the drive, talking to a constable.

An hour later, when Karol had concluded the examination and the mortuary van attendants had left with the zipped body bag, a white-faced Arthur was given permission to leave. Graham watched him drive slowly away. "I wonder if I've just given him a chance to destroy something."

"Don't know what it could be," I said.

"Let's pray we don't find out the hard way. Lynch! I want a thorough video of the house interior, too. Don't miss a thing."

Margo's 'Sir!' was as good as a raw recruit's. A moment later she called, "Mr. Graham, sir."

"You have something else, Lynch?"

"Yes, sir," Margo said, standing a bit taller. I knew she was dying to complain about the space suit and face mask, but she kept her eyes on Graham. "In the process of lifting Miss Van Dyke, with the ground beneath her now exposed to view, I am able to discern a small twist of hemp fibers."

"What's the ground like, Lynch?"

She pressed her palm against the ground, feeling its condition, then said that it was wet. She backed away when Harry came over to video the area.

"Not so odd, Taylor. After all, it rained last night."

I remarked that I had heard something about it, then said, "Ground would have sponged up the water, no matter if she was out here before it started or afterwards. That doesn't help us much. You think that's what she was groping for?"

"Seems absurd, doesn't it? A barely discernable strand of rope."

"Coincidence?"

Graham called to a constable, who hurried over to Margo with a pair of tweezers. As Margo entered the tent, Karol said, "So, does the plot thicken?"

"The plot *sickens*, perhaps."

"Lot of rope around this village."

"Enough to hang someone with, if hanging is required after we've finished."

"Hung for a sheep, hung for a lamb."

"Or lambs to the slaughter," Graham said, grimacing. "Thanks, Lynch." He accepted the clear plastic bag from Margo and stared at the encased rope fragment. "Do anything for you, Taylor?"

"I hate to jump to conclusions, but it sort of brings to mind another piece of rope we've seen with another recent Upper Kingsleigh death." And, I thought but didn't mention, another series of rope incidents that I was involved in. Three, to be exact: my personal Guy, the string tied around the wren, and the nooses drawn on my photos. So what was the connection?

Turning so he now faced the back garden and the dotting of bundled tree branches, Graham murmured, "It does indeed."

Chapter 20

"Isn't it rather odd," I said after a few moments of amazed contemplation, "that we have two cases involving rope?"

"We don't know if this death is a case yet," Graham reminded me. "'Case' refers to something other than natural death, Taylor."

"But if Karol finds something," I persisted, staring at the bundles of tree branches. "If it turns out to be —"

"Murder?" He stepped back, making room for a constable who was bringing Harry a tape measure. "Who'd want to kill a respected, well-liked woman like Ramona?"

"Who'd want to kill a respected, well-liked man like Steve Pedersen? You know as well as I do, sir, that motives run deep. Especially in villages."

"Well, I hope we can rule out Arthur. I don't think I can stand the thought of a besotted lover killing his intended. I was brought up on tales of Robin Hood and King Arthur."

"Fortunate for us that Ramona fell where she did."

"Why?"

"That piece of rope... If it is murder, and the rain obliterated any footprints or small clues outside, the body, by falling on the rope, protected it."

"Sounds planned. Look, Taylor, I'll go along with your murder suggestion. I hate rushing fences, but it looks suspicious with the whitened skin of her lips. Killer had to be a local. Would she come outside at night for anyone but a local, someone she knew?"

"Unless she was carried outside after death."

Graham called to Fordyce, who then cut a sample of rope from the nearest bundle of branches that still lay where Talbot had left them. "What say we earn our pay and take on the questioning of my two favorite suspects?"

"Talbot and Uncle Gilbert."

"Who do you want?"

"Surprise me. You thinking of Talbot and Uncle Gilbert because they seem to like rope more than anyone else in the village?"

"Yes. I'm for Talbot, then. You tackle the ever-inebriated uncle. You seem to have such rapport with the less fortunate."

"That motherly touch again."

"Everyone should have such a mother. We'll meet back at the incident room."

While Graham was questioning Talbot, I was trying to get a sober, straight answer from Uncle Gilbert. Arthur had practically torn apart the house before finding his uncle in the ballroom. It was a cavernous room, as such rooms are. Satin-cushioned chairs lined its perimeter, ready for foot-weary dancers. A half dozen crystal chandeliers polka-dotted the ceiling, their rows of diamond-like pendants glittering in the morning sun. I crossed the hardwood floor, conscious of my footsteps.

Gilbert, amazingly enough, was conscious of them too, for he looked up at my approach. He was placidly sitting in the middle of the vast floor, putting together a jigsaw puzzle. Though all five hundred pieces were scattered about him, only a few dozen were assembled. And very creatively. One piece in particular buckled drastically from the forced fit. Still, I gave him credit. Both pieces were blue.

Gilbert's eyes were as blood-shot as the last time I had talked to him. And as unfocused. He craned his head back to study better who was standing beside him. Upon seeing me, he laughed and gestured toward the bare floor.

"Just the person I need! You must have been sent by Athena herself, Sergeant."

It might have been more appropriate if Gilbert had said Dionysus sent me. Old Dion probably knows his way here by heart. Paid a recent visit, too.

"Just who I need — a cop, a 'tec to lend her great wisdom, to snoop out the errant pieces! Say you can find the missing amongst all this!" His arm flapped haphazardly in the direction of the scattered pieces. "I'm working on this tricky bit here. Need a knobbly bit on the right. Blue and a funny little red stripe. If you can locate our missing member, I shall personally write a letter to your chief constable, advising him of your superior traits and recommending immediate promotion!" The puzzle piece fell to his lap as he leaned backwards in his roar of laughter.

"While you're at it, mention I need a raise."

Another blast of mirth roared over me. Suddenly serious, he said, "Wages are a hell of a thing, aren't they, Sergeant? Money's going to be the death of civilization. You see if I'm not right. The rich get richer, and the poor —" He sniffed. "Wages, Sergeant. We're all wage slaves in one form or another. Work and wages. Four-lettered words if there ever was. I, myself, for all the grandeur about me, am reduced to a wage. Yes, a wage. Supplied to me by my kind nephew. Not as regular as I should hope, nor as much as I should hope, but there you are." Without any concern for matching color or shape, he wedged a piece into an accommodating area, then hammered it flat with the side of his fist. Looking up from his work, he said, "Oh, it's you. Back again? More questions?"

"I'm back, yes, but it's over a different matter."

"Different? What the hell do you mean?"

"Ramona Van Dkye was found dead this morning."

For all of Uncle Gilbert's advanced alcoholic state, the news of Ramona's death appeared to sober him quickly enough. He watched the placement of my puzzle piece with no sign of awareness. His head raised slowly until he was nearly eye to eye with me, his mouth dropped open, revealing yellowed teeth and an alcoholic odor. I eased backwards as Gilbert expounded his innocence. "I didn't do it! I had nothin' to do with it! I was here. Asleep. Ask Arthur. Ask —"

"I'm not accusing you of anything, Mr. Catchpool."

Gilbert asked what had happened. When I had told him, he slowly shook his head. "Awful. God awful."

"When was the last time you saw her?"

"What's today?"

"Wednesday."

"Ahh, yes. Well, it'd have to be. Ramona saw Arthur for dinner, but that was last night."

"I'm asking about *you,* Mr. Catchpool."

"Me?" He blinked slowly. "Me and Ramona? Well, that'd have to be at the bonfire. Sunday."

"Do you know of any reason Ramona might have been killed? Grudges, old love affairs that didn't end amicably, debts never paid..."

"Other than her short-lived marriage, I can't think of any old loves. And that left her a widow, so you shan't have to look for a husband."

"Married to whom?"

"Don't know. Ask Arthur. Ask Ramona. *She'd* know. Can't remember."

I sighed and tried another line. "You were seen Sunday before the bonfire in the vicinity of the effigy. Are you interested in rope? Did you ask Talbot for the loan of any remnant he had, perhaps?"

"Loan of rope? What the hell are you on about? I didn't ask for any rope — then or later. Not from anyone. And I didn't buy rope, either. We've got enough about the estate. Why you asking? She wasn't hung, was she? Rope! That's why —" His shaking hand swept uncontrollably across his mouth, trying valiantly to moisten his lips and tongue. "That's what you mean! There was rope on her body. She was hung or tied up. Or else you'd not be asking me about rope. Oh, God, I had nothin' to do with it. Nothin'! I swear, I *swear...*" He lowered his head, cradling it in his hands, and repeatedly groaned his innocence.

I left him to his suspicions and denials.

"ANYTHING REVEAL ITSELF to you, Taylor?" Graham sat at a table in the incident room, his long legs extended in front of him, his heels pushed into the floor and angling his chair slightly backwards. His arms were bent and his interlaced fingers supported his head like a pillow.

"Nothing to get me a promotion. Uncle Gilbert, as you will not be surprised to hear, both denies thought of borrowing rope or knowledge of loan of rope. He seems to have minded his own business for once. You?"

Graham shook his head, telling me that Talbot admitted tying Ramona's bundles during the weekend, but that he ended the job Monday. "And you could have told me that much. I believe anyone could have done it. Talbot's rope isn't uncommon, and it's lying about, most likely, contrary to his claim to have it under lock and key."

"Not much help. Although I was told again that our Ramona had been married. And, no, I don't know her husband's name. A job for Fordyce."

"Maybe Uncle Gilbert and Talbot are related. Do fraternal twins share similar cerebrations?"

Death of an Ordinary Guy

"Don't know about that," I said, momentarily thrown by Graham's word choice, "but Uncle Gilbert's not too strong on the headwork."

"The only interesting item I came upon was Tom in the middle of the road. He was taking photos of the pub and post office reflected in rain puddles."

"He's certainly creative. Wonder if it's instinctive or if he walks around his subject before he shoots."

"Wonder how many rolls he goes through on holiday," Graham said, probably thinking of the film incident. "Well, he's bound to have an interesting album. I tire of snaps of Aunt Edith reduced to a dot in the middle of a Sahara-like stretch of beach."

"Or the wedding party and guests — none of whom I know, but should find interesting because so-and-so's niece was a flower girl. Why is a photo of the bride and groom stuffing wedding cake into each other's mouths so fantastic? Icing all over her makeup, fingers sticky... I should think a bride would want to forget it."

I waited for a murmur of agreement, for a commiserating word. Instead, Graham sat mute, as though he had not heard me. Or as though he was thinking of a similar situation, for his eyes stared past me, focused on something beyond the window. I watched his face, trying to read his thoughts, wanting to understand the private world into which he slipped periodically. There was a slight lowering of his eyelids and a tightening of his jaw muscles, which I knew happened when he was angry or impatient. A phrase, hardly above a whisper, escaped his lips.

"Beg pardon, sir?" I said.

He stirred, as if the sound of my voice broke his mood. Shifting his eyes to my face, he seemed startled to find himself in the incident room. "Pardon?"

"I didn't catch what you said. Sounded like 'till death do us part.' You want me to check up on Ramona's marriage?"

Graham rubbed his face and said no, that he had just been thinking of weddings. I wasn't so sure. I thought he had mentioned Ray again. A brother or uncle? Perhaps a best friend. Someone who had bested Graham in love? I busied myself with the papers in front of me. As much as I longed to ask him about Ray, I refrained. Graham would tell me when — if ever — he wanted to.

"Driving a car requires a driving license. Doctors and architects need to pass their exams. So do plumbers. Why can't potential photographers sit through instructional classes? All the film that's wasted on dot-sized Aunt Ediths..."

I agreed that I tend to doze off when viewing my uncle's photographic attempts. I had just suggested bringing in some lunch when Graham's mobile rang. He muttered that it was getting as bad as mealtime at home and punched a key. After uttering a few oaths, he hung up and said, "Care to guess who that was? I won't even make you lay a wager."

"Your few choice euphemisms didn't give me much of a clue. I don't get much from 'The hell you did.' Leaves a bit to the imagination."

"On executing constabulary business, our valiant constables found a turquoise thread."

"Turquoise," I muttered, recalling the puckered threads in Ramona's nightdress. "And where was this found?"

"On a bush outside the back door."

"Not meaning to play devil's advocate, sir, but couldn't the thread be old? Days, months ago?"

Graham conceded the possibility. "Unfortunately, Taylor, I've had many a case that hung by a thread."

Death of an Ordinary Guy

Chapter 21

WE WERE NEARLY finished with our meal in the public bar — a break Graham and I admitted we needed — when Derek limped into the pub's large room. He nodded at us before joining a group at the bar. It was evidently one of their usual meeting places, the stretch of empty tables patiently waiting for tourists or villagers.

"Derek!" Evan threw his damp towel beneath the bar counter, drew a pint of bitter, and set it down in front of Derek. "We were just saying before you came in that we're starting up rehearsals. The walk-around's just five weeks away, right?" Evan turned to one of the older men leaning against the bar. Receiving an affirming nod, he said, "Right. Five weeks."

"Not much time."

"Not much time, you may well say. So, we've got to get at our carol rehearsals."

"Hope it's not as damned cold as it was last year." One of the men lowered his head, hardly lifting the glass from the counter top, and took a long drink. "Damned near froze to death before it was over. Bloody snow. Like as froze me feet trudgin' through that muck."

"Aye," another of the group agreed. "Never knew the wind so fierce as it was up at Leadlove's farm. God, it was like I had bloody well nothin' on. Cut right through to the bone, that cold did. Ain't much better tonight."

They paused, turning toward the front door, and listened. The wind moaned between the door and its frame, rattling the brass knocker. A tree branch bumped against a window, as though it wanted to come in from the cold. Returning to their drinks, the men seemed suddenly colder and talked quietly of a past snow storm. "Never found Andy's body till next spring, it were," one man reminded the group. "Found him up around Fenig's Hill, near the pool. Frozen solid as a board and twice as stiff. 'Course, it's near always certain death up there that time of year, isn't it? Cold."

Silently, I agree, knowing that patch of Thunor Moor. It was desolate, wild land, planed by fierce wintry winds that left nothing growing taller than grasses. Sheep refused to graze there, seeking instead the warmer, more sheltered dales. A pool of bracken-infested water along a walking track further chilled the wind as it swept across the pool's black surface. Frost and ice, always thicker and more abundant on the pool's eastern shore, seemed to linger into the summer, when it took refuge in the crevices of ruined stone walls. 'Cold' hardly described the moor.

"At least it's not snowin' tonight," someone said as the tree branch scratched again.

"Maybe not," Derek said, "but there's the smell of it in the air."

"I can feel it more than smell it. Gets into my bones. Missus says it's neuralgia, but I don't hold with that. Seeps into my body, cuts right through my flesh when it's about to rain or snow, don't it?"

"Maybe we should bypass Leadlove's," Derek suggested. "I don't know as they would miss us all that much, anyhow."

"Not as though they was regular Churchgoers. Wouldn't think they'd miss the carols, them not attendin'."

"Will be our twenty-fifth year of caroling," Evan said. "Can you believe it? Quarter century, same group. Regular as clockwork we showed up."

"I wouldn't have given us that hope when we started," one of the group confessed.

"No," admitted Byron, walking up to the bar. "Sounded awful, we did."

"I wouldn't say 'awful,'" Evan returned. "No one ever sounds like Kings College Choir right off. It takes a bit of work."

"We've done all right," Derek said. "Improved each year."

"That's where the hard work comes in. Makes it enjoyable when folks appreciate us," Byron agreed.

Evan nodded, then snapped his fingers. "We ought to have some kind of celebration after finishing at the last house. Yes! After Leadlove's farm. We'll stop here at the pub for a drink and a bite, and toast another twenty-five years of the Upper Kingsleigh Carolers."

Death of an Ordinary Guy

"Ought to have some kind of plaque made," suggested another of the locals. "Hang it here on the wall — if you aren't of a mind to say no, Evan."

"I'd be honored. Maybe get a few more to join, if they see how we've fared."

"We'll have all our names engraved," Derek said. "Show our spirit —"

"Speaking of spirit," Byron said. "If I may interrupt your meal, Mr. Graham...."

As though on cue, every head in the room turned to us. I felt their curiosity, their eyes darting between Graham and me.

Byron said, "You any nearer to an arrest?"

A few throats cleared, a few feet shuffled as the Interested waited for the news.

Graham eyed me as though we shared a secret, then turned to the men. "The Constabulary, although dealing with many dozen cases simultaneously, has utilized all its available resources for the swift and successful conclusion of this case. It has received the top priority of the Chief Constable, since murder receives priority status. The expeditious completion and apprehension of the miscreant, although an honorary pursuit, must also be tempered with lawful procedures, else we should be confronted with a vigilante episode. I have conferred both with the Assistant Commissioner and the Chief Constable and we feel that an arrest, while being of major concern to the emotional and mental well-being of the citizenry — not to mention their physical survival — is imminently pending."

Did he take a course on officialeze, I wondered, sharing a wink with him, or had he a natural talent?

The men nodded, mumbled that they had thought so all along, and occupied themselves with their drinks.

Evan wished us God speed and Derek mumbled that this was one November 5th they would not forget for many years, so it didn't make any difference to him — other than the seeing of justice served — what happened.

"You don't mind that it's upset your wife, then?" asked one of the men.

"'Course I mind," Derek said, his voice strained, his face flooding with color. "But what's done is done. Can't undo it. Calendar turns to Guy Fawkes night next year, Kris and I will be reminded of this mess, certainly. But other than the police finding the killer and someone being satisfied with the trial outcome, it doesn't make a difference in our lives, does it? Will it yours, George?" he said, confronting the man. "Or yours, Byron? Or Evan? I doubt it one bloody bit."

I felt like saying, "More tea, Vicar?" but after an awkward moment Evan cleared his throat and asked the group if they could get back to a more pleasant topic. "If we're going to do this plaque, we haven't much time. We must make our decisions. There's bound to be something we can order from Buxton or Chesterfield."

"You thinking of donating it?" Byron prompted.

"Worried about the cost, are you?"

"Not more than the next. It's just that, with Christmas coming..."

Evan frowned. "Might've known you'd let a few quid come between you and our anniversary. Never seen anyone so fretful over a penny."

"What were you thinking, then?" Byron leaned across the bar, eyeing the man. "I can't see you parting with that kind of lolly. Must be talking of fifty quid or so, with the engraving — if we do it up right. Nothing cheap."

"If you're so money shy, what say we all contribute toward the cost?"

Murmurs bordering on consent greeted Evan's suggestion.

"You can always grab a spare job washing windows or making up beds at the Manor," someone joked from the back of the room. "Maybe earn a few pence washing Arthur's Jaguar. 'Course, you'd have to sign away the remainder of your salary in precaution of your scratching it."

"Better yet," Evan declared, grinning at Byron, "get your boss to donate the plaque. Save us poor working chaps doling out our own meager savings. Then we could have a proper party."

Talbot, the lone occupant at a table, coughed loudly, drawing the carolers' attention to him. He drew his handkerchief across his mouth. "You can have your party if you want. I'm not the man to stop any of you. But it's kind of silly, if you ask me."

"Well," Byron said, kicking a nearby chair and sending it crashing into its neighbor, "nobody's asking you, then."

Evan shook his head slightly at the man, as if silencing him, and asked Talbot what he meant.

Talbot stuffed the handkerchief into his pocket, picked up his glass and stared at it. "It may be twenty-five years for you, Evan Greene, and most of your others, but Mr. Derek Halford, here, has

Death of an Ordinary Guy

only been out carolin' with the lot of you for twenty-four years. Wasn't here in '73, or don't any of you have the intelligence to remember that?" He finished with a sort of flurry, dramatically draining his glass.

"What the hell are you talking about?" demanded one of the men.

Evan's hand went out to the man's arm. "It's true. I'd forgotten. It's not the sort of thing you normally make it a point to recall each year, is it? Derek was back by the following spring, but anyway, it's the group that's been going for twenty-five years, and that's what's being celebrated, not the individual members."

Talbot stood up, pushing back the chair with his leg. He remained at the table, staring at the men. "You can give out whatever the hell you like. Might as well do it. Next milestone's fifty years. That's another twenty-five years, Evan, and you're in your sixties now. You probably won't be 'round then to enjoy it. Didn't you learn your tables at school?"

Ray of sunshine, I thought.

"Thanks for your permission, Talbot."

"Lot of nonsense, all this time spent on singin'. The telly's got whackin' good programs on. So's the radio. I can hear better on records any day of the week than I can from you lot. Who needs you?" He grabbed his coat, struggling into it as he stomped out of the pub amidst an array of angry protests.

Graham murmured, "What an extraordinary exhibition."

I nodded and emptied my glass. "The lady doth protest too much, methinks."

"Truer words, Taylor. Come on." We followed Talbot at a more leisurely pace.

We were several yards behind Talbot when the connecting door to the vestibule banged open, revealing Vernon Wroe. Upon seeing Talbot, Wroe grasped the handyman's arms in affection.

"My boy!" gurgled Wroe, all excitement. "I was going to drop by later this evening, but you've saved an old man a trip. How are —"

Talbot shrugged off the unwelcome hands and stepped backwards. "I'll save you a trip anytime, then, for I won't let you in. And I'm *not* your boy. I wish to hell you'd stop natterin' on like that. I asked my dad once 'bout you and him. Know what he told me?" Talbot squinted through the smoke of his cigarette, studying the man before him. "He said he never knew you. You were in the same regiment, all right, that you and Kris's dad was mates, but that was it. So bugger off afore I get good an' mad." Talbot brushed past the colonel and slammed the outer pub door in his exit.

Embarrassed at being caught in a melodramatic pronouncement, Wroe averted his eyes from us, mumbled something noncommittal, and slowly entered the public bar.

"Amazing," Graham said as we walked to the stairs leading to our bedrooms. "What's it mean?"

"What'll come of it is my question."

A chatter of raised voices inside the public bar turned our attention to the commotion. Peering through the door's glass panel, we could see Wroe getting friendly with a group of women seated at a table.

"Amazing," repeated Graham. "Rebounds from rebuke by his pseudo son and transforms to amorous octopus in less than five minutes."

"The man's got stamina."

"Or hope. Ooh, that hurt!" Graham said, referring to a slap the older man just received from a middle-aged blonde. Wroe's back was towards us but the woman's face told us her attitude to the colonel's strategy and attack. Graham grimaced, but for whom he was feeling sympathy, I didn't know. "Serves him right, I don't doubt. They don't look very happy with his technique."

"As good as a Buster Keaton film," I said, pressing my nose against the glass, trying to hear.

"Don't insult Keaton. He had class and dignity while being funny. Wroe's just funny, in a pathetic manner."

We watched Wroe approach another member of the group, only to receive the same answer, though delivered differently. Wroe finally seated himself at a lone table and occupied himself in studying the fire.

It was my turn. "Amazing."

"You can dream about the second reel. Good night, Taylor."

"'Night, sir."

Death of an Ordinary Guy

Chapter 22

I LIKE TO WALK in the early morning, and while in Upper Kingsleigh I saw no reason to discontinue my habit. The walk not only focuses my mind on the day's activities but it also gives me a chance to bird watch.

I followed a much-used trail, entering the woods by Arthur's estate. The quiet, cool blend of sanctuary and November morning enveloped me. Old leaves and pine scented the air. I zipped up my jacket against the cold.

Several yards away a green woodpecker hopped among the branches of a dead tree. Despite the bird's large size, he had been difficult to see at first, for the sunlight had not fully penetrated this section of the woods. He was resplendent with red crown and nape that magnificently offset his practically all-green body. I watched him pursue his breakfast until a noise eventually disturbed him. He rose in a flurry of flapping wings and loud laughing call, settling somewhere out of my sight. The tree seemed oddly vacant without him.

Farther along the trail I came upon several nuthatches. A bit of fluff on the wind, this small bird — half the size of the green woodpecker. But size did not diminish its beauty: it was equally as striking with its subtle blue-gray back and orangish belly. Neither bird was on the endangered list, but I was thrilled to see them.

I crossed Rams Dyke Creek. In the village the stream announced its presence by vociferously clambering over moss-slick rocks and gurgling around half-submerged logs. Here in the midst of the woods it slowed. Perhaps it had no reason to impress the villagers with its frantic pace. Perhaps the land lay flatter here. The channel widened and filled with leaves. The stream, it seemed, needed the earlier white water rush to clear itself of strangling vegetation. I stopped, dipping my hand into the water. Pure liquid ice. I wiped my hand on my slacks and crossed the stream. A growth of burdock, withered by frost, clung to the bank and brushed against me as I reclaimed the forest floor. Beneath my feet, fallen leaves and twigs crunched, scaring the birds into loftier branches.

As I came to the farther edge of the wood I saw the noose.

It hung from a tree limb, barely stirring in the slight breeze. I stopped abruptly. My heart beat racing, I glanced around the area, waiting for a cry of "Surprise!" or a laugh or a rush of kidnapping hands. When nothing happened, I finally approached it. There was nothing to indicate a connection with me or the Pedersen case. Yet, why was it here?

It was a new rope, still smelling of hemp fiber. Was it another warning? Or some local kids playing at their own Guy Fawkes hoisting? Perhaps Mark was joking with me, having somehow learned of the other episodes in my room. Perhaps he had been the original instigator all along and this was just Chapter 4 in his bag of pranks. I stared at it, wondering what he had waiting for me at the pub when I returned. Another dead bird? It would be like him to do this, I thought, grabbing the noose and savagely tugging it from the tree. Some strange trial to see if I was on a level with the boys. I peered at the rope's cut end. Of course without the lab's help I couldn't determine how long it had been weathering here. And a call for their expertise would raise questions. And I was still determined to keep all such incidents quiet. So, I was stuck. Damn! as Graham often said.

I threw the rope onto the ground and kicked it against a tree. The dull 'thud' did nothing to lessen my anger. I picked it up, hit it against the trunk, then flung it onto an open patch of ground where I stamped on it. After burying it beneath armfuls of leaves and rocks, I emerged from the woods near Talbot's cottage considerably happier.

The village was also in the midst of its early morning routine. There was the usual clank of bottles as Evan set out the empties for pick-up, and a car accelerating as someone left for their job. A voice called out a last-minute message to someone. A door slammed and two dogs barked. But it was quiet on the whole. Much quieter than the morning rush at Buxton.

The Conways and Talbot stood near the edge of the lane at Conway's Gift Shop. Eleanor was leaning on her broom, evidently taking a break in her morning chore. Talbot turned as I approached and, for some reason known only to him and God, called out 'good morning' and tipped his cap to me.

"If the murder hasn't scared them away, we'll have tourists," Mason said, his face flushed. The first rays of morning sun fell upon his features, revealing his paper-white complexion.

"Christmas brings many folks out," Eleanor said. "You'll see. They like a piece of the past — connect with ancestors, see how our customs evolved. It's too soon to worry, dear."

He rubbed his nose so vigorously that I was half expecting to see blood when he stopped. I tried not to stare as I approached.

"Lot of folks do like the pageantry. Kind of puts a spark in their ordinary days, I agree. And in ordinary years we do all right. We get — what would you say, Ell—half our profit for the year?"

"I'd have to look at the books to see."

"Doesn't matter. Something close to that, anyhow. The point is —"

"The point *is*," Talbot said, his index finger poking Mason's chest, "we can build up the trade here, 'stead of seein' it die. With a little education from the right people, in the right spot, we'll be put on the map and have nothin' to fear. And they'll take us serious — you'll see."

"What *are* you talking about? Who's doing this education, as you put it, and where?"

"Never you mind that." Talbot took a cigarette from his jacket pocket and lit it. He was about to throw away the match when he held it toward Mason. "Like this match, now. Unlit it's no good. Just a bit of useless wood, for all its potential. But strike it at the right time and apply its flame to the right place —" He imitated an explosion. "Whoosh! You got somethin' movin' and dramatic, and all from a bit of education. Same thing here in the village. Trust us, lad."

I glanced at the Conways as I passed. Evidently they were as nonplused as I was. Mason opened his mouth but Talbot said, "You'll see. Once we get goin' you won't have to worry no more."

Without appearing obvious, I couldn't slow my walk. I was out of listening range in seconds, wondering, along with Mason, what Talbot was planning.

I HAD JUST entered the incident room when Fordyce called me to the phone. "The Vicar, Sergeant. He asked for you or Mr. Graham, and since Mr. Graham's not here...."

I nodded and took the receiver. Lyle's voice shot over the phone and bore into my ear. "I know it's dreadfully early. I hope they haven't pulled you out of bed." He paused, as if expecting me to reveal my schedule. I assured him I was fully dressed and had breakfasted. "Really? I suppose I could have waited, but I wanted to catch you up before you left for the day. I didn't now if you'd be about, if I'd see you —"

"Has something happened, sir?"

"What? Oh, no. At least, not to me. I suppose I'm an alarmist, but there was that poor American, you know.... Well, there's always the doubt if one keeps quiet."

"It's always best to tell the police anything connected with a case, sir, no matter how trivial you may think it."

"Yes? Well, that's good to hear. Perhaps I shouldn't say anything, but in light of what happened with Ramona...."

I nodded my head, took a few notes, and hung up assuring Lyle that I did not consider the call a waste of time.

"A witness to Steve Pedersen's murder?" asked Graham, who had strolled into the room mid-way through my non-cipherable grunts, and who was now searching for his pen among the papers on the table.

"We should be so lucky."

"My fantasy," Graham said rather dreamily. "Just once. Just one time before I retire, I'd like a witness who was at the scene, who took a video, whose word won't be doubted, who —"

"I think you're wanting Moses again."

"And what's wrong with him?"

"Nothing. Just a little hard to get a hold of right now. Unless you're not telling me something."

"Taylor, I tell you absolutely *everything*. That's the only way a good police team can work."

I must have eyed him rather dubiously, for he said, "I had porridge, toast and tea for breakfast. Now, what say we deal with something a little less palatable. In case you've forgotten, we were working on that wonderful year 1973. We have Byron stating that because he had that tragic car accident in December, he left the village. Talbot spouts off last night about Derek's absence from the village during the winter of 1973. Doesn't that do something to your curiosity, Taylor?"

"To tell the truth, sir," I replied, suppressing a yawn, "it didn't keep me up last night."

Death of an Ordinary Guy

"And you call yourself a detective. You have something for us, Salt?"

Mark nodded, handing the page to Graham. While Graham skimmed the paper, Mark moved slightly so he stood behind Graham. He raised his eyebrows, pointed upstairs and to his watch. Not only could I read his pantomime, I could read his mind. I made a face at him and shook my head. Mark tossed out a dazzling smile before returning to his computer. I breathed deeply, hoping to cool my anger, and looked at Graham.

The vehicle accident records for the area around Upper Kingsleigh in 1973 showed a fatal accident in December, attributable to the extremely hazardous conditions of the roads. Two people were named as occupants of the car: the driver, Byron MacKinnon, and a passenger, George Alton. "Well, well," Graham said. "Here's something unexpected. A Good Samaritan stopped by. Care to venture a guess?" He smiled at me from over the top of the printout.

"Derek Halford."

"First rate, Taylor." He tossed the paper onto the table. "How'd —"

"I didn't guess, if that's what you're accusing me of. He doesn't say what he was doing out in the wilds of Derbyshire, I take it. Though it was a few weeks after the pomp and ceremony of the dole. Suppose he was coming home from Christmas shopping?"

"More likely blew his wad in a Buxton pub. He was a bright, young bachelor in those days."

"Don't think he spent his loot on anything for his place. Could do with a new coat of paint and a few covers on the chairs. What's he been doing with the money all these years? Three hundred quid is a nice bit of change. Not only that, does his wife question what happens to the money?"

"Maybe she's the one who's been running foot loose through his wallet. You know — equality in marriage. He works hard to earn it, she spends it."

I ignored his sexist statement. "How long have they been getting the benefits from that dole? Since the 1960s or '70s, isn't it? Over twenty years, at any rate. Twenty times £300...." I stopped to calculate the total. "Six thousand pounds!"

Graham suggested that Derek might have used the money in a different way.

"Such as?"

"Such as a new car, telly or fridge, lessons at the Open University, bill at the dentist, get the dog spayed —"

"Doesn't have a dog."

"Maybe he did twenty-five years ago. Anyway, if Kris doesn't question the suspicious dwindling of their fortune, why should you? Evidently Derek is of a philanthropic bent."

"Charity starts at home."

"He can give some of it to charities and still have some left over for his dog. What now?" Graham groaned as I snapped my fingers.

"Remember our first interview Sunday night? Arthur Catchpool, when he was telling us about how he had to turn part of his mansion into the B-and-B establishment? Well," I said, hurrying on after Graham nodded, "he mentioned in passing, though I've my idea he was rather proud in a one-up-manship sort of way, that he'd made Derek a loan. Remember? Arthur tossed it out when he told us Pedersen stayed Friday night at the house and left Saturday to stay with the Halfords."

"He didn't let drop the generous amount of his loan, did he? No, I don't recall it either. But I do recall Arthur mentioned the Halfords had enlarged their home. Something about it able to accommodate several guests, now. But if that's not it, I don't know what he's using his money for."

"I thought you liked his dentist. Or vet." I picked up the phone, dialed the Constabulary, and asked the obliging listener at the other end to fax us information on any planning applications made by Derek since 1973. When I'd hung up, I said, "She'll phone the planning board and let us know."

"Your idea being...."

"We'll at least know the extent of any alterations or whatever in his house, and make a fair deduction of the amount of the loan. If it's a whole extra room, it probably set Derek back a bit. I don't expect he makes all that much at his present position. And, inheritance aside, he can't have paid back the loan all that quickly if it was a nice, fat sum. At least it gives us something to go on."

"A simple coat of paint and those seat covers wouldn't have warranted Arthur's pocket-dipping."

"You don't suppose," I said, "that Derek used the loan money to help Kris with her dad's funeral. If she was financially strapped, it'd be one way to win a hesitant maiden's heart." The background noises of ringing phones, computer printings, and convivial conversations receded into a whisper as I waited for Graham's Judgment.

"But she was engaged at the beginning of November to Byron. Why wouldn't Byron do the funeral favors?"

"Couldn't afford it?"

"I wonder...." Graham gazed at the report before saying, "Do you think it just a little too pat for Derek to be present at the car accident?"

"Unusual, perhaps, but it's a main thoroughfare. Be more strange if they happened to meet in the middle of the A838 in Scotland."

"Damn it, Taylor, this thing just doesn't smell right. Kris' father dies, and Derek steps into Kris's life as her husband, supplanting Byron, who'd been engaged to her up to that point."

"Byron said he didn't feel he could marry her after the accident."

"That's it. Byron said. We have no witnesses. The obliging statement given to our man-in-blue at the time of the accident says that Derek was passing by and stopped to take up his Good Samaritan role. He was there before our boys were."

"You think it was planned, then?"

"I don't know if it was planned, but something's sticking in my throat. Pedersen, as former fiancé, turns up here in Upper Kingsleigh, and two days later *he's* dead."

"You think Kris is responsible for both deaths? Why should she want to kill her father? And Pedersen —"

"I don't think it's *Kris* we have to focus on, TC. I think it's *Derek*."

"*Derek?* Why him?"

"Nothing concrete, I'm afraid. That's the problem with the entire supposition."

"Usually your instincts are correct, sir."

"I was wondering if Derek could be unsure of his wife's love, maybe even jealous of Pedersen,"

"Wonder what it feels like to know you're third best."

"Exactly. Can't do much for anyone's ego."

"So you're thinking Derek eliminated his old rival?"

Graham rubbed his forehead, the strains of putting motive to action starting to tell. He eventually looked at me, his dark eyes serious as he explained. "Derek planned his conquest, if you want to call it that. First he eliminated Byron — probably slipped him a hefty check to get him out of the running. Then Derek gets rid of Pedersen and substitutes his body for the effigy. Neat, succinct. He's taken care of both rivals, and feels relatively secure with his wife's affections."

"*Absit invidia.*"

"'Let there be no envy,' indeed," Graham muttered, his mouth tightening.

"We can't prove it, though. You said it was your instinct. I've worked with you on enough nebulous cases to trust you, but what set you off?"

Graham tapped the case notebook. "What your friend Talbot said last night at the pub."

"His ranting about the caroling? What's a bit of caroling got to do with —"

"Not the caroling per se. The expounding about the group's gala anniversary. Or, one of the group who isn't entitled to the silver loving cup."

"Derek?" I said. "Evan said he'd only been with them for twenty-four years."

"Derek was absent from Upper Kingsleigh from December '73 until the spring of '74. Three months. What did he do in that time? Where did he go? I need to find out. There's no such thing as coincidence in a murder investigation, Taylor."

"That soul of discretion should be able to tell you, sir."

Graham grabbed his mobile and punched in the vicarage number. Almost immediately he was speaking to Lyle. "My day will be much better, thank you, sir, if you can give me a bit of information. I know I've bothered you enough with this dreadful affair, but if you have a moment —"

As they talked, I had an image of the vicar sitting at his desk, his bald head warmed by and throwing back the yellowish light of his desk lamp, his round cheeks expanded like air-filled balloons as he held his breath in expectation.

After several minutes, Graham whistled, a slow, low tone, and thanked the vicar before hanging up.

"What's up? Did the vicar remember Derek's absence?"

"Derek left them rather abruptly. Just phoned the vicar one day to tell him he'd be leaving."

"And where did he go?"

"Derek told the vicar he was going to do some hiking and skiing in Germany."

"Nothing so unusual in that," I said, feeling let down. "My cousin's wife has been to —"

"The point is, Taylor," Graham said, rather abruptly, "when Derek returned he brought Lyle a Bavarian stein."

"Wonder if it's the kind with the hinged lid. I always think they're good for —"

"There are other places than Germany in which to buy German gifts, Taylor. A stein doesn't prove he was there in '74."

"And your idea of his hideout is..."

"I'm gong to find out. He had to have been *somewhere* for those three months."

"Just because a man lies about a trip, whether to impress his neighbors or the girl he loves, doesn't mean he's guilty of murder. You can't take him in charge for Pedersen's murder on your suspicions of a twenty-five-year-old unsubstantiated holiday."

"Maybe not, but I can find out what our efficient government records show about his passport."

Inwardly I groaned. I knew Graham's bulldog tenacity, the way he set his jaw once his teeth were into a case, the way his back stiffened as though protecting his soft, vulnerable belly. He wouldn't release his bite or drop his shoulders until either he had his suspect in charge or had been declared dead by a doctor. And even then, I mused, listening to Graham's tackling of the poor official on the other end of the phone, I wouldn't put it past the man to haunt the guilty party into insanity or confession. A *real* Holy Terror.

The minutes ticked away as Graham stayed on the phone, waiting for anything the computers could find.

"No Derek." Graham slammed down the receiver and glared at me. "So where the hell was he?"

Chapter 23

"WHY MAKE SUCH AN OBVIOUS LIE when it could be checked so easily? Why not just say he wintered at Brighton or some other place?"

Graham groaned, running both hands through his chestnut-colored hair and down the back of his neck. He kept them there, clasped, and leaned his elbows on the table top, speaking more to the pile of papers in front of him than to me. "1973 will take a bit of research, I agree. Not like a crime committed last year, say, and the information easily accessed via computer."

"I doubt if the villagers really cared that much where he went. We'll have to employ that army to look through boxes of old files."

Mark came up to us again, this time all Police Officer. "Excuse me, sir, but Fordyce is on his way over with a post card. Said you'd most likely want to see it right away."

"What's so important about a post card, Salt? Is it the only post card unread by a postal employee?"

Mark glanced at me, probably unsure if Graham wanted a response. I just smiled. Just figure it out yourself, Mr. Superior Being, if you're so sure of yourself... Seeing I wasn't going to help him, Mark addressed Graham. "The card, sir, was displayed rather prominently in Ramona's front room."

I swallowed slowly, feeling my heart rate increase. "If it's a gilt card," I said rather quietly, "I remember seeing it when I talked to her."

"That's it," Mark said. "Fordyce said that during his examination of the room he found it and thought it a bit strange. It's from Coventry." He turned smartly on his heel, leaving me to bear Graham's reproach.

Death of an Ordinary Guy

I nodded. Would Graham demote me for overlookng the clue? I could feel my throat closing. I wiped my palms against my slacks and said, "Home of Lady Godiva's infamous cold-catching ride."

He didn't seem to consider the post card rank-breaking. "Though not in the same stature and certainly not as provocative, it's also the boyhood home of Talbot Tanner. The place where his adoption proof resided."

"You think there's some link in all this?" I said, feeling a bit better.

Graham tossed his pen at the stack of papers obscuring the edges of the table. Silence closed around us while we considered it.

"So where's the motive in all this — Pedersen or Ramona? In all these happy villagers and tourists, someone hated either Pedersen or Derek, if you want the mistaken identity theory. And enough to do something about it."

As though the Olympian gods were directing the affairs of humans below, Fordyce entered at that precise moment. There was something in his face — a glint of triumph in his eye — that suggested to me that this was not a normal report. He strode over to Graham, stood stiffly by the chair, and handed over a sealed plastic bag.

"It's been printed, sir," Fordyce said. "Hargreaves figured it was useless after all these years, but...."

"No doubt we'll have *your* dabs on this, Taylor." Graham said.

I felt as though I was going to be sick.

Fordyce frowned, then said, "Found it in the front room. Propped up on a small wooden plate rack. Almost tossed the thing aside, there was so much in that room."

Graham muttered that he had heard about it.

"Yes, sir. But if you'll look at the message —"

"Thank you, Fordyce."

The man's shoulders inched backwards slightly as a blush of pride colored his cheeks. He answered Graham's remaining questions, then left.

"No expense spared," Graham said, angling the card so its band of gilt edging caught the light. This same brilliance had been applied to the subject's hair, for the card showed a romanticized rendition of Lady Godiva, sitting quite ladylike on a white horse.

"Nearly as good as a French post card."

Graham turned it over to the message area. "You read Conan Doyle as a child, Taylor?" He leaned forward, positioning the card between us.

"I was reading them when most kids were reading Pooh Bear, sir."

"I bet you were." He read aloud, "'My month's nearly up. I'd like to stay longer, but I need to leg it at the end of the week. Been hunting in all the antique shops for that pre-war tie, but I can't find it. Beginning to think it's been bombed out of existence. Could Cain have felt happier?'" Graham looked up, slightly amused by the apparent code.

"Who's Cain?" I said.

"Cain and Able, Taylor. Surely you know enough bible to know those two."

"What's he mean about Cain feeling happier?"

"The obvious thing that comes to mind is murder."

A silence settled over us as we studied the card's possible meaning. "Who sent it?" I picked up the card, scrutinizing the postmark. "March, 1974. Long time to keep a post card. No signature. Ramona supposed to know who was in Coventry in March, 1974?"

"That's why I hoped you were up on your Conan Doyle."

"And this bit about a tie...."

"Not a silk one, if that's got you confused. My guess is a family one — that adoptive tie Derek's so hot over. Look, TC, it all fits. Antique shops are just Derek's clever way of telling Ramona he's been hunting for Talbot's adoption papers — the 'antique' part referring to old business or Talbot's age or something. I'm assuming for the moment it is Derek who sent the card, yes. Don't know anyone else interested in disproving Talbot's adoption."

"Arthur? He provides the dole money."

"Can't see Arthur particularly interested. So what if Talbot proves he's the rightful heir? According to the will, Arthur still has to fork out the money. Either way, he's out his yearly £300. No, it's got to be Derek who sent this."

"But the reference to Cain, sir. Why talk about Cain if Derek hadn't committed murder? And he obviously didn't. 1974 was a long time ago. Talbot's walking around, healthy as can be. Same with Derek and Arthur. Why Cain?"

"Perhaps," Graham said slowly, "Derek meant it symbolically. Since he could find no trace of Talbot's adoption, Talbot has no legal or family ties to the money. He's dead. Gone. Buried. Derek had nothing to fear from Talbot."

"Good riddance to a potential brother."

"Like Abel. No more brother. Or.... Perhaps Esau and Jacob would have been a better comparison than Cain and Able."

"Pardon?"

"The two sons of Isaac," Graham reminded me. "Jacob stole his older brother's birthright. Old Testament."

"Never was too strong on the bible. Sir, if Jacob stole his older brother's birthright, do you think —"

"Talbot is older.... I don't know, Taylor. We're getting into more speculation than we should. It's so easy, so tempting to build a case this way."

"The Super will have your guts for garters if you do, sir."

The expression was not lost on Graham. He sighed. "Unfortunately, he doesn't need much provocation."

"So, if Derek was the original driver, he no doubt got his game leg from the car accident, wouldn't you say?"

Graham nodded and patted my hand. It was in a careless manner, as though praising a dog for correctly executing a trick. I wish it had been more heart-felt.

Graham's voice heightened as he vocally talked through the scenario. "If he got his limp from the accident, he couldn't let the villagers see it. It would take a bit of explaining how he ended up with a limp by playing the Good Samaritan."

"So he ducks out of Upper Kingsleigh, holes up to rest, thinking Germany's as good an alibi as any. No one'd be looking for him on the continent. And the skiing accident would sound logical."

"But he goes to Coventry — that town that keeps popping up in Derek's and Talbot's pasts like a thorn in the foot."

"The dates, fit, sir. March, 1974."

"And Lyle said that Derek returned in the spring."

Like pigeons to roost. Or a sparrow to a waste bin, I thought. Bedecked with homecoming flowers to mark the errant loved one's welcome and to speed the dead to heaven. Home to spend your final days. I looked out the window, at Evan waving to the Conways, at Colonel Wroe talking to the American tourists. How many final days did any of us have? The chirping of the birds on the window sill broke my reverie and I asked, "You think Kris knows anything about all this?"

"Derek's Coventry holiday?" Graham shook his head and picked up the post card, staring again at Lady Godiva. "That was before he had married her, Taylor. Even if the 1973 dole went straight into Byron's pocket, Kris wouldn't know. What's his wouldn't be hers until the wedding."

I was about to remark that money didn't necessarily have to be communal property after a joining of two households when P.C. Byrd hurried into the incident room. He came directly to Graham and handed him an impressive assortment of official documents, each one consigned to constabulary paper.

"Lab report on the rope fiber found beneath Ramona Van Dyke," Byrd said, his voice as even and emotionless as if he were choosing a piece of cod from the fishmonger's. Graham looked up and took the papers held out to him. "And the p.m. report. They've found something slightly unusual at the deceased's cottage. A small glass jar. Might have been for marmalade or some such. Found near the back door, under a bush, sir."

"And what is this jar holding, or have the contents washed away in the rain?"

"Not completely, no, sir. Diluted somewhat, but the smell's still there, and we're about to take it to the lab. Turpentine. Smells like it, anyhow." Byrd allowed himself a slight smile when Graham praised their work. "And Sergeant," Byrd said, almost as an after thought, "here's the information you asked for."

I thanked him and opened the envelope, not bothering Graham, who was occupied in his own pursuit of knowledge. It was a report of the Halford's bank account. Even with the generous handout of the dole money, it was little better than mine. I scanned through the pages, back through a decade of deposits and withdrawals. It was all fairly steady. No drastic money juggling anywhere. I thanked Byrd again and laid the paper on the table. Byrd turned smartly and made for a paper-laden table, whistling under his breath.

Would you have expected turpentine, Taylor?" Graham was reading the reports as he talked to me, yet relinquished their fascinating hold when I replied it was common enough in most households. "Could have been cleaning something."

"Or Talbot may have done. He is the odd jobs man for the village."

"May have been a very odd job," Graham grunted, handing me the reports. "What does one use turpentine for? Removing paint, cleaning off grease, asphyxiating Ramona."

Death of an Ordinary Guy

"Damage to kidneys, intense congestion and swelling in the lungs and brain...." I turned briefly back to the report to make certain of the facts. "Died within minutes, from Karol's estimate. Got to be murder, sir. No one, even the most determined suicide, would use turpentine. It'd be far too painful to swallow, and more than one sniff...."

"Aside from the fact that she was intensely happy with her forthcoming marriage, why commit suicide? It was murder. The killer no doubt doused a rag, clamped it over her nose...."

"That whitish skin around her nose. That was the area where he held the rag."

I could envision the struggle. The man — for it had to be a man. Who else would have the muscular strength to hold a turpentine-soaked rag to a struggling woman for minutes while she inhaled lungful after lungful of this odor? Ramona, whether inside or outside her house, would have clawed at his hands, trying to break his hold. He had worn gloves, for no one I had seen in the village had scratches on his hands. And he had been callous. A swift gunshot in a heated argument is one thing, but to deliberately hold a kicking, struggling woman for minutes.... I shuddered. Graham hadn't noticed. He was intent on the post mortem report. Facts were what solved murder cases. Not emotions. And I had started to get as emotional about Ramona's struggle as I had about my dead sparrow.

"No doubt, Taylor. Karol also suggests the body was moved sometime prior to its discovery. The blood is stagnant in the upper body cavity, not along the back as we would expect since she was found lying on her back."

"The blood settled in her chest area," I said, standing up and reading aloud over Graham's shoulder. "And fixed lividity generally occurs six to eight hours after death." I looked at him, a long, emotionless stare. He returned it, unblinking. "Fits our time table, since we know she was lying there during the midnight storm and found at seven the next morning."

"So sometime during those seven hours her position, if not her entire body, was shifted. Why, Taylor?"

"To place her outside, or to extract something damning?" I tried to voice my nebulous thoughts. "Something incriminating from the struggle, perhaps. Something like a button or whatever that could point to the murderer."

"You think she was killed inside, then, and her body arranged in the back yard?"

"Karol's report pushes me in that direction, yes." I tried to convince him. "And her slippers were free of mud. Even if it rained like Hell — which it did — it wouldn't have washed her slippers completely clean of her stroll outside. *Something* would have clung, no matter how miniscule."

"And our ever-efficient though underpaid lab boys would have found it." Though he had jested, he looked serious. We were nearing the wrap-up of the case and he was anxious to end it. He may have joked with Byron at the pub, but for all his near-nonsensical verbiage, his emotions had been poured into his statement. Being close to naming the murderer propelled him ever faster in his work. I tried to understand him, tried to read the man within. His eyes gave me no information other than his solemnity. Yet, there was something else in their depths that I couldn't read. A second later, it had vanished and he sighed. "If not carried outside, Taylor, we at least know she was moved, though why...."

"Could it have to do with her hand behind her back?"

"The rope fiber?"

I nodded while he assessed the possibility.

"We have no proof, Taylor. Although I hate coincidences —"

"Perhaps we should go about this as to who could have killed her, which might lead us to the reason for the body shift."

"So whom do you favor as the murderer?"

The incident room was quiet this morning. Most of the officers were either at the scene or on errands. In the silence, the sounds of the village sifted through the pub's walls: a dog barked, people talked, an occasional car horn honked. Common, everyday sounds. Sounds far removed from murder on a cool, tranquil evening.

"Well," I said, a bit too eagerly to show Graham I could put two and two together as perfectly as he could, "it occurs to me we have focused on Derek due to the dole money."

"And you are suggesting we are off track, then." Graham's eyebrow was cocked slightly, his head tilted to one side as he studied my face.

"Yes, sir, I think we are. He loves his wife. Of course, no one can decipher the inner emotions of another," I said, coloring. I averted my eyes from Graham, pretending to refer to the bank account statement. When the blush had subsided, I continued. "I think we can take his love as real."

"Even with Pedersen, the ex-fiancé showing up?"

Death of an Ordinary Guy

"Kris made no move to go with him," I reminded Graham. "She could have said something to Derek, granted, but she's still here. And Derek is devoted to her. And if you're thinking that Derek paid off Byron annually with the dole money so he could slip the wedding ring on Kris's finger, that's another dead end." I handed him the bank statement and waited until he had read it before I said, "The £300 is deposited in November or December for the past dozen or so years."

"So he wasn't keeping it out for Christmas gifts," Graham said, tossing the report onto the table.

"If Derek was paying for Kris, as I said, why suddenly quit? We have to focus on a different motive."

"Then, if you don't like the love rival elimination —"

"There's money involved, yes, sir," I said, watching Byrd as he took out his wallet to make change for Mark. When I began again, my voice cracked. I coughed, covering up my anger, and said, "It's the money of tourism."

Chapter 24

"THE FOREMOST TOURIST enticer is Arthur. You saying *he* killed Pedersen?" Graham said, a note of disbelief in his voice. "*Motive,* Taylor. *Why?* He didn't even know the man."

"Not Arthur. He's involved in tourism, yes. So are Byron, Eleanor and Mason Conway, and Evan. They all have a lot to lose if tourists side step this village."

Byrd had replaced his wallet and was again tackling the computer. Mark, I was glad to see, had taken his change and left the room. The door hadn't closed completely and I could hear his loud laugh in the pub's entryway. He was busy flattering Paula, one of Evan's staff. Either he got a quick 'yes' or was just passing the time of day for once, for his voice faded as he left the building. I saw him pause just outside the front door and consult his watch. Calculating how much time he'd have to kill before his bedroom rendezvous, or seeing if he could rig up Surprise Number Five before I finished up with Graham? I grabbed the bank statement, crumbling it in my hand.

"And there are others," I said, "indirectly, whose livelihood would be threatened by the loss of tourists."

Graham said, "Ramona, by marrying Arthur, would have had her fortune linked to his. And Uncle Gilbert, who clings to Arthur's wallet tighter than any cork ever did to a wine bottle."

"Arthur admitted he needs the B-&-B business to keep his head and hall above water. Byron also needs the B-&-B, for as Arthur's fortunes go, so does Byron's living."

"The Conways have their gift shop, which depends 100% on tourism."

"And Evan, though not totally dependent on the tourists, certainly gets a strong percentage of his yearly income from them."

Death of an Ordinary Guy

"Seven people whose lives hang on the whims of tourists," Graham said, staring at the names he had scribbled down. "But why eliminate a tourist? We just agreed these seven people *needed* tourists."

"They do. And Pedersen's murder is coincidentally connected to tourism."

"Guy Fawkes Day, yes, since he was dressed as the Guy. So who among this chummy list committed the great *faux pas?*"

He asked it as one colleague to another. There was no mockery in his voice, as Mark would have done, taunting me to explain, to lay open my heart and then shred it with laughter and ridicule. Graham wanted to know my reasoning, to see if I had thought logically and applied the clues and facts of the case to my choice. He was writing something opposite one name on the list. Probably writing down his own deduction, I thought, for he finally raised his head and looked at me, ready for me to continue. As student looking at teacher.

"Byron." I had said it louder and more forcefully than I had intended. One word, so simple, crashed into the silence of the room like a pistol shot. There had been no derisive laugh, no mocking rhyme. Graham angled his head, interested in my logic, and waited patiently for more, knowing I would explain when I felt ready.

"Yes, sir. Arthur told us during our first interview Sunday evening that Byron had been near to bankruptcy about 15 years ago."

"His business had failed," Graham recalled. "And Arthur was extolling Byron's virtue in repaying his friends who had lent him the business money."

I nodded and smoothed out the wrinkled bank statement. "This confirms it. Derek was probably paying Byron the dole money for those 15 years — there's no sign of it in the account. But after that, the Halfords suddenly become richer by £300 each year."

"Byron had repaid everyone and, being the virtuous fellow Arthur insists he is, refused anymore of Derek's dole money. Fits." He chewed on a pencil, waiting to see if I had pieced together the rest of the scenario.

"So, if Byron's money need is legitimate and verifiable — which it is — we turn to a different angle. If Pedersen wasn't killed for himself —"

"We'd be daft to say he was," Graham concluded. "No one except the Halfords and the American couple knew him. And we've eliminated them."

"Then perhaps he was killed — not so much as a symbol proper — but as result of a symbol. As a result of loving that symbol and depending on it to bring guests to Arthur's B-and-B so he could be assured of employment."

Graham was drawing the effigy along a margin of the bank statement, rendering a remarkably lifelike face. He decorated Pedersen's shirt in the stripes of the Union Jack flag. "This whole weekend was peppered in symbolism, Taylor. The Guy itself, Derek with the symbolic crutches at the dole...." He threw down his pencil. "So what's the motive, if you're going along with this reasoning?"

"I was on bonfire duty Sunday," I reminded him. "Early afternoon Byron, with considerable pride, was explaining the history of Guy Fawkes to the Americans, who —I'm sad to say — didn't quite take it seriously. Pedersen was the worst of the lot. Byron got offended. Probably got into a fight with him later that day. As we worked out earlier, sir, the bruising on the jaw indicates Byron probably KO'd Pedersen with his fist. Once on the ground, he kicked him. Doesn't know his strength, if you remember him kicking the chair in the pub. Anyway, if Pedersen had merely stumbled, there would be more general bruising, as on hip, knee, palm, places where he'd break his fall. But the concentrated area of bruises, plus the cracked ribs, led me to conclude he was assaulted as he lay on the ground. Byron probably then hit him with a stone or stick. There were a lot of nice-sized pieces of wood about. One correctly-placed hit...." I shut my eyes, sickened by the imagine before me. Of Byron, overcome with anger, striking out in a moment of patriotism, pushing Pedersen, perhaps a little too hard, picking up a stone, not meaning to kill....

Graham was staring at me when I opened my eyes. His voice was soft, as though not wanting to frighten me. "Some people have more homeland love than others, I agree."

Like Colonel Wroe, I wanted to say, but I knew Graham was thinking of the man.

"There's also one other bit of evidence. The hoisting itself."

"Byron and Ramona switched jobs this year."

"Normally Ramona raises the effigy and Byron lights it. But Byron couldn't let her raise it."

Graham nodded. "She would have discovered immediately the difference in weight between a straw effigy and a man. But why dress Pedersen as the Guy? Why not leave him on the ground, say?"

Death of an Ordinary Guy

I nodded. That had thrown me for quite a while. "Byron probably viewed Pedersen as a sort of defiler, an uncouth, ignorant bloke who didn't even try to see another point of view, who ridiculed the other fellow's beliefs."

"Rather like our original cast of characters in 1605, I assume."

"For someone like Byron, who loved the village and was struggling out of debt, the Guy was the perfect symbol of a traitor, a fitting shroud for such a despoiler."

Graham sat, just looking at me, studying my face. There was no hint of mirth or ridicule or puzzlement in his eyes. I wondered what he was thinking, what he was going to say. We had no proof of Byron's part in this, other than the conflicting weight of effigy and corpse. But it was common sense to anyone's logic. And it certainly made sense to clothe the object of Byron's anger in that handy shroud. Graham finally leaned forward, put his hand on mine, and squeezed it. He said in an even, warm voice, "Well, Taylor, first class bit of reasoning. It all fits — motive, opportunity. Byron knew everyone's time table and jobs... And he would lose just as much as Arthur would if the B-and-B guests stop coming."

"I don't think he thought of that at the time. I think it was a crime of passion originally. He just struck out at Pedersen in anger for ridiculing the ceremony."

"Remember, remember...." Graham began, then let his voice die away as though he was remembering something dim and past and painful. "Since you've done so well, Ray —" He colored, hearing his mistake, and coughed as though to hide it. I pretended not to notice. Graham said, his voice forcibly brighter, "You've done a first-class job, Taylor, with Pedersen. What are your views on Ramona?"

I dismissed the possibility of an amorous Wroe; even if he had come for a fling and been thwarted, he wouldn't have come prepared for murder. And Arthur didn't make sense, for he was engaged to her. And a 'Sorry, old girl' would be a more sensible way to break the engagement, if he had wished it, than murder. And Talbot, though the rope fiber and ropes tying the twig bundles in her yard were the same, anyone could have cut a piece from the rope... I bent my head, massaging the back of my neck. I was tired of thinking about the two murders and about my own dilemma. I wanted a good night's sleep and a holiday in Jamaica. Instead, I said, "I really haven't thought that far, sir."

"Yes, you have, Taylor. You're just not using your head. Mind if I give you a hint? The body wasn't as we're used to seeing it." He folded his arms, leaned against the back of his chair, and waited for me to continue the reasoning.

Again I could see the scene at Ramona's. Although it had been the darkest of nights, I could see it clearly in my mind. The man with the limp body in his arms placing it on the ground, then coming back much later to shift it, placing something beneath it. My voice was barely audible as I said, "Ramona's sprained wrist. She wore no sling. She had been ready for bed."

"And?"

"And we know that she was pretty helpless, that Arthur or Byron brought her meals, looked in on her."

"Bingo! Our player and logical house access."

"Good so far?"

"First rate, TC. What else?"

"Byron stumbled into her Sunday, causing the sprain so she couldn't raise the Guy — I checked with Evan and the local doctor. Anyway, he would have had to somehow keep her from raising the dummy, else the weight difference would be obvious."

"And who do you favor for her murderer?"

"Has to be Byron, sir."

"Why?"

"Ramona must have known about the '73 accident. Of course! In the pub, when she and Derek were talking.... We didn't catch much, but she said at the end something about 'your secrets' being safe. Could be singular 'your,' but I don't think so. Not when, in the same breath, she wished him and Byron —"

"— a good evening," Graham finished, his voice taking on a hard edge. "She knew about the role reversals from the accident. Only reason that makes sense. But Byron, like most amateur killers, got scared."

"Probably thought he couldn't trust her in light of the Pedersen murder investigation and all the questioning, though I agree that if she hadn't said anything in all this time she was probably good to retain her silence. Still, murderers get scared."

Graham added a crutch to his effigy sketch. "It's easy to let loose a bit of information you intend to keep secret. If Byron was afraid she'd say something, he very easily would have killed her."

"He has his own quarters at Arthur's. He could easily slip out. He'd stick to the edge of the woods. It's unlikely anyone would see him at midnight. Arthur, the only one to ask embarrassing questions, had just returned from dinner and was bunked down for the rest of the night."

"All the little birds to their nests," Graham murmured. He had wandered to the window during my speech. We had been asking questions and dealing with possible motives and suspects for hours, unaware that morning had slipped into afternoon, impervious to the waning of precious autumnal daylight. Graham now stood looking out the eastern window, staring at the saffron-tinted light of late afternoon, stretching his chair-weary muscles. I bet he could sit by the hour and watch the changing light. He loved the late afternoon, the early evening when the growing darkness creeps into sunlight-splashed regions. At the light-flecked fringes of the fire area, giant, bare arms of the oak stretched out, canopying the burnt wood beneath it, scratching at the lilac-hued clouds above. Graham's voice came slowly, as though drugged from sleep. "Ever notice how dark it is in these villages with no street lights, Taylor? Dark as the grave." He turned from the window — rather reluctantly, I thought — and looked straight through me. His eyes were vacant, as if he saw something other than the pub room.

He'd rather be out there, I mused, wondering what captured his attention, what private world held him. Was it his broken engagement, some ministerial tie or past trouble, boyhood memory? I wished he would tell me, include me in his world, let me hold him. He seemed so alone, so vulnerable, so melancholy. Twilight does something to him, pulls at his soul or memory. Perhaps it's the link with something ancestral to all of us, of Homo sapiens huddled protectively around the midnight fire. Or something whispering to him of holy things. It's as though all the sadness since the world began had poured upon him. And he feels every tragedy: lost loves, betrayals, conspiracies. He's feeling this tragedy, too — as cop and as minister — as valiantly as he's trying to detach himself from it. He can't rid himself of compassion. And really, that's not so bad. I focused on his face, and tried like so many other times to envision Graham in clerical garb. I was never happy with the image. Not that he wouldn't have lent a sympathetic ear, but there had to have been more restraints in the church — even if it had been the more radical Methodist religion — than he's been subjected to with the Force. And for the impatient, incautious Graham, the dogma and rules of religion must have been frustrating.

"Byron would have known Ramona wouldn't put up much of a fight." I was talking again to Graham's back. He didn't turn around. I continued. "He knew she was taking Mogadon. She might have been groggy enough not to put up much resistance when he —" I couldn't finish the sentence, the image of Ramona struggling against Byron's assault too nauseating.

I closed my eyes. Sunday evening's scene burst into my mind. I was back at the village green. Evening spread across the sky. A cloud momentarily masked the moon. From somewhere in the darkness, a match scraped against something rough. The smell of sulfur filtered downwind, and a small blue and ochre flame flared in the blackness. A stronger scent of kerosene as the batting ignited, and the vicar's face leapt out of the dark, bathed in crimson, gold and yellow. He ignited the torch and handed it to Ramona. Byron smiled at her, kissed her on the cheek in condolence, and pulled the dummy off the ground, stepping back into the blackness beyond the fire so his effort wouldn't be noticed.... I shuddered, opening my eyes to find Graham gazing at me, back to being all cop, all concerned that something was wrong with someone else. I smiled weakly.

"Byron and the effigy. It was so easy. He had the woods close by. He could drag Pedersen into the woods, redress him there, then easily drag him out when no one was looking."

Giving me a final appraising look, Graham said, "If anyone happened to see him, he could say he came upon Pedersen and had stopped to render help. It wouldn't matter if Pedersen was dressed, half dressed or nude. It's his word against anyone else's."

"It was dark, probably near tea time." I suddenly trembled, imagining the clothing switch that had happened in the woods a few hundred yards in front of me that late afternoon. Like a damned, incompetent first-day constable on the job I had let him get away with murder.

"Anger is a strong force in murder, Taylor. Nearly as powerful and prevalent as love and lust."

I was afraid to respond, afraid my voice might betray my burgeoning feelings. Instead, I asked about the knife.

"Byron, you don't need reminding, is virtuous. On the way from delivering meals to Ramona, he stopped in to console Kris. And while he was fixing her a cup of tea perhaps, he got the idea and the implement. Sitting somewhere, I'm sure, was the box of goodies Pedersen had brought with him from Kris's mother."

Death of an Ordinary Guy

"The opal ring," I volunteered, "and her dad's scout knife. Looks about that vintage."

The telephone rang as Graham uttered a complimentary remark about my reasoning. I let it pass, assuming I would soon hear an uncomplimentary remark about letting Byron redress Pedersen. One emotion at a time.

Graham picked up the receiver, listened for a minute or so, made vague, responsive sounds, then said, "Meet us there, will you? I'll phone you back," and hung up. As he dialed, he said, "That was Tom Oldendorf. He said — Oh, Vicar," Graham declared as the phone was evidently answered. During Lyle's response, Graham mouthed 'I'll tell you in a minute' to me, then spoke a few sparse sentences to the vicar before ringing off. He angled his body so he could look around the room. Byrd was still there, lingering over a report. As soon as Graham called him, Byrd dropped the papers and came over. Graham consulted his watch before saying, "Byrd, hate to ask, but would you mind running back to Buxton for a search warrant?" He jotted down the particulars, handed the note to the constable, then turned back to me.

Graham leaned back in his chair, his eyes closed as though he was concentrating. He was silent for such a long time that I thought he had fallen asleep. I was about to cough when he said, "Yes, Taylor, a jug of wine, a loaf of bread, and a terror-inducing warrant beside me in the wilderness. My apologies to ole Edward Fitzgerald, wherever he may be."

"Pardon, sir?"

"Fitzgerald. The poet of *The Rubáiyát of Omar Khayyám* — that piece I just mauled. Whatever happened to Fitz?"

"Dead, isn't he, sir?" I smiled as Graham opened his eyes and cocked an eyebrow.

"We'd best fortify ourselves, Taylor — physically as well as legally — before we pick up the vicar and see what our muscleman has to say."

Chapter 25

HOURS LATER OUR prime suspect looked vaguely uneasy and surprised at seeing us at his door, but he welcomed us. A batch of posters — freshly printed in vibrant graphics — leaned against a wall opposite the doorway. A mockup of a brochure, along with architectural sketches for display cases and room arrangements lay scattered across his desk. Paints, brushes, and a sketch pad leaned against a battered easel. An electric teakettle whistled madly on the counter, and Byron asked if we would like something.

"I was just going to have a cuppa," he said, pouring the water into the teapot. "Sure I can't get you anything? Beer?"

Graham, I thought, sighed. It was just discernable above Byron's chatter. His jaw muscle was tensing, for the scar shone prominently against his skin. He wants to get on with the arrest, not play at tea parties.

As though sensing Graham's impatience, Byron said, his voice faltering slightly, "Guess that's the wrong thing to suggest, isn't it? This has to be an official visit. Forgive the mess." He blushed, obviously embarrassed by the paper and books stacked around the room. "Kind of caught me behind my chores. I've got a little project on. I and — well, we want to develop a visitor's center." He caught me staring at an unwashed mug, the interior of which was ringed with tea leaves, a section of the exterior rim stained by a lipstick mark. Gesturing toward the table he asked if we'd like to have a seat.

Graham shook his head, saying we'd only be a minute or so. He let Byron finish his tea making, then asked where he had been Tuesday night.

The spoon rattled suddenly against the sides of the cup. He gently removed it, set it on the countertop, took a sip of too-hot tea, and tried to smile. It was forced, the kind that is used in awkward

Death of an Ordinary Guy

situations and accompanied by a quick change in subject. This time Byron could not change the subject. He coughed lightly before replying, "Tuesday night? Why, here, I should think. Or in the office. Wait just a bit.... Yes. Here. I had been to Ramona's to deliver lunch, and Arthur went down for dinner. Even if she could had fared for herself, what with Pedersen's —" He flinched at the subject, stared at his cup, then said rather softly, "I just sat around, read and listened to music. Why? Because of Ramona?" Graham nodded and Byron gushed on. "Well, you would ask, wouldn't you, seeing as how it was probably someone in the village. I suppose you want to know if I saw anything. Can't say I did. The Manor's too far away to see anything. Sorry I can't help." He waited, probably hoping we'd gathered what we wanted and would leave.

We didn't. Instead, Graham delivered the murder theory. The hot tea splashed onto the tabletop as Byron jerked sideways. He stood open-mouthed, his eyes bulging, his cheeks flooding with color. "You're — you can't mean it!"

Graham issued the usual warning. "You do not have to say anything —"

"Nice to know the individual has some rights left to him in this country," Byron muttered.

"You do *not* have to say anything," Graham repeated, as though forcing Byron to listen.

Byron's eyes fixed on Graham's face, his fingertips attempting to dig into the cup. "You're damned right I don't. And if you think I'm going to say anything without my solicitor —"

"— but it may harm your defense," Graham continued, rolling over Byron's bluster, "if you do not mention now something which you later rely on in court."

"Not bloody likely to, am I?" Byron said, his anger stronger than his discretion. "You've got it all thought out — the howdunit, the wheredunit, the whendunit. Mighty clever cops you two are, aren't you? Watch a lot of 'The Bill' on the telly? It's obvious, you two are so adept at this fictionalization of my completely innocent actions. Should have spent your time watching 'Police Action Live,' see how reputable, responsible coppers work, instead of slandering us innocent chaps."

"Anything you do say," Graham went on, "may be given in evidence."

"You two wired, then?" Byron gestured with his free hand toward Graham's jacket. "Your cronies back at the station, or perhaps parked outside the gate, listening to all this over a mike, jotting it all down? That how you use my words in evidence against me? Hold on!" He snapped his fingers as though the truth exploded before his eyes. "You have a tape recorder in your pocket. Perhaps secreted inside your pen. Or fashioned to look like a warrant card. Your lab boys are so ingenious these days. Bloody marvelous!" He laughed, his voice full of irony and resignation at his situation.

"You have a right to legal advice, should you choose," Graham added, although it was unnecessary. "I suggest you send for him, Mr. MacKinnon. Your situation is very grave. This really is not a laughing matter. Murder isn't. I'm confident we have a water-tight case against you."

The laughter died abruptly. His eyes widened as he mumbled, "Well, you would say that. It's all part of the plan. Scare me into confessing. Make me think things will go easier if I own up. It just won't do, Lads. So, unless the heavy gang is lingering about and ready to beat a confession out of me, I'll take my chances with the judge. Unless you've already got to him and bribed —"

"You're probably safe with a trial, Mr. MacKinnon," Graham said, his words sharp in his anger. "Though I can't guarantee it. I couldn't afford much of a bribe. Just the minimum acceptable."

Byron's gaze shifted between Graham and I, as though judging which of us would be the more sympathetic. He focused on me. He whispered, "You can't really think I killed Pedersen and Ramona."

"I'm sorry," I replied, "but we do."

"We don't rank this as fun and games," Graham said, his voice full of the hardness that claimed him when about to make an arrest.

"But —" Byron fumbled for the back of a chair. A laugh, tinted with the rudiments of hysteria, burst from his throat.

I handed him the cup of tea. "Perhaps you'd feel better, sir, if you had a sip of this. Need to sit down?" I pulled out the chair nearest to him, offering him the physical support and emotional breath-catching he needed.

Murmuring something that might have been 'no,' Byron ignored both offers. He turned his gaze from my outstretched hand to Graham's eyes. The hardness that lay in his voice also lay behind his unwavering look. Byron swept a none too steady hand across his lips, letting his teeth nibble slowly at his knuckles before responding. "You haven't any proof. You can't have."

"Why can't we?" My lower, quieter voice contrasted greatly with Byron's rising pitch. I turned to Graham, wondering what

Death of an Ordinary Guy

would happen if Byron demanded to see our evidence. "You know of any reason why we can't have any proof, sir?"

"I can't come up with any, no."

"What's my motive for these murders?" Byron said. "Isn't that a usual consideration? My motive is damned thin if not nonexistent. The man was a stranger. I didn't even know he was going to be here. He arrived with the Oldendorfs. Two separate rooms booked. Under their names. And you're insisting I planned this whole thing and killed him? A bit thick, Graham. You're clutching at straws." Having recovered from his shock, he delivered his first defense.

"Strange you should mention straw," returned Graham, pulling the unencumbered scout knife from his pocket and holding it in front of Byron. "This whole case wallows in straw, you might say. Seen this before?"

Byron barely glanced at the knife before replying smugly, "Yes. In the corpse."

Carefully laying the knife on the table, Graham asked if Byron was certain he hadn't seen it elsewhere, prior to the murder, and urged him to look at it again. The rivets, dotting the wooden handle like eyes in a potato, stared at him. Blood had dried to a brownish smear and imprinted the brass section separating the blade proper from the handle. The corroded release mechanism faced Byron as though silently urging him to close the blade and obliterate the revolting spectacle.

Shaking his head, Byron denied he'd seen it in any other setting. Once he'd glanced at it, however, it mysteriously held him.

"Murder motives take many forms, Mr. MacKinnon. It can be triggered by many things, too. In your instance," Graham said, forcing patience into his voice, "perhaps Pedersen's rude scoffing about the Guy was the last straw in a stressful week. National pride is a powerful motivation. Especially when foreigners do the ridiculing." He paused, studying Byron's face, the hand still crammed into his pocket.

Byron lifted his head and returned Graham's gaze. The initial fright was gone; his voice was steady when he spoke. "I don't know what you're talking about."

Graham reached for the folded piece of paper. Holding it out to Byron, he said, "This is a search warrant, Mr. MacKinnon. If you read it, you will see it gives me full authority to search your home and remove just this sort of thing." He gestured toward the can of turpentine sitting on the floor beneath the easel. Then, tapping lightly on the warrant, he said, "You want to change your story about Tuesday night?"

Though visibly shaken, Byron managed to keep his voice calm. He sniffed, drawing in his upper lip as though he was smelling something rotten. "You arresting me because I've got turpentine? I bet most houses in Upper Kingsleigh have turpentine. I use it to clean my paint brushes — or haven't you noticed? I'm in the middle of a project, as I said. And anyway, I was home, like I said. All night. You think I'd go out in that hell of a storm?"

I excused myself and exited the office area by the front door. A few moments later, I reentered. Byron's fingers gripped the edge of the countertop as Tom Oldendorf came into the room.

Tom glanced at Byron, then took a deep breath as Graham asked him to relay what he had seen Tuesday around midnight.

"I saw," Tom began haltingly, "a man at Ramona's house a little after 11:30."

He took another breath, as though to finish in a rush of facts, when Byron's tirade stopped him, "You saw a man at Ramona's. Big bloody deal. I suppose I'm that man. That's why you're here, right? How could you see any man, how could you identify me as this man if it was as late as you say? Ramona doesn't have a driveway lamp. How you going to beat that, Inspector?" Byron turned to Graham, his eyes enlarged by his anger.

Graham quickly asked Tom to continue. "I was standing on the main road. It was just after eleven. I had a flashlight with me, but I'd turned it off because I wanted absolute darkness for my photos. I do nature photography," he explained to Byron. "That's why I'd chosen that spot. I'd driven down, parked in the pub's lot, then walked about the village for a bit, glancing at the sky, noting where the lightning flashes were. I liked the looks of the road Ramona lives one. It's quite dark — no street lights, no driveway lights. I walked down the lane, then stopped opposite Ramona's driveway because the Halfords have that marvelous old tree in their front yard. I thought it'd make a great photo if I could get the bare branches of the tree with the lightning flash behind it. So I waited there in the dark, my camera set up on the tripod. I'm a very patient man. Well," he grinned slightly, glancing apologetically at Graham, who remained straight-faced, "you have to be patient if you do nature photography. Anyway, I saw the lights go on and off twice in Ramona's house. Ordinarily I wouldn't think a thing of a light going on or off, but twice in rapid succession? That sort of drew my attention. I looked to see what was going on. I thought maybe something had happened and someone was signaling. When the lights went out for the last time I saw a man slip out of the front door and practically run up the road."

"And if I'm that man," Byron said, "how come I didn't see you?"

"I was farther down the road. Angled toward the tree but farther past her front door."

Byron grumbled something about this sounding rehearsed and everyone but he having a ready-made answer.

Graham nodded for Tom to continue. "Well, I got my lightning flash photo. Two of them, in fact. By that time, it was just beginning to rain, so I scrambled back to my car. Carla, my wife, knows I came back around midnight because I woke her up and she heard the rain start." He waited, watching Graham, who still remained rooted near the table.

Byron broke the silence, his voice high and his words rapid. "You saw someone slip out of Ramona's house. Doesn't prove it was me. It could have been —" He fumbled for another defense. "It doesn't mean a thing. Dark shapes — Jesus Christ! You've all met to concoct this, because you can't think of anyone else to pin it on. If I'd suspected what was going on, I'd have invented some iron-clad alibi. Else why am I the only one —"

This time my movement to the door and signal to someone outside stopped him. The door swung open and Lyle walked in.

Chapter 26

LYLE BEGAN IN his usual haphazard way, saying he hoped he wasn't inconveniencing anyone and apologizing for his duty as he phrased it, but eventually told of his errand of mercy Tuesday evening. "Arthur rang me up close to 11:30. Worried about Gilbert. The man had been drinking all day, evidently, and was now hallucinating. You know how he gets."

I mumbled that I did indeed know, even after knowing the man for so short a time.

Lyle grimaced, as though reliving the scene. "Screaming that he saw the devil and was scared to death of going to hell. He kept calling for a vicar to save him. So Arthur phoned me up. It was the only way to calm the dear man." Lyle's fingers stroked the edge of his jacket as he paused in thought. "I went, had a talk with Gilbert — well, trying as hard as I could to make him understand God's love and that he should forsake his drinking. I finally got him calmed down a few minutes before midnight. As I was leaving the manor, I saw Byron."

"And how'd you see me?" Byron said, cocking his head forward as if to catch every word.

"By the light from the front door," Lyle said simply, evenly. "When I opened it, the light fell across the yard. I saw you just entering the door to your suite here." He stood there, suddenly quiet, aware of his identification, aware that he was helping the police identify Byron as a murderer.

"So," Byron said. His eyes darted from Lyle, who was looking very uncomfortable, to Graham, who was looking decidedly comfortable. He nearly bit off his words in his anger. "As inane as the first piece of fiction! So you saw me enter the Manor. Doesn't prove a thing. I enter it each day. Most people do enter their homes. That doesn't make me a killer."

"No, it doesn't," Graham said slowly. "However...." He waited for what seemed minutes. In the quiet I could hear Byron's labored breathing, the call of a cat outside and the tap of Graham's fingers on the tabletop. I knew it was a waiting game to test Byron's nerves, but it was tensing my already taut emotions. As I was about to motion to Graham he said, "By your own admission, Mr. MacKinnon, you have stated before Sergeant Taylor and me that you were home all night. We have this witness, however, who will place you at the crime scene at the exact time. We have another witness who saw you arrive home. And before you can flip us off, we also have something else that will prove definitely that you murdered Pedersen."

He stepped back slightly, as though giving me the floor. I watched him walk over to the clothes dryer. Folding his arms, he leaned against it. Byron, I noticed, was interested in Graham's movement. When I cleared my throat, Byron jerked his head back to me. His eyes were wide and wild looking, like a trapped rabbit. "This year of all years," I said, "*you* raised the Guy at the bonfire. This year of all years, Ramona had a sprained wrist and couldn't do it. You conveniently stumbled into her in the pub, injuring her so she couldn't do her usual job. It would have been awkward if anyone but you hoisted the Guy, for then they would have felt the weight of a real person instead of the straw effigy. Anyone else would have been surprised and called out. But you didn't because you knew it was a person."

The room turned deathly quiet. The teakettle, shiny and squatting on the counter, had hushed. On the desk, the electric clock whirred noisily in preparation for the hour, then sank back into anonymity. Outside, the tomcat had relinquished his serenade, seeking more fruitful pastures elsewhere. The wind, underscoring Byron's anger only minutes before, now merely sighed, as if exhausted or surrendering to the futility of denial.

I looked at the group. Lyle was fidgeting with his collar, running a finger along the inside of the fabric, as though the subject was too vivid or recent for his comfort. Tom eyed the posters, his artistic eye perhaps evaluating the placement of graphics and text. Byron sponged his forehead with his hand, then blotted it on his jeans. Graham, I was inwardly amused to see, leaned against the clothes dryer. His long legs were crossed at the ankles, his arms folded across his chest, as though he had all the time in the world. He looked at Byron, silently urging him to speak.

"I didn't mean to kill him," Byron said with sudden resignation, his eyes on me. He sighed, knowing his own cleverness had trapped him. When he spoke again, it was nearly *sotto voce* and with a gentleness strangely in contrast to his earlier violent outbursts. "It was an accident. I was damned angry with him, which I admit. Mocking our national symbol. But I only mean to push him. I swear that's all! He came back later, checking the lanterns and torch for fireworks."

"Must have been when I was walking around and was stopped by that French couple to answer questions," I muttered, my stomach tightening. If I had returned minutes earlier, perhaps... But Graham, I saw, was not reproachful when he glanced at me. What had he said earlier, about understanding that I had had to walk about? He did not hold me responsible, even now as Byron was relating the fight time table.

"He got into it with me then, and I got angry. I pushed him. He pushed back, then threw a punch. Something snapped in both of us. He started swinging his fists like all hell had broken loose. I couldn't get away from him and so I pushed him again, but he came back at me. I picked up a large, heavy limb and..." He lowered his head, wiping his eyes. When he raised his head he said, "I ought to have left him there. I know that now. I'd walked away after the fight but I kept thinking of him, so I went back a bit later. No one had found him. He was still sprawled on the ground, his arms and legs all at different angles. I dragged him into the woods and clothed him as the Guy. I heard a couple of kids run around the fire circle so I squatted in the woods till they'd gone, then dragged him out and strung him up. No one'd seen me. I was mad as hell at the time, but now...." He looked directly at me, pleading with his eyes for me to understand. I shook my head very slowly, envisioning the scene. Tom must have had a war flashback, if he fought Byron so savagely. As if understanding I wanted proof, Byron rolled up his sleeve and showed me the bruises. Not that it proved Pedersen had done it, but I believed him.

"I killed Ramona, too. That was planned. I admit that, and I'm sorry I did it. But I had to. You see, I was afraid she'd tell about the car accident, about how I took money from Derek to pay off my earlier business debt. I owed them and didn't want to see them suffer bankruptcy due to my own failure. I loved Kris — still do. But I had to give her up. What are two people's happiness when compared to all my friends' financial future?"

"And after you paid back your friends," I said, "you let Derek keep his dole money."

Byron lowered his head. A great shudder claimed his body and he grabbed Lyle's hand as though any contact with God would steady him. "I don't say it was a gallant gesture in taking the dole money and abandoning Kris, but I had to chose between that and my friends. Derek's turned out to be the best friend I ever had."

"But why kill Ramona? Even if you were nervous, as you say, it has been twenty-five years since this all happened. Why would you fear she'd talk now?"

"She had told her husband. You didn't know him, of course. He died years ago. *And* she told her mum. She lives in Denmark, I know, but when someone's that talkative, and there are police all about asking questions.... Well, I couldn't take the chance, could I? I couldn't risk she wouldn't talk. Her tongue is such an undisciplined thing."

I could understand his anger and fear. There's a desperation that claims those who kill, an imagination that hears footsteps and gossip. The surest way to silence both is to eliminate both sources. I heard Byron's voice and wondered what I had missed.

"I hadn't planned to kill Ramona until Tuesday evening. I'm sorry about that murder. But I was scared she'd say something about the accident in 1973." He didn't elaborate, assuming we knew all about it. "I'd waited outside for a long time. Nearly an hour and a half. Arthur had been there for dinner, and the bastard didn't leave until eleven. I waited for a few minutes, making certain he wouldn't return to reclaim some forgotten item, then banged on her door. I had the turpentine all ready for her, you see. Poured a bit onto a cloth when I saw the light go on. She was surprised to see me. I grabbed her arm, pulled her outside, and —" He hesitated.

"I carried her to the middle of the back garden. I turned off the light when I went inside her house. I was afraid someone would see me. Then I had an idea about making it look like burglary, so I turned on the lights again. But when I realized the police always see through that I quickly changed my mind." He glanced at Graham, silently acknowledging the Force's talent. "I came back later. Not for the turpentine jar. I figured I was safe there. I'd worn gloves, so there were no fingerprints to connect me with a common glass jar. *She* might've dropped it there, for all anyone would know. But I did come back much later — I don't know what time. When I first returned here, after killing her, it was beginning to rain."

"That was when Lyle saw you," Graham said.

Byron nodded. "I didn't know anyone saw me. I was thinking about — well, anyway, it was then that I got the idea of implicating Talbot with a fragment of rope. Everyone knew he'd done that job of work for Ramona. He made no secret that he always had rope. I thought it rather a brilliant idea. But I waited for an hour or so before returning to her place. It took a lot longer than I thought, setting up that fiber bit. Several times while I was sawing away at that damned rope I'd hear a dog bark or a noise in the woods. I kept glancing back at her, half expecting her to get up. I thought I'd never get out of there. Ever try cutting a thick rope with a dull knife blade in the dark?"

"You got the knife from the Halfords, thinking to implicate them?" I asked.

"Yes, from Kris and Derek," he said, "but I didn't think they'd be suspects. The knife was awfully old."

"And awfully common," Graham said.

I tried to envision the strange scene — a corpse lying on the cold ground, a stormy sky with occasional bursts of ominous thunder and lightning, a desperate man cutting a rope in near pitch blackness, his hands encased in clumsy gloves, looking over his shoulder, perhaps, for the damning witness. And all the time that damning witness was out there in the dark, waiting to catch a flash of lightning, never realizing he was going to help catch a murderer.

"I knew you'd find the rope." Byron went on, automatically, hurriedly, as though he was afraid of running out of time. "I didn't realize you could tell she'd been moved, though. That was a mistake. I see that now. But I had to kill her." His voice slipped into a sort of whine, pleading for understanding. "I had to stop her menace. She was like that, you know. *Teasing.* She said she wouldn't tell, but you know how things get out."

I nodded, my eyes fixed as if by hypnosis on Byron. I remembered Ramona's laugh at the pub, the way she had teased Derek.

"I understand your action," Graham said, his voice low and strained, "even if I don't condone it. Now, Mr. MacKinnon...." Slowly, almost as though he was offended by everything that had been revealed, Graham laid his hand on Byron's shoulder.

Death of an Ordinary Guy

Before Graham could take him outside, I took a breath and said, "It was you, Mr. MacKinnon, who rigged those atrocities in my room, wasn't it?"

Graham looked at me in surprise, having no idea what I was talking about. I said quickly, "You wanted to scare me into leaving the case because I had heard the episode with Pedersen on Sunday at the bonfire. You were afraid I would remember your anger and deduce you killed Pedersen."

Byron nodded, turning toward me.

"Arthur mentioned on Sunday evening that you take group photos of the guests here." I nodded toward the camera on the counter, next to the sketches. "I also saw it when Mr. Graham and I questioned you the day you were talking to Talbot. Expensive model. You go in for all the gadgets, including telephoto lens."

"I was afraid to get too close to you, afraid it would give me away if you saw me."

"Actually, sir, your career gave you away."

"Being secretary to Arthur?"

"No, sir. Bookkeeper. You also keep Evan's books. You work in his office. Mr. Graham mentioned it Wednesday morning."

Graham was about to say something but I cut him off, not wanting his praise in public. I wanted to finish with Byron. "You have access in that office to all the pub's keys, Mr. MacKinnon. They're probably conveniently labeled and hanging on hooks. I do admit," I said, my excitement ebbing somewhat and needing to take a breath, "I originally thought of two other people as possible perpetrators." I mentally made a note to be nice to Mark, now that I had cleared him of my suspicions. And Talbot, running a close second, had no room keys. While emptying waste bins in the pub, he had had to knock on people's doors, leaving the rooms that didn't answer. I smiled. "I was confused for quite a while before I eventually heard that you were in the pub's office. But, as Chief Inspector Graham keeps reminding me, a good police team always tells each other absolutely *everything*."

A month-long trip to England during her college years introduced Jo to the joys of Things British. Since then, she has been lured back nearly a dozen times, and lived there during her professional folksinging stint. This intimate knowledge of England forms the backbone of the Taylor/Graham mystery novels, of which DEATH OF AN ORDINARY GUY is the first. Her two cats, Dickens and Chaucer, share her St. Louis home.